THE CRYSTALLINE JAWS OF DEATH

Costa sat enclosed by a webbed mesh of hand-length crystals, eight-sided, rectangular with pointed ends, no wider than her finger. Despite the seeming fragility of the formation, she could not snap it.

Then a single musical note, of such volume and purity it brought pain, struck through her. Clasping her hands to her ears, she reeled back, falling just as the crystal mesh of the enclosure shattered around her. Tiny shards embedded themselves in her arms as she cringed, covering her head as best she could. Hot little rivulets of blood ran down her cut arms, but she barely noticed as the things rushed at her.

She cried out as she was pressed into the frozen ground, cutting her cheek on the shards of crystal littering the earth like snow. She felt fierce stinging, and smelled blood, her blood, as though her skin was being peeled away. The scraping came again and again, almost eagerly, and she felt it rasp bone.

It was feeding upon her!

Ace Science Fiction Books by Jay D. Blakeney

THE CHILDREN OF ANTHI
THE OMCRI MATRIX

THE OMCRI MATRIX

JAY D. BLAKENEY

ACE SCIENCE FICTION BOOKS
NEW YORK

To Dad,

who's the best

in this universe

or any other.

This book is an Ace Science Fiction original edition, and has never been previously published.

THE OMCRI MATRIX

An Ace Science Fiction Book / published by arrangement with the author

PRINTING HISTORY
Ace Science Fiction edition/March 1987

Cover art by Neal McPheeters.

For information address: The Berkley Publishing Group, 200 Madison Avenue, New York, New York 10016.

ISBN: 0-441-62353-0

Ace Science Fiction Books are published by The Berkley Publishing Group, 200 Madison Avenue, New York, New York 10016.

PRINTED IN THE UNITED STATES OF AMERICA

CHAPTER ONE

Surprisingly, Janal received her in the small, steel-lined cubicle which was his true working office, one where precarious stacks of disk cards coded in every category from classified on down to published ceep reports vied with each other for space on his granite slab desk. A waist-high shelf to one side supported four viewers shimmering with full screens of data; across from it on a similar shelf blinked a formidable communications bank. Disk racks hung from the rest of the available space, giving the room a closed, cluttered, strictly utilitarian atmosphere. Janal saved the displays of his art objects and valor medals for the spacious office of muyar wood and living carpet, where he received dignitaries and handed out commendations.

Costa, her heart thudding and her eyes aflame with eagerness, did not care where he received her. Dressed impeccably in her fawn honors uniform, boots shining and strifer snapped firmly out of sight beneath the holster flap, she entered the office and came precisely to attention before him.

"Sir."

Looking harried, he glanced up and shut off the viewers with visible reluctance. Centuries of pure ancestral breeding on protected planets had marked him with high cheekbones and eyes of one color. Janal's were gray, and they looked right through her with a stony bleakness that stopped her heart.

"The Directors have met, Lieutenant. I'm sorry. Your petition was denied."

"Denied!" For a moment her intense hopes would not let her believe it. "But, Commander, it was so certain! I—" She swallowed hard, her eyes narrowing to a cool green. "I made a mistake in presentation perhaps. If I register an appeal—"

"No. The Directors meet only once a year for special petitions. You have no justification for bringing this before them again. They'll only penalize you—"

"I don't care! It is my right to—"

"Can that!" he snapped, dropping his momentary sympathy. "You signed the full-life contract. They have every right to hold you until you die."

She nodded bitterly, unable to hold back the resentment that had been building for so many years. "Yes, and what other choice is there? Only full-lifes can advance to officer rank, and only officers can be granted contract releases. I've served, Commander! I've done my duty and more! I've given the Directors everything I have, and now they hold me back! Why? The last time I petitioned and was refused, I expected it. But this time should have been a routine agreement. Almost everyone is granted release on their second petition. Why not me? *Why?"*

"Costa." Glancing impatiently at the chronometer, Janal shoved aside a pile of flagged disks labeled "Nogales" and leaned forward, resting his elbows on the desk. His eyes met hers firmly. "I have followed your career ever since I awarded you your first commendation. And I have approved of your desire to leave Playworld and enter the Fleet—"

"The Rangers," she broke in passionately. "I'm good enough to meet their requirements. You have said so—"

"Yes, you're very good. Too good." He sighed at her quick frown. "You are the best squad leader in the patrol, planet-wide. That happens to be a tremendous asset to us, one which the Directors are unwilling to release."

Her frown deepened with her anger. "You mean—"

"I'm afraid so. You rocketed through the ranks to become an officer in record time. You'll continue to be a squad leader until your ten years are up, at which time you'll pass through standard promotion to a captaincy and to a position as a training instructor, with all the benefits—"

"Damn the benefits!"

"Lieutenant."

Her eyes dropped at that quiet rebuke, but terrible rage engulfed her. She said bitterly, "This is all *flin,* sir. You've always been honest with me. What's the real reason for refusal?"

"Your breeding, for a start," he snapped, looking annoyed at being pinned down by her question.

Shocked, she met his gaze and could imagine the thoughts sweeping his mind: half-breed, savage, subhuman. She had never expected to find prejudice in Janal. "Sir, that is beyond unfair."

"I thought you were above a petty persecution complex, Costa."

"No, sir! Not when—"

"You had better discipline it."

She shook her head, past caring if she were reprimanded. "I do not understand how the Directors can fear an adapt. They—"

"No one is afraid. The Directors implemented the adapt program for sound reasons. Frankly, Lieutenant, you are one of the best results that program has ever produced. Aside from the fact of your extreme usefulness here on Playworld, the Directors do not want you off-planet lest you prove to be an embarrassment."

Costa's mouth fell open. "How—"

"Oh, not that you would fail any duty assigned to you in the Fleet. But the Galactic Space Institute doesn't look kindly upon the breeding of adapts which they have not authorized."

"We are not under GSI's jurisdiction."

He gave her an unforgiving look for speaking the obvious. "No, but the Directors prefer not to attract GSI's attention. You would blaze across the galaxy like a comet."

She frowned in bewilderment, unused to being derided for doing her best. "But other adapts have been released."

His gray eyes regarded her steadily. "So this is what it takes to make you whine."

She flinched as though struck. The iron discipline of the service cracked down on the rawness in her soul, and she stiffened back to attention. She must leave, get out at once before her protests deteriorated into begging. Janal would do nothing further on her behalf lest his own neck get chopped. It was pointless to keep prodding him.

"Is that all, sir?"

Janal nodded, looking relieved. Damn him!

"You have your orders regarding the Kublai?"

"Yes." Snarling in her heart, she forced her voice to be cool and professional. "His Supreme Glory lands at 0400. The arrangements have all been ordered and confirmed, except for the mustering of my squad. The harem will be settled into its quarters tonight in Beros under escort of the city patrol, and we'll move out in the morning, standard time."

"Basic security procedures. He'll be bringing quite a contingent of his personal guard, and we don't want to get in their way."

Costa nodded. "In short, I'm in charge of selecting a campsite, but otherwise to stay clear."

"Yes. There are always assassination threats hanging over a Kublai, and lately the United Worlds of Drugh have been a touchy subject for the entire Commonwealth. If anything should happen to the Kublai, civil war would erupt among those planets, and the Commonwealth's best shipping lanes would go right out of commission. Even though we aren't a part of the Commonwealth, we would certainly find our heaviest passenger routes cut off. Visits would have to drop; prices would fall; our economy would suffer." Janal sighed. "If he were coming here merely to hunt game it would be trouble enough, but this religious pilgrimage could be the start of something the Directors do not want on Playworld."

"The Directors could have avoided this problem by refusing to allow the Kanta Archives to be built on the middle continent," said Costa dryly.

"Perhaps. It is not our place to debate their wisdom in that matter. What *we* are concerned with, Lieutenant, is that all things go smoothly. The Ishuts have been causing more trouble than usual; Demos alone knows what those damnable Kanta priests have been telling them."

"Ishuts!" said Costa in surprise. "They do not matter—"

"Every element on Playworld matters!" he retorted. "You forget, Lieutenant, that any disturbance planetwide is routed through this office. Now, the Directors want everything concerning the Kublai's visit here to go well. That's why you've been given oversight of the expedition." Janal's smile did not reach his eyes. "As always, you will do your duty."

"Sir!"

Snapping out a salute, she spun on her heel and strode out, cursing the commander and the Directors in the five ways. In the outer reception area a tall, obese man with a scarlet cape held over one arm waited impatiently. Costa flicked him one swift, surprised glance as she swept past the reception drone which chimed a polite farewell after her. Wob Nogales, owner of all the amusement park licenses on the bleak north continent, coming here to see Janal like a normal citizen? As the doors opened for her, she dared look over her shoulder and caught Nogales winking at her. She shrugged and strode on.

Not for anything did she intend to leave headquarters by the usual route, where half her squad and various other friends lay in wait. The celebration for her offworlding was already planned, requiring only the go light from Janal today. Well, there would be no celebration, she thought savagely. She was trapped here just like everyone else born on this gilded dustball, a slave to the Directory for the rest of her life regardless of talent and ambition.

The best squad leader on the planet. Mercy of Moii! Did Janal think that dry bit of praise would soothe her? A muscle in her wrist twitched, close to the butt of her strifer.

She skirted the engineering section of the building, knowing her friend Arto had docked duty to wait for her in the main lobby, where a mobile of the galaxy hung suspended in the air against the backdrop of black walls and floor. A miniature replica of Playworld spun in the forefront, and tiny ships even came and went through the star systems in a dazzling display of suspension technology. Arto had designed it; he would wait for her there because he knew she could never resist the chance to look at it. But today the sight of those twinkling little stars would make her long to smash the thing to bits.

Taking a janitor lift down, she cleared the security drone and strode out into the crisp, perfectly controlled air of the city. Only then did a ragged sigh escape her, and she dodged down a service alley to crouch out of sight behind the loading dock of a fashionable boutique that sold quesquet furs and Sihh tears. There at last she was free to press her forearm over her stinging eyes: one proud, much-decorated officer of the Planet Patrol sniveling in the dirt over the ashed remains of a lifetime's hopes. She might as well go back to wearing a loincloth in the desert, living each day as it came without a single thought for the wealthy tourists who came here to play from all over the galaxy.

"Costa?"

She jerked up, slapping away the tears furiously. "Duval! How dare you follow me?"

He frowned at her. Stocky, with gray touching his hair, and his middle beginning to thicken from his favorite wife's prized cooking, Duval wore his desert uniform with an air of competence and pride. They had served together in the Planet Patrol for years, and when she was promoted ahead of him he showed no resentment but instead remained steadfastly loyal, taking no advantage from being her elder brother. Unlike her, he was content with his rank and his life; he had no ambitions to see the rest of the galaxy.

"The Directors turned you down?"

She nodded mutely, still choked with disappointment. "After all I've done! I—"

"What did Janal say?" asked Duval angrily. "Did you just accept the denial? Didn't you demand an explanation?"

"Of course I did! He said I'm too good, and that the Directors are afraid the GSI would notice me and start snooping into Playworld's adapt program."

"That's *flin!* The GSI knows all about the special breeding programs here. Why, they even sell the Directors access into specified gene pools. I remember our parents discussing it before you were born. No, Costa, the Directors just want talent like yours to stay on this dustball for Dhurrie wages. Can you appeal?"

"No." She looked away, struggling to stay in control. "Can I never escape? I've spent my life trying to be the best, trying to utilize my abilities to the fullest, and my reward is to be called a freak. Moii! They made me this way, both more and less than human. They use me, but I will always be subclass, something shameful, something they will not—"

"Costa, don't." He crushed her shoulder with a sympathetic hand. "Don't ever call yourself a freak. There's nothing shameful about being able to hear a tawn-snake slither over the sand at fifty meters, or being able to follow a cold trail by its scent alone, or being able to see through gloom that would blind a regular patroller. Demos, it takes a major plague virus to even give you a sniffle. I wish we could all be like you."

She smiled bleakly. "Thanks, Duval. But you'd better not

say that in public. You'll be branded an adapt lover."

"I've been called worse things."

She shrugged, grateful for his sympathy. For a moment she longed to rest her head on his shoulder as she had done in childhood, before taking on the pride and obligations of a warrior. "Cancel the party for me."

He nodded. "Look, I've got leave for a few days. Why don't you come home with me? Everyone would be delighted to see you."

She thought about his sprawling, comfortable *sieghr* on Lilliput and shook her head regretfully. "Not this time. I've got to muster a squad."

"Janal put you back on assignment? Where?"

"Jungle expedition. Large party. The Kublai of Drugh."

Duval whistled. "Not a good time of year for the jungle. All right. I'll call Aimlee and tell her I'm canceled. Then I'll find Puce and—"

"No." She held out a hand, trying to soften that sharp negative. "I . . . it's just better if I take out a squad of strangers."

"You need good people in the jungle, Costa."

"I'll get them. But . . . I don't want sympathy on this assignment," she said almost fiercely, wanting him to understand. "I need some time before I can face my friends. I bragged too much about the Rangers. Now I—" Her voice broke.

"Understood." He held up his fourth finger to her. "Moii go with you, Lieutenant."

She returned the gesture, and watched him walk away.

It was nearly 0400. She had better get a squad mustered and on the field before the Kublai and his party arrived. At this hour in the afternoon, the crowds were heavy as they dispersed from the shopping districts and queued for the lifts that would take them up to Stratum Four suspended overhead, where the luxurious villas, casinos, restaurants, and pleasure gardens were located. Costa made her way to a call booth, where she stood impatiently for the scanner to read the ID grid surgically implanted in the skin over her sternum. A light blinked on in readiness as the scanner switched off, and she rubbed her stinging chest through her tunic as she punched in her call. Seconds later she had a duty roster on the viewer, and she made her selections for muster quickly. Headquarters would contact them with their orders to report to the south landing field at 0400. She was free until then.

Leaving the call booth, she pushed her way through the gaily dressed crowds to board a crawler heading downward, incurring more than one curious glance at her dress uniform with the interlocked Ps on the right arm and the strifer on her hip. Normally it boosted her pride to stride through the tourists as a walking emblem of authority; now her skin crawled beneath her tunic and her muscles burned with the need to strike out at anyone or anything. Her pride was a useless, pathetic thing. She wanted no reminder of it.

To her relief, the crawler was relatively empty. She did not think she could stand being crammed into the midst of a crowd of civil servants on their way home. The crawler whined and jerked along its descent from Stratum Three to Two, where row after row of low-income housing alternated with enormous generator plants and small, grubby little shops humming with sonic bars across their entrances. This was the underside of the fabulous capital city which tourists never saw; this was what kept Beros going. Costa stayed on the crawler all the way to the ground, where the slums of Beros sprawled nearly out to the space port.

Here, the temperature was not controlled, and dust and heat fogged over her at once, sticking her tunic to her back and marring the shine of her boots. She unsnapped the flap over her strifer and held her wrist close to the butt as she stepped off the crawler into the crowded maze of the bazaar. The noise of hawkers, skin-sellers, and haggling women struck her at once. Interspersed through the babble came the smells of unwashed bodies and herendi dung. She threaded her way through grimly, trying not to listen to the dozens of conversations which her keen hearing sorted through automatically, uninterested in watching the street acrobats performing feats of agility while pickpockets ranged swiftly through the gawking onlookers. A city patrolman lounging sleepily in a shaded doorway lifted his fourth finger to her in casual greeting, and she returned the small salute. The sun blazed down on her head, heating the fine black strands of hair which she wore cropped strictly just below her earlobes. Snapping down an inner eyelid against the glare, she swallowed more dust, grimaced as she stepped around a bleating flock of herendi darting this way and that, and decided to seek out a wineshop instead of the traditional blessing of her duty amulet.

Tall, graceful Dhurries squatted regally along the street in their loincloths, tarlarl sticks smoking between long, nervous fingers as they gambled with brightly colored splits and argued among themselves. Once aristocrats of the ancient tribes, they now waited for hire as bearers and scouts for the daily expeditions heading out from Beros. Ulangs, thickset and belligerent, with bristling crests of coarse ash-colored hair, refused to demean themselves by pandering to the tourists. *Yulies* was their word for the rich people who flocked to Playworld for a few weeks of idleness. Rather than catering to them, they flung themselves instead into commerce where they were known to be fierce, shrewd, and ready to cheat anyone who was not sharp enough to catch them out. Then there were the Ishuts, most primitive of all. Only outcasts of that tribe ever drifted into the Beros slums, and they always caused trouble.

Two were causing trouble now, circling an alarmed peddler and nipping at his heels with their pointed sticks. The thronging crowd parted around this disturbance, pausing with intent curiosity, and in the hush a Ulang merchant's reedy voice rang out:

"Twenty *guillens* for this fine rug. A fine rug, sir. Woven by deft . . ." His wheedling trailed off as the peddler screamed and cowered down with his tray of wares clutched in his arms.

Frowning, Costa scanned the crowd swiftly for a ceep, but as usual whenever trouble erupted in the bazaar, no city patrollers were around. The one she had passed a few streets back was too far away to intervene here. She reached wearily for her strifer, ready to draw it if one of the Ishuts went for the peddler's throat. With another scream, this time of rage, the peddler threw down his tray of painted balls and fled. Ishut laughter mocked his flight as his tormenters scooped up the balls and bore them triumphantly away.

Children, thought Costa with contempt, letting her wrist swing away from her weapon. Dangerous, superstitious children. Ishuts should be kept out of the city, they and their Kanta priests. With narrowed eyes she watched the two thieves race up the street to gleefully deliver their loot into the hands of a black-robed priest with a double crossing of dried blood smeared on his shaven brow. He praised them, and when they raced on with laughter he let the tribute roll indifferently from his hands.

Costa shrugged and turned to stride on, but in that instant as the crowd pressed around her a hand seized her from behind, crushing her arm and dragging her into a narrow alley between two shops. Something thin and sharp pricked her forearm, making it sting. She snarled in fury, her free hand striking with a sleeve knife. It split through thick cloth to stab at nothing solid. Startled, Costa stared wide-eyed at the Omcri holding her. A chill pierced her to the second part, and if long established cynicisms prevented her from making a visible sign of warding, she wished uneasily in her heart to do so.

"Loose me, faceless one!" she said with a snap to hide her fear. "You detain an officer of the—"

"Identity known," said the double-timbred voice that issued from no living throat. Yet Omcris were not machines. The grip tightened on her arm, cutting off circulation. "Ambition comes hard on Playworld. We sell. You buy. Talk now, yes?"

How did it know? Her topaz eyes fell swiftly from the obsidian void swirling beneath the cowl of the Omcri's robe to the black-gloved hand gripping her arm. Rage and indignation stormed through her. Janal's working office was supposed to be snoop clean. Obviously it was not! Nameless, faceless, untraceable Omcris were often used as couriers of death, placing assassination orders across the galaxy. And the Kublai of Drugh was to arrive in less than an hour.

Her head lifted. "You won't hire me to chop the neck of His Supreme Glory. Now loose me, devil-thing, or eat strifer fire."

In silence the Omcri released her arm and glided rapidly through the crowd, which moved aside with revulsion. In moments it had disappeared from sight. Her arm tingling as circulation returned, Costa drew in a breath through her teeth, shaking from the adrenaline still pumping through her gut. Mercy of Moii! She had never been that close to one of the things before, and she hoped she never would be again. Jerking up her sleeve, she swiftly examined her arm. A tiny red prick marred the flesh. The skin around the spot was oddly cold to the touch. She frowned with a shiver.

Wiping the sweat from beneath the warrior braid coiled over her brow, Costa entered the first wineshop she came to. This one was large and of a certain reputation. Here, ruffians of countless systems gathered in dark corners to plot and barter. Normally she never entered the place, but she wanted a drink desperately now. Strifers were worn openly in defiance of the ordinances, so the only thing which set her apart from the rest of the company was the patrol uniform she wore. Hard looks of hostility hit her when she walked in.

The burly door guard stepped forward to intercept her. "Oi, Pepe," he said in toneless Unise. "You coming in on business? Maybe the ceeps won't like that, eh?"

It was too late to retreat without incurring jeers that would bounce off any patroller setting foot in the place for the next several months. Costa overcame the urge to ease out, and looked the man in the eye.

"What the vice squads do is their business. My business is a dry throat," she said and walked past him with her back itching, expecting him to plant steel in it at any moment. No one in here would mourn or report the death of a nosy patroller. But the guard let her pass, and after a moment the rigidity in her spine eased.

The tables were filled, save for one. She stopped in dismay as she saw the Omcri sitting before her in solitude. Disdaining a chair, it floated as though suspended on antigrav units. The small rip in its robe killed her hope that it might be a different Omcri than the one that had accosted her. She cursed beneath her breath, and snapped up all her lids to penetrate the farthest reaches of the gloom in hope of one small, overlooked, and empty table. Nothing.

"We talk now, yes?" said the Omcri.

The queer coldness in her arm intensified. She gazed at it, troubled, then sat down at the low table with her back to the wall. She kept one hand on her strifer, her heart thundering as she strove to understand how she had been manipulated into this. Worse, spies ran rampant in the bazaar. At any moment the extraordinary conduct of a patroller seated in the close company of an Omcri could be reported. She had taken an oath to uphold the service, the Directory, and the standards of Playworld; she had spent her life conforming her wild nature to rigid disciplines, taking care to let nothing mar her record. Yet now, after all the work, sweat, and sacrifice, she still could not advance. The patrol had been a toehold for her ambitions. Now it was an abyss. And maybe she didn't care if a spy reported her.

A waiter sidled up with the drinks of cheap tinsel they had to pay for and stood ready for them to order what they really wanted.

"I'll have slow-water, if it's fresh," she said, nervously flinging back her warrior braid.

The Omcri lifted the back of its hand, and the waiter departed hastily.

"Now we talk," said the faceless one, leaning slightly toward her.

In the smoky gloom, the place where its face should have been was an unworldly black emptiness. But now and then she caught a faint, greenish glimmer through the swirling patterns, like dim starlight seen through nebula clouds. The coldness of nonexistence hung upon the creature. And a slight, tainted scent struck her nostrils. She shivered again.

"I am not an assassin for hire, Omcri," she said, fingers curling more tightly upon the polished butt of her strifer. "Mark that. I came in here to drink, nothing more."

"Anger, great. Heart, flame. Emotions, unimportant to he who speaks through this one. Do nothing. Be gone in jungle at appointed time, and death will come to the protected one."

Costa drew in a breath slowly. Maybe she should pretend to go along with this for a while, if only to learn more for her report to Janal. "I understand now," she said. "But my squad will just guide the expedition. His Supreme Glory will have his own guards."

The Omcri made a derisive sound. "Palace guard worry us not. Planet patrol not same. We know warriors. We know of *you*."

She warmed to the compliment even as the third part of her warned great caution. "Whose courier are you?"

The Omcri drew back abruptly. "Not know. Not say. We

buy ambition. You sell service. Yes?"

She slumped back in her chair, fighting for time. "What price?"

The Omcri drew a short slender wand from its wide sleeve. The wand was banded in many different colors, and the faceless one adjusted these into a pattern of descending hues of lavender before extending it. Her hand jerked, oversetting the tinsel which flowed in a muddy stain across the table. The offer was generous enough to make her head spin, enough to pay for a vacation here on Playworld, and certainly enough to enable her to leave the planet forever. Temptation burned her throat, but she curled her cold, shaking fingers into a fist and did not touch the wand.

She frowned. "Money can't be spent in a detention ward."

"Ambition, great. Ambition, known. Ambition, fulfilled," said the Omcri.

She flinched. "Moii's oath, death-dealer! You can't hand me a release from my contract here. You can't get me into the Rangers. And you certainly can't obtain for me a new ID grid implant."

"All things can be done. New identity acceptable condition for contract. You have sold. We have bought—"

"I haven't touched that wand," she said swiftly, panicked by this attempt to seal a bargain.

The Omcri bowed its head. "No need. When time comes, you will do." Gloved fingers gently touched her arm, making her flinch. "Ambition, great. Emotions, known. *Et*!"

It rose swiftly from the table and glided away just as the waiter brought her slow-water. She sipped the drink thoughtfully, a pulse beating hard in her throat as the stuff burned down to her stomach. All her instincts were twisting knives within her. She had checked once on the cost of a new identity. She had even hired a spy to find out what a smuggler charged for lifting living cargo off-planet. The costs for both were astronomical, and back then, of course, she had been confident of her own abilities and of the tradition of granting a good officer release after two cycles of exceptional duty. Not for her, however, never for her!

She slammed *guillens* on the table and strode outside angrily into the blazing heat to find a call booth. A beep sounded in her ear, and in seconds a bland voice responded over the tinny connection:

"Beros HQ. Command Central. Specify section."

"Commander Janal's office. Priority call."

There was an infinitesimal pause, then: "Clearance code please. Stand by for reading—"

Mercy of Moii! Was she a fool? Costa cut the connection and ejected herself from the call booth. A snoop had intercepted that connection! And she had checked the call booth herself before using it. Clean on her end, which meant Janal's office was not. Someone had expertly broken his security. She glanced at her chronometer and cursed loudly enough to make a veiled passerby leap quickly to one side and scurry on. There was no time to find an alternative way to reach the commander now. She had to get out to the landing field. Damn and damn again! This left her out in the cold completely, without even her good squad, thanks to her stupid, bruised pride. Costa squared her chin. She would manage somehow, and, by Demos, that Omcri would find he had made a poor bargain indeed.

CHAPTER TWO

A hot raw wind blew across the open field of the auxiliary port of call. Reserved for local, small shuttle, and racing traffic, the auxiliary port lay cupped in the wide bowels of a sharp-edged lava canyon, isolated and lonely, with Beros cut off from sight by the towering black cliffs. Only the incessant roar and turbulence from scout craft and cargo loaders landing and taking off in screaming arcs destroyed the illusion of desolation.

Bolts of light flashed from the aqua-tinted sky as the brazen, low-hanging sun reflected off metal. Costa squinted and stepped away from the shade edging the side of the elegant reception building. All three inner lids snapped down over her eyes and she gazed intently upwards at the incoming craft, noting the unusual slant of trajectory which marked it as Drugh, even before it came close enough for her to see the wide, low-slung body of the shuttle.

"Squad." She glanced briefly at the six she had mustered. One was female, a taciturn Ulang of habitually bitter expression, dried to leather and bone, with lazy blood-red eyes, a short-cropped hair crest, and a well-ashed tarlarl stick drooping from her lips.

At Costa's gesture, they all pried themselves from the shade and made a slight effort to straighten rumpled tunics. Their boots were scuffed, their strifers unpolished, their fatigues hard worn. They were all strangers to each other and lacked any *esprit de corps.* As a group they weren't much, and the perfectionist in Costa writhed at the thought of presenting this sorry band to His Supreme Glory instead of a handpicked squad of her best. Then she gave herself a bitter shake. What did it matter? She could stop trying; she wasn't going anywhere.

The shuttle made its final approach. In silence, well aware of the two Directors and their entourage standing inside the polarized windows of the reception building, the squad followed Costa out to the edge of the landing field. Costa shouted and waved an arm at the Dhurrie bearers in their scarlet loincloths, and slowly they unfolded their long-muscled limbs off the dust-whipped ground to line up behind the squad. Costa's eyes ranged across them all. She spoke sharply once again, and the Ulang spat out her tarlarl stick.

Close up, the Drugh shuttle was enormous and squat of line. Bold royal insignia emblazoned the sides. The engines whined down and cut, giving the official Beros welcoming delegation time to file out into the sunlight and heat at a decorous shuffle. Costa waited poised, her topaz eyes locked on the hatch. As soon as it opened with an abrupt rush of air, she barked the order, and the squad snapped to attention.

The ramp folded out smoothly as the hatch locked open. A figure stood just within the shadows of the interior. His Glory was impatient, she thought, but then the man minced down the ramp into the light. She saw the gray uniform and the silver stripes before she saw his face, and the sight hit her like a sharp blow to the stomach. A Ranger!

Behind him, tall, heavily muscled guards in harness and light armor lined up on either side of the ramp with ceremonial gold-tipped spears held at ramrod attention. Costa took no notice of them. Her eyes could not leave the Ranger as he approached her. Only now as he drew near, she saw she had been mistaken. The elaborate shoulder padding, flared cut, and expensive fabric betrayed the tunic to be a fashionable parody of a uniform. Her eyes narrowed to an icy green as this creature halted before her.

His own gaze, jaded and cynical, swept across her contingent. Annoyance twisted his face painted with lines of rank, and he glared at her. "I am Bessam al-zk. Mah to the household of His Supreme Glory. Identify yourself."

"Lieutenant Costa, sir."

He lifted a dark, delicately plucked brow, and his painted mouth tightened. "And you are in charge of this . . . squad?"

She heard the thinly veiled derision, and anger pounded a hard pulse through her throat. She lifted her chin a fraction higher. "Sir!"

"Who is your superior?"

"Commander Janal."

He pointed to the communicator on her belt. "Get him. I

wish to request another officer."

"On what grounds?"

"Sex. A female cannot be permitted to guard His Supreme Glory." His eyes shifted to the Ulang. "She must be replaced as well."

For a moment Costa could not believe she had heard correctly. Then her eyes heated to a bright topaz. "There is no gender in the service. You violate my honor as a warrior."

"Zuthat ma dal!" He swept out his hand in anger. "The laws of pilgrimage are strict. This defilement cannot be permitted."

"I wasn't notified of your authority, sir. My superiors have given me this command, and, aside from the personal guard of His Supreme Glory, I am in charge of the Kublai's well-being."

"No."

Her hand moved by reflex for her strifer, but iron-hard discipline guided it instead to her communicator. She thumbed open a channel, cutting across the drone's standard reply. "Squad four-niner requesting priority channel to Commander Janal. No coding. Open, please."

"Lieutenant, what is the meaning of this delay?" demanded one of the bureaucrats assigned to the welcoming delegation now wilting in the heat. "What is the difficulty? The Kublai must not be kept waiting for any reason—"

"His Supreme Glory must not be defiled," snapped Bessam, quelling the man.

"Defiled? I-I do not understand."

Costa glanced up while the communicator crackled on delay. "Apparently females cannot be present. We were not informed of this cultural difficulty in our briefing."

The bureaucrat exclaimed and made ineffectual little shooing motions with his plump hands. "Then you must leave and quickly. We must not offend His Glory."

"I do not absent my post without authorization," said Costa through her teeth, and turned away as the bureaucrat gobbled in affront.

"Janal here," came the static-filled voice.

Costa lifted the communicator and reported in a tight, emotionless voice. This should have been foreseen and handled properly, she thought, while blood-shame burned through her strongly enough to make her hand shake. The Kublai was nothing but a gilded boy without even so much as a battle scar; she should have taken up the Omcri's offer, shipping lanes and interplanetary war be damned.

When she finished, Janal remained silent for so long she wondered if communication had been cut.

"Let me speak to the Mah," he said at last.

She handed over the communicator and stood aside. The courtesy proved unnecessary; Janal and Bessam spoke in Drugh Dialect I, which she recognized but did not understand. After a few minutes of heated argument, Bessam broke off and handed the communicator back.

"Costa?"

"Yes, Commander."

"Your assignment remains."

She grinned. "Yes, sir!"

"There is one adjustment. Consider Mah Bessam your temporary commander."

"But—"

"No protests, Lieutenant. The Kublai's presence here is potentially explosive. We can't afford to create an incident. I know you will do your duty. Janal out."

She hooked the communicator back onto her belt, expecting Bessam to smirk. His expression of relief surprised her.

"At last, that duty is over," he said, pulling out a brightly colored cloth to fan himself.

She frowned. "You mean this was all for show? That it meant nothing?" Belatedly, she realized she was being openly discourteous and tried to alter her tone. "Do you always—"

But the Mah no longer seemed offended as he raised his hand casually in a signal to the shuttle. "Face," he said, fanning himself. "One is required to go through these formalities of ritual. They mean nothing, of course. Will this delegation be long-winded? I find myself soiled and thirsty. Your planet is much touted, Lieutenant, but I fear my appreciation of untamed nature is small."

"No doubt," she said tersely.

With a shrug he walked back to the shuttle, while the delegation muttered and mopped brows and shuffled about. The heat grew more oppressive as the wind died down. Costa endured the delay stoically, pulling in all her senses to tune out her surroundings. She needed rest. She was being too emotional in front of the Directors.

Then the anger sparked again. *What did it matter?*

Finally the Kublai appeared, slim and graceful of body despite his arrogant stance. His elaborate headdress was embroidered with gold that flashed in the sun, and he wore exquisite, tissue-supple leather that wrought a faint gasp from the Dhurries behind Costa. She could have cut off her warrior braid in disgust. No one was more respectful of his superiors than a Dhurrie, but no Dhurrie respected poverty and even the despised Ishuts did not wear animal skins in public display. The Kublai could not have appeared in anything more calculated to cause passivity, laziness, and the theft of his possessions in the jungle. Unmindful of these problems, the delegates swarmed His Supreme Glory, who received their fawning welcome with a faint, slightly bored smile, then broke away to approach Costa's squad.

"We have always desired to take up the hunt on Playworld," he said in a soft, sibilant voice that could not quite pronounce consonants. "Alas, this time must be devoted to that which is greater. Serve us well, and all shall be amply rewarded. When do we depart, squad leader?"

Not by so much as a flicker of an eyelid did Costa breach protocol by glancing at him. Her gaze remained correctly distant. "1700, Glory."

"Which is?"

"Dawn."

He beamed, clapping his soft hands together. "Splendid! My friends, do you hear? We begin at dawn. Oh, do not moan, Bessam, my lazy companion! We have the privilege of serving the great Kanta. And when we have finished our sacred duties, then we shall go hunting. Yes, hunting in a true wilderness. None of the ceremonial, boring displays of tame animals more ready to die than we are to kill them." He turned away from Costa to gesture at the bowing Mah. "Arrange it, Bessam. We are certain Playworld will be delighted if we stay longer than our original plan."

"Thy wish is done, Glory," said Bessam in a toneless voice,

which contrasted flatly with the Kublai's enthusiasm.

Under the aegis of the welcoming delegation, the Kublai, his richly dressed friends, and the personal guard were conveyed to Beros, while two more shuttles bearing auxiliary guards, servants, the Companions of Delight, and their attendants roared in swift descent over the field. Costa grimaced at her aching ears and blinked at an unwieldy, rectangular metal box being unloaded from the royal shuttle.

"At rest, squad," she said and strode over to Bessam, whose expression had pinched into sour displeasure as soon as his ruler had departed. "That container . . ." She pointed. "If it holds valuables, it should be stored in a security compound on the east side of the landing field. Shall I have it registered for you?"

Bessam stared at her in astonishment, then tittered. "Oh, you ignorant parochials! How amusing! No, no, Lieutenant, you may not register our sacrifice to Kanta."

"Sacrifice!" Involuntarily her nostrils quivered, seeking the scent of whatever lay inside the box. "Do you bring a live offering, Mah Bessam? This will have to be reported."

"Why, Lieutenant," he said blandly, spreading wide his tinted palms. "We are well aware of your regulations. No violations have been made. You have the word of the Drugh government." For a moment his eyes bored into her skeptical ones, then he shrugged and fluttered his handcloth. "What can we do but humor His Supreme Glory in this quest to revive the Kanta religion? He believes that in coming here to the ancient ruins of the original temples he will accomplish something profound. The belief is harmless, Lieutenant. Humor His Glory with us, please."

With a shrug of distaste, she drew back. "My orders oblige me to do so, sir. Is there anything else?"

At his negative, she turned on her heel and went back to the squad. "Dismissed," she said.

They had already been given their orders for tomorrow. The squad dispersed as swiftly as the desert wind, and only then did she allow her straight shoulders to sag wearily as she left the field alone, choosing to walk back into the slums rather than take transport.

• • •

Four days later, she ducked the angry whine of strifer fire and rolled beneath a bush just as the bolt meant for her split a sizable chunk of wood from a muyar trunk. The stench of burning wood mingled with that of ozone and rotting earth as she buried herself lower in the undergrowth.

"Hobra! Noyle! Fan out—"

She sprang and rolled again as strifers mowed down her protection. Agonizing fire scorched her leg, which gave under her. Choking back an outcry, she grasped the thin line at her belt and threw the tiny grappler up into the thickly laced limbs overhead. It curled around a branch and held, and with a grunt she hauled herself up, a perfect target for two seconds. Then mercifully she was hidden in the treetop.

Puffing, she crouched low and sprang to another limb, moving with care. A shaking limb would betray her position to the attackers. No one blew her out of the sky, and with a gasp she sank down, wincing as she put a probing hand to her leg. It was just a graze; she need not fear serious loss of mobility, but oh, Moii, the pain!

She wiped a sleeve across her face, smearing dirt, sweat, and tears on it, and listened helplessly to the screams of rage and agony as men died all around her. *Take to the trees, the trees!* But they had no jungle lore. They did not know what to do except stupidly stand their ground and fight in the Drughan way while snipers mowed them down. She had lost the positions of her squad. She dared not thumb open her communicator. But neither could she just squat up here, quaking in terror. She must do something!

Gathering her line in a small coil, she clipped it to her belt and hauled herself up a sawtooth vine, grimacing as it pricked through her heavy gloves. The attackers had encircled the camp and opened fire just as everyone gathered wearily for supper. They had heavy strifers and bolt rifles, outgunning everything in the camp, and even the staunch bravery of the Drugh guards could not hold out much longer against such odds. She swung into the next tree, landing noiselessly above a pair of men in dark jumpsuits and armored helmets busily preparing a small deton-bomb.

Costa's strifer erupted with two needle-thin spits of death, and the bombers fell. She dropped off the limb to the ground beside them and pulled their bodies aside to crouch in their place. Swiftly she reset the deton, fumbling with the trajectory meters, working more by instinct than expertise. Aiming it across the camp where the bolt rifles seemed to be massed most tightly, she fired the bomb and threw herself flat in the coughing backlash that shook the earth beneath her and drove all the breath from her lungs. For a moment she lay stunned and deafened, her head ringing dizzily, then she pushed herself up and grimly surveyed the flames shooting through the heavy undergrowth. No more bolt rifles fired, and she nodded in satisfaction.

As she started to load another bomb, however, strifer fire exploded in her face, knocking her back. Only a swift leap saved her as more strifers raked the spot where she had crouched a moment before. She slithered far back beneath a thornbush, shaking uncontrollably with the need to cough out the fire in her lungs. Strifers swept rapidly overhead, trying to drive her from her scanty cover. She dragged herself to her knees beyond the bush, clutching her stomach in desperation. She was going to be sick; no, she dared not stop moving, not for an instant! Somehow she scrambled on, flinching from each sweep of death, yet somehow escaping by dodging again and again. Coughing overwhelmed her, and she fell on her face, writhing in agony as a wave of nausea swept over her. She retched violently, then threw herself to one side as the strifers fired again. They were toying with her, anticipating her every move, driving her easily along into whatever trap they had waiting.

She must get back into the trees! But how? She would be picked off the moment she left ground cover. A death cry shrilled nearby, making her start and whirl around on her knees. Panting, she looked frantically about, unable to clear her singed nostrils to scent out anyone who might be close. Her nerves sang like wires; she needed nothing to tell her that she was well in the trap. But from which side would it spring closed?

Gathering her rubbery legs beneath her, she reached for the line coiled at her belt, determined to try to get up even if it brought her death. The wind shifted, and suddenly she no longer smelled death and fire and blood, but something cold, tainted, and infinitely evil. *Omcri!*

Her heart leapt into her throat as one of the creatures lifted noiselessly from the matted undergrowth a meter or more into the air and began to glide toward her, the long robe billowing out. Costa froze, fear hammering through her. She could not even breathe. The line fell from her nerveless fingers, then as the devil-thing rushed toward her with outspread arms, she snatched at her strifer and fired point-blank.

The thick robe smoked and charred, falling open in long tatters to reveal nothing but a dark, shapeless cloud. Coldness touched her sweating face, and with a scream she ducked to one side, barely eluding the creature. It circled and flew at her again, the cowl falling back as it swooped faster. She saw the knife in its gloved hand, a long, translucent blade filled with a milky substance that swirled and glowed eerily in the failing light. Desperately Costa reached for her own cutter, snapping out the three toothed blades with a practiced flick of her wrist. She threw hard, slicing off the Omcri's knife hand at the wrist, yet although the knife fell for a moment the creature merely plucked it from midair and came at her again, unimpaired.

Oh, Moii, why hadn't she struck a bargain with the Omcri in the wineshop? She could be far away from this by now with her money and her new ID grid. But even as she dodged, unsuccessfully this time, and cried out as the Omcri wrenched her arms behind her and lifted her into the air with it, she knew she would have died no matter what bargain she made. Assassins of this caliber needed no loose ends to talk after the deed was done on a different side of the galaxy.

The Omcri enfolded itself about her, and she screamed again, struggling vainly against a force she could not resist. Coldness invaded her body, seeping through her as a horrible finger of thought slid inside her brain, probing, invading, violating. Pain jerked her ruthlessly, and she was freezing, congealing, growing rigid and unable to struggle. But she would not go easily to the death this faceless one planned for her. Grimly, forcing stiff fingers to obey, she grasped the butt of her strifer and drew it, turning it upon herself. Another scream ripped from her throat as her brain seemed to shred apart, then she was falling, spiraling down into oblivion.

CHAPTER THREE

Costa awakened slowly to a throbbing pain, astonished to find herself still alive. With difficulty she sat up, then drew a swift breath and listened to the silence surrounding her. The battle was over! It was just twilight, so she could not have been unconscious long. But why hadn't the Omcri finished her? With a shudder, she cradled her arm against her middle, trying to work out the coldness which had invaded her through to the bone. After a moment the arm felt better, but she could not force away the sensation of having been tainted by that *thing* invading her mind.

Her strifer lay at her side, the charge nearly drained. She picked it up and holstered it with trembling fingers, remembering how close she had come to using it upon herself. Then she wondered if anyone else had survived.

Standing brought her pain. She could barely straighten, and her bruises were terribly sore. Her wounded leg gave under her on the first step and only a hasty grab at a tree trunk saved her from falling, but after that she gritted her teeth and hobbled on, every sense straining as the twilight thickened.

A flock of carpals fluttered into the tree branches overhead, squawking and tearing at each other with their blue, razor-sharp beaks and talons. Relief swept over Costa. If the animals were beginning to gather in to feast on the carnage, the attackers must be gone. She hobbled faster to the edge of the clearing where the camp had been pitched yesterday evening. Well-worn game trails led down to a brackish stream, and she had not wanted to camp in this place. But since orph mating did not commence for another month and the big beasts were unlikely to be running amok, she had given in to the Kublai's desires. Sonic protectors had kept the kicats roaring in frustration all around the perimeters during the nights, but His Supreme Glory had slept undisturbed. Now he probably slept forever.

Angrily Costa pushed away rising guilt. Janal might have

assigned extra protection had she ever reported in her conversation with the Omcri courier, but even an army of patrollers would have found it impossible to deal with jungle snipers.

Crouching by the edge of the clearing, Costa scanned the camp with care, her heartbeat quickening at the sight of purplish blood and entrails strewn everywhere. Tents, collapsed and burning, sent dark plumes of acrid smoke into the steamy air. She coughed, startling a half-grown kicat which had trotted into sight. It crouched a moment, lashing its tail, then snarled and leaped on the body of a guard to rip off a leg. Costa stood up with a shout, and the beast sprang away, snarling, but she knew it would soon return with more of its kind. The jungle moved swiftly to a feast; she did not have much time.

Overhead the carpals screamed and jostled each other on the lowest branches. She cursed them for their noise. As rapidly as she could, she hobbled across the camp, fighting to keep her stomach from heaving at the sight of so much death. She found no one alive, but neither did she come upon the body of the Kublai. Hope flared within her. Had it been an abduction instead? If so, she would bring him safely back or die in the attempt.

In the wreckage of the supply tents, she found a small sonic protector that seemed undamaged and soon filled a pack with a medikit, rations, and fresh charges for her strifer. Then she started a count of the bodies, forcing herself to finish the grisly task. None of her scouts had come through. Some of the braver guards had died beyond the camp along with their attackers, who wore nondescript mercenary tunics carefully lacking any identification. She traced each trail of blood out to its end, using her keen sense of smell as the light failed even more. In the distance a kicat coughed, bringing her upright with an exhausted sigh. She could look no longer. Only Bessam and the Kublai were unaccounted for. Costa rubbed her forehead wearily. She would make camp in the safety of the trees, and in the morning at first light she would mark the trail of the attackers.

She turned away from the game trail to push quietly through the undergrowth in search of a suitable muyar tree where she could sleep safe from predators and the trilid parasites that bored through wood or bone with equal appetite. Nothing ate muyar wood. The wind shifted again, bringing her an unexpected scent of chemicals. She stopped and glanced over her shoulder at the camp, snapping up her innermost eyelid in an effort to pierce through the gloom. Drawing her strifer, she turned back cautiously. The smell came from the sacrifice box which had tumbled out of a transport sled during the battle. It now lay dented, its closure seal broken. She eased up to it, not certain she wanted to face another unpleasant surprise today. Against the deepening pools of shadow, she could see an escaping curl of mist rising from the edges of the lid.

Costa frowned and gripped her strifer more tightly as she tugged at the lid. It sprang up against her palm with a sudden rush of air, making her flinch back. As she did so, the box tipped further, crashing over onto its side. A body rolled out at her feet. She cried out as a limp arm slapped around her ankle, then she caught hold of herself, panting and ashamed.

The raw scent of human blood curled through her nostrils. She knelt and rolled the body over. It was a man, cold and damp from chemicals, but breathing. She could barely see now; she had no time to delay here further. The jungle was coming alive around her.

She glanced back at a faint rustle behind her and abruptly switched off the torch. Slinging the pack over her shoulder, she tied one end of her line about the man before tossing the other up into the branches. Her blind aim seemed to go true. After an exploratory tug she dug in her heels and started hauling him up into the treetop. It wasn't a muyar, but it would have to do.

Animal musk fogged her nostrils, and she stiffened at the soft pad-pad of big paws. Consciously she overcame panic and kept pulling until the man was safely up in the branches. She anchored the line with a spike driven into the trunk, and sprang up into the tree seconds before a low cough warned her of the kicat's spring. One gigantic paw brushed her back, the claws ripping her tunic as she hauled herself desperately up to the low branches. The kicat growled loudly, snarling and slapping the heavy metal box about. Costa climbed higher until the tree swayed from her weight, then clung there trembling for a long while, her face mashed against the rough bark which stank of mextle droppings.

Not until the kicat left did she find the strength to set about pulling the man up to her level. Her back ached, and her muscles were so spent they trembled uncontrollably. Twice she slipped and nearly let him plummet to the ground below, but finally she got him wedged safely into a fork of the tree and tied him there with her line. Sinking down on a narrow branch with her back against the trunk and her legs dangling, Costa wiped her streaming face with her arm and opened the pack. Seconds later she found the switch on the sonic protector, and the little unit hummed into life, making her teeth itch and her frayed nerves unravel more. But at least now she could relax her guard against tree predators.

She switched the torch on the man for her first good look at him. He was still wet, and in the steamy heat of the night he was unlikely to dry. His dark head was tipped back, dangling past the fork of the tree, so that all she could see of his face were the sharp angles of his cheekbone, nose, and beard-stubbled chin. But he wore the plain gray uniform of a Ranger, a real one this time.

"Mercy of Moii," she breathed, her eyes widening as she counted the stripes of silver braid on his sleeve. She touched his hand. He was slightly warmer than before.

He stirred, moaning, and her grip tightened on his arm.

"Easy, Major."

Blood seeped up through the gray tunic, dulling the silver braid with an ugly stain that looked black in the dim light of her torch. His lean, hawkish features twisted with pain, but as she pulled open his tunic he opened his eyes.

"*No,* Garth—" A shudder ran through him, and white suddenly ringed his clamped lips.

"Don't talk." She frowned, hot blood running over her hand as she pressed it to the spongy mess of his side.

Obviously the box had possessed some sort of stasis unit to keep him alive, and now that he was out of there she had better work fast if he were going to live long enough to give her any answers. Unbuckling her belt, she pulled off her tunic. The cloth was lightweight but tough, fashioned to withstand the abuse of her profession. With a grimace she took her cutter to it, slicing the cloth into strips which she knotted together. The sleeves were torn off and folded into a pad which she bound over the wound, pulling the edges as close together as she could. After an initial jerk, the Ranger passed out again, to her relief. She was no medic, and the less he experienced of her rough handling the better.

He lay stuffed into the tree fork like a rag, but short of untying him she did not see how she could make him more comfortable. And if she did untie him, he was likely to roll out and fall. Desperately she crouched beside him, staring at his pale, drawn face. He was very bad. With a sigh she dug into the medikit, searching for something, anything she could give him that might help.

"Damn it!" she said aloud, becoming frantic. "Didn't those fools pack anything useful?"

"Droxyhyazine," he whispered, startling her into dropping the kit. Only a quick snatch saved it from falling to the ground below.

She stared at him. "What?"

"Droxyhyazine will stop it from spreading," he said, his eyes shut and his voice barely audible. "Blue nodule . . . usually clipped in with the painkillers."

Her hand closed on it in puzzlement. "You need a coagulent, not a stimulant."

"Both, then. But the droxyhyazine first."

"Look, Major, you don't—"

He gripped her wrist with a hand that was icy cold, and opened his eyes to glare at her with an arrogance that even pain and loss of blood could not diminish. "Am I cold?"

"Yes." She frowned. "You're losing blood—"

He grimaced with impatience and forced her hand against his side. "No! There! Am I cold there? You know what Omcri poison does. Did they get to me?" A shudder ran through him, and he fell back with a ragged gasp.

His torso was lean and rock hard with muscle. Several white scars marked the skin, but there was nothing more. She scowled, deciding he was delirious, and gave him a full dose of coagulent.

"You have a hole in your side big enough for me to put a fist through, but that's all I see."

He mumbled something she could not understand, but the relief in his voice was plain.

She crouched there on the limb beside him for a moment, then said, "Will you identify yourself, Major?"

He moved restlessly, but did not reply.

"Please!" She shook his arm. "It is important that I find out all I can about the Kublai. Why were you an intended sacrifice? How were you captured? And where? Can you answer any of my questions? Please try!"

Somewhere in the distance an animal screamed in death, then silence blanketed the jungle once again. The major was unconscious. Sighing, Costa crouched down on the limb with her back against the main trunk and gingerly stretched out her wounded leg. It throbbed viciously, but she made no move to attend to her hurts or even to dig through the pack for rations. Exhaustion washed over her. The man was probably dying; by dawn she would be alone in the wild, always hostile jungle.

The sharp bite of a needlewing jerked her awake. She sat up, wincing at the crick in her neck, and exclaimed in anger as she realized she had fallen asleep with the glowlight shining wastefully in her lap. Another needlewing bit viciously. She slapped at it and dug out a spare tunic from the pack. Her singlet was glued unpleasantly to her skin, and the failing light of the torch made the sweat shimmer on her bare arms like drops of oil. The pinprick on her right forearm had become an angry spot circled faintly with a thin dark line. Alarmed, Costa touched it hesitantly. The skin was cold and slightly withered as though it had received a freeze burn.

Omcri poison? She regarded the major as she pulled on the oversized tunic. Then at the buzz of more needlewings, she hastily switched off the light.

For an instant the darkness made her feel as though she had been swallowed by something feral. A dozen different musks marking territories warred with the fetid scent of rotting earth, yet when it stirred the warm breeze brought her the clean, spicy smell of muyar leaves. By feel she fumbled through the pack and managed to pour herself a welcome cup of cold gel.

The weight of the communicator on her belt recalled her at last to her duty, and she was just thumbing it on when the major moaned.

"Water?"

Guiltily she choked on the last swallow of her gel. Switching the glowlight back on, she poured out more and held the cup awkwardly to his lips. He gulped avidly, then coughed and spat part of it out.

She grinned. "I know. The taste is something you learn to ignore. Drink it all. It's full of supplements."

He obeyed her, grimacing, then let his head fall weakly back. His eyes were dark hollows in the muted light, and a clammy sweat glistened on his forehead.

"Identify yourself."

She looked at him. "That was my request first, Major."

He shrugged. "I wear a Ranger's uniform with the stripes of a major on it. That's enough data on me for now. Who are you, and what planet is this?"

She didn't like being on the receiving end of an interrogation, but she supposed, considering the fate that had been recently intended for him, that he deserved to have a few of his questions answered.

"This is Playworld. I am Lieutenant Costa, of the Planet Patrol. From appearances, the Kublai of Drugh intended to offer you as an illegal sacrifice in the ancient ruins of Kanta, which are located about fifteen kilometers from this point."

He frowned, obviously trying to fight off his weakness. "And you rescued me? But how did you know—"

"The expedition was attacked and massacred this afternoon. The Kublai appears to have been abducted. In searching the remains of the camp I discovered you."

"Oh." His eyes flickered. "Lucky chance, then. Thank you, Lieutenant."

"No, it was *not* lucky chance," she said through gritted teeth. "The Kublai was set up for today's attack. And as squad leader, I am responsible for his safety. Now, identify yourself, Major, and tell me how you came to be in that box."

He laughed weakly. "Report to a local Pepe? Slinny-loo,

you are out of your mind. I don't fall under your jurisdiction."

Her eyes heated to a bright, hard topaz. She glared at him, swallowing down the insult because she had to, and thumbed on her communicator to far range.

In the distance an orph bellowed to a chorus of answers. The moon, so renowned for its beauty, hung far overhead as a pale, useless sliver, but the wind had risen slightly, lifting some of the oppressive heat.

"Squad four-niner to Beros Central."

"Don't report in!" he said sharply enough to make himself wince.

"Why?" She lowered the communicator to look at him suspiciously. "Since I have no jurisdiction over you, Major, perhaps you will find my commander—"

"No," he said through his teeth. "This is a security matter."

She frowned in exasperation. "You can't slap security over this. Squad four-niner to Beros Central—"

"Don't be a fool! This isn't some common tourist you've lost and must report in—"

"There are no common tourists on Playworld," she said, losing her patience. "But, yes, all the more reason to report in to Janal. Someone has got to get out here before the carrion eaters remove all clues of who these attackers were. A team needs to be dispatched after the Kublai. And the ports have to be sealed. We—"

"He won't be taken off-planet."

"You sound very sure."

"Does Playworld have Kanta archives?"

"Yes, a socio-religious study group was given permission last year to come in along with a team of archaeologists. But the origin of Kanta temple worship has nothing to do with—"

"It has everything to do with this. Stop meddling in things you do not understand." He tried to sit up and failed. "Why am I trussed up like someone's dinner?"

"So you won't fall out of the tree." She shone the light briefly into his face and saw the sheen of fever there. Needlewings swarmed in, and she slapped violently as she boosted her communicator and tried again.

Finally a crackle of static answered her.

"This is Beros Central, four-niner. Limited communications from this mark."

A low beep sounded, infuriating her as she realized she had been relegated automatically to a drone connection. Throwing aside caution and code regulations, she said tersely:

"Emergency priority to Janal. Mark: Kublai abducted. Mark: four-niner expedition destroyed. Repeat: four-niner expedition destroyed. Respond priority requested."

Static replied, and she grimaced impatiently as she waited for the message to be routed. Janal was probably at home in bed. But, by Demos, if she got hooked up to that idiot subordinate . . .

"Lieutenant?" Janal's clipped, unmistakable voice responded faster than she had expected.

"Lieutenant, you're writing your death warrant if you mention me," said the Ranger very softly.

"Commander, this is four-niner," she said without glancing at him. She rubbed her gritty eyes and wished for stolid Duval at her side now, Duval and Puce and Rebo.

"Costa, switch to open channel beta."

Costa jerked to alertness. "Commander, I do not advise. Monitored communications—"

"Disregard and switch, Lieutenant."

She had no choice but to comply, uneasiness crawling through her gut.

"Now, what the devil is going on out there?" demanded Janal, suddenly coming in much more plainly. "I thought Central could depend on you to keep that expedition out of trouble."

"Uh, sir!" she responded blankly, disconcerted by the oddness of that remark. Janal must know he was being snooped, and if so, he was warning her in the only way he could.

"Is Mah Bessam there? Put him on!"

"That's a negative, Commander. The Mah has apparently been abducted along with the Kublai."

"The *sule* of the Kublai's guard?"

"Dead. Everyone else is dead, sir. However, I did find an officer of the Rangers inside the box marked for the official sacrifice—"

"What was that?" he asked through a sudden blast of static. "Repeat transmission."

She frowned, her uneasiness growing. Interference on an open channel usually meant someone was monitoring it. The attackers had obviously thought they left no survivors. Was she now informing *them* otherwise? "Sir, on this channel I prefer not to—"

"That was an order, Lieutenant!"

Sighing, she relayed all that had happened. "As for this major, sir, he refuses to identify himself or explain—"

"Put him on."

She pulled herself upright, teetering slightly on the branch, to hand the communicator to the Ranger. But his eyes were shut, sunk in deeply in a face that had gone gray.

"Major!" She shook him in annoyance, but he made no response.

"I find it hard to credit such a report . . ." Janal was saying through another burst of static. ". . . unlikely. The Kublai had cleared all points of the ceremony with our regulations. Where is this Ranger, Costa? Put him on, if he exists."

"I'm sorry, sir," she had to say. "He's unconscious and severely wounded. Sir, please. This massacre must be investigated as soon as—"

"Yes, massacre is a very good term for it," said Janal coldly, clipping the words. "Did you sell the planned coordinates of the expedition to the Omcri in the wineshop, Lieutenant?"

"Sir!" She gasped, the accusation hitting her like a punch in the stomach.

"That expedition was the only one cleared for Jungle Sector C. No one could have possibly tracked you so quickly or so easily had they not been given the coordinates. I realize that you've been bitterly disappointed in your ambitions, Lieutenant, but I thought the Directors could count on your loyalty. Instead you have permitted a small personal setback to destroy your good sense. Not only have you exchanged the safety of an important personage for your own gain, but you have sacrificed the lives of your squad as well."

"Commander, I—"

"You will of course be stripped of all rank and privilege as soon as you return to Beros. At that time I expect you to surrender yourself to security for trial. Also, you will—"

Costa thumbed off the communicator with a snarl, her insides heaving as the hurt and bitter anger plunged deep. She stared blindly at the communicator for a moment, then smashed it to bits with the butt of her strifer.

"Wasn't that a bit drastic?"

Her head jerked up to find the major's eyes glittering at her. She started to lash out at him, then threw the ruined communicator into her pack with force. "Janal set me up. For years he was my mentor, almost a father to me. He knows I would never betray my duty. *He knows!*"

"But you were tempted?"

She stiffened. "Ranger, you dare too much! A warrior is tempted often, but seldom bites. You, on the other hand, have many things to account for. You are here on a non-Commonwealth planet without authority. Your physical condition may gain you some leniency for this infraction of treaty, but when I take you back to Beros, *you* can stand in the Hall of Accusations."

His eyes, opaque and smudged into deep shadows by pain, never faltered from hers. "But you aren't taking me back, are you? Because you aren't going back yourself."

Blood thundered in her ears, and she bared her teeth grimly. "I will not be framed by those *flin,* whoever they are! No, Ranger. I will not go back until I have found the Kublai and my justification."

A mirthless smile just barely pulled at his lips. "Good. Those who are out in the cold rarely fail, do they, Lieutenant?"

"No," she replied and bleakly switched off the glowlight.

CHAPTER FOUR

Jillian Nogales hastened down the deserted Street of Souls, afraid of the dark pools of shadow where anything might lurk in this hour before dawn, but determined to let nothing stop her. The silence was absolute as though only death lay cold within the windowless buildings lining the stone-paved street. And in that unnatural quiet her straining ears could clearly hear the soft whir of the suspensors artfully concealed beneath her town robe. Her hand clenched within its wide sleeve . . . concealment, artifice, dependency. How she hated this gnarled, rippled body which imprisoned her with its defects! But soon, very soon, she would be free.

Impatience clawed at her throat, but she could go no faster without upsetting the gravity balance of the suspensor which evened out her limping gait into a smooth sway. Some of her father's numerous acquaintances found her odd walk seductive. Others of more perception looked at her with pity.

She hated pity! She would kill to keep it away!

A red door glowed at her. She halted before it, panting, and rapped once. Stone grated quietly on stone as it slid aside. She lurched through, her weak heart hammering painfully against the delicate walls of its sealant, and the door grated back into place with a thud that boomed against the total darkness surrounding her. The place was cold enough to make her shiver despite her body temperature regulators, and the air she breathed in was still and ancient like that of a tomb. Was it to be *her* tomb?

Panic made her whirl back to the door, but with an effort she caught herself, forcing up her head and drawing in deep breaths until she grew calm again. No one must see her fear.

She waited another minute to make sure her resolution was like armor, then she pressed the small button on her wristband. There was no immediate response, and the darkness stood around her like a wall. But at last, just when she grew angry at the delay, a dim glowlight flickered to life before her like the opening of a blood-red eye. She squinted at the hooded shape which formed from the shadows and approached her soundlessly. It passed within centimeters of her, chilling her as the cold of its being touched the flesh of her cheeks. Her nostrils wrinkled at the musty scent of ice and dried leaves, but when the creature lifted an arm to beckon, she followed it across the blood-shadowed courtyard into a low tunnel and the flame-illumined chamber beyond.

A still figure in the umber robes of Kanta sat there. The unsteady fall of light gleamed off his shaven, blood-crossed brow and threw his face into deep shadow from which two eyes glittered with an intensity matched only by Jillian's own.

She stepped forward, funneling her nervousness into anger.

"I have been kept waiting too long," she said, her shrill voice echoing stridently off the circular archways. "My power units are seriously drained—"

"You came alone?" asked the priest in a deep voice, rough with enough menace to make her heart thump hard against the walls protecting it.

"Alone," she said, clinging to the arrogance she had adopted long ago as protection. Better that those around her should hate her than pity her, or underestimate her. "My drones wait with the lytcar."

"That which was discussed . . . you will do?"

"If you meet my price."

The priest turned his head. "Anran?"

A tall figure stepped through one of the archways, booted feet scraping grittily over the stone. He stopped beside Jillian, towering over her. His skin was extremely pallid as though no blood of any color coursed through his veins, and his eyes . . . She shivered, her heart lurching as Anran stared down at her. His eyes were two black voids. To gaze into them made her dizzy as though she were spiraling into infinity.

"Omcri," she whispered, drawing back.

The priest smiled, revealing a row of filed teeth and gums stained scarlet. "Not at all. Anran is one of the chief researchers at the Archives here. He is also a fine surgeon."

She gasped, her eyes flying back to the lean giant beside her.

"There are many ancient surgical techniques in the Kanta rituals which require study," said Anran in a toneless voice.

"You are the one?" she said doubtfully. "You are to be my

doctor? The finest physicians in the galaxy have examined me, and the result is that I now stand here at the mercy of machines. Half of my organs are artificial. I walk only through the assistance of suspensors. I represent the finest work of eminent cosmetic surgeons, neurologists, and medical engineers, and still I am nothing but a deformed mess of clanking parts subject to replacement every four months. Can you restructure me as this representative of Kanta has promised? Can you make me a whole, normal, functioning human being? I want the truth, Anran!"

Anran flinched, then regarded her with a disquieting lack of expression. "It can be done."

She flung open her town robe. "Then begin now!"

"Wait!" said the priest, rising as Anran reached out to her. "First, good lady, let us finish the business at hand. When our task is done, you may have the services of Anran. Surely, you can find within yourself the patience of a few more days."

How many? she nearly screamed, but curbed herself, drawing in several deep breaths before she could finally nod.

"Very well," she said reluctantly. "I see I have no choice."

"We do not coerce you, good lady."

"You do not have to." She lifted her chin. "What are your instructions?'

Anran turned and abruptly walked away as though he had received a dismissal.

The priest ignored his departure. "Do you know exactly where your parent has imprisoned the Kublai?"

"In our villa."

"On the northern continent?"

"No. Our villa in Beros. On the Street of Harmony, Stratum Four." She blinked, recalling the jerk from sleep as her father woke her to show her his prisoner. Until that moment she did not have the faintest inkling of how desperate Wob Nogales was to stop the Kublai's expedition from succeeding. And if he found out that she was now betraying him . . . She swayed.

"What is wrong?" The priest caught her arm with a hand that was dirty and rough enough to snag the costly fabric of her town robe.

"My heart . . ." She shut her eyes, letting herself lean upon the priest as her regulators struggled to readjust to the leap of metabolism. "I must sit down. I . . . there are spare power cells in my lytcar. Summon my drones."

The priest gave an order to one of his silent minions and dragged her to his chair. "If this is a clever ploy to betray us, good lady, you will—"

"Don't be absurd!" She gasped for breath. "What need have I to betray you?"

"You are betraying your parent. One act of treason begets another—"

"My father is taking a foolish risk. Even the neutrality laws of Playworld will not be able to protect him from extradition if he is caught abducting the Kublai."

The sound of approaching footsteps made her look up eagerly. It was R7, coming at last with the precious power cells.

Jillian glared at the priest. "Replacement requires disrobing. Where may I have privacy?"

His eyes narrowed distrustfully as he tucked his stained hands into his sleeves. "We shall vacate this chamber for a few moments only."

"It will be sufficient. Go!"

They left in silence. She drew in a desperate breath of air tainted by the faint smells of death and rot and opened her garments for R7.

"Hurry!"

The drone worked swiftly, removing her suspensors which left her sagging helplessly in the chair, and switched her power unit to auxiliary in order to remove the expended cells. She hated auxiliary with its ten short minutes of capability. Suppose R7 suddenly developed a malfunction and could not complete its task? She had been drilled in the procedure to free her from this fear. But the anxiety persisted, even to the point of convincing her that she would make a fatal mistake were she to rely on herself.

"Hurry!" she said again, gripping the stone arms of the chair. Time seemed to rush away from her, even though the rational part of her mind assured her only a few seconds had elapsed.

R7 chimed agreeably, never faltering in its work as it replaced one power cell, tested it, then replaced the other. It switched her off auxiliary, and Jillian closed her eyes as she grimly passed through that hellish moment of absolute helplessness before the new cells booted power back up to nominal levels. She felt her heart lurch, falter, then resume a strong beat. Sighing, Jillian lifted a shaking hand to her brow while R7 replaced the power cells in the suspensor units. It refitted them around her and helped her rearrange her clothing.

"Do not return to the lytcar, R7," she said. "I do not know how long I must remain here. It may be necessary to replace the power cells again."

"Accord," chimed R7, with one of the few words of vocabulary she permitted in its programming. Unlike her friends, she hated chattering drones and was never amused by their synthesized accents.

"You have recovered, good lady?" inquired the rough voice of the priest.

Jillian straightened herself at once. "Yes, but I warn you that I cannot survive many such shocks. Will this take much longer?"

"Only long enough for you to give us the plans of the villa and the exact location of the Kublai inside it."

"Never!" she said sharply. "Our security system is both elaborate and expensive. I will not give you the access code."

A scowl creased the priest's face. He came up to tower over her chair. "What games do you play?"

"No games, fool. I will bring the Kublai out."

"You?" The priest showed his filed teeth. "You, good lady, are unlikely to manage such a feat."

"My drones are programmed to obey me independently of my father's servants," she said, barely holding onto her temper. "Choose a rendezvous point. I shall exchange the Kublai there for Anran."

"You distrust us? You would not bring His Supreme Glory here?"

"The distance is too far. Neutral ground is reassuring for *both* of us."

"Cleverly spoken, lady. But I think we shall stick to our original plan."

"No!" She gestured in anger. "My father will know if the villa is breached. He will—"

"And what, good lady, will your parent do when he finds the Kublai gone without any evidence of a break-in? He will suspect you. We seek to protect you from suspicion."

She sat there, her breathing ragged with stress. "And what will he suspect when he finds his infallible security system broken?"

"Nothing is infallible," said the priest with another smile. "For your peace of mind we shall leave Omcri traces behind. Your parent has employed Omcri couriers in the past; he knows they can enter many places denied to creatures of . . . other . . . species."

She shivered at the thought of an Omcri in the house. Perhaps she had been a greater fool than Wob. Perhaps she should never have come here. But then she looked at the expended power cells in R7's hand and shuddered with loathing. No. She must be free of this useless husk of a body. She must not back away from this opportunity.

"Very well," she said slowly, frowning. "I shall have to obtain the code which unlocks the main systems. The Kublai is being held in the north wing, second floor. An additional security system has been engaged around his suite, and he is heavily drugged for his own protection."

"Excellent. Our appreciation is great, good lady, for this assistance."

She looked hard at the priest as she stood up to go. "I should be able to get the code within a day, possibly two. Do not grow impatient and doubt me."

"When you have it, do not transmit it," he said sharply, his eyes glittering at her.

She drew in a breath. "When you send someone for it, be sure Anran accompanies him. And Anran must be prepared to stay with me. I shall see that he has all the facilities he requires."

"Agreed," said the priest. He beckoned a shadowy figure forward, and with a start she recognized the pale-robed figure of an Omcri. "Now . . . To be sure you do not change your mind in the next two days, good lady . . ."

"No!" She drew back as the Omcri approached her. "Keep that thing away! I'll not change my mind. Fools! R7, protect me—"

The Omcri lifted a gloved hand, and R7 froze in mid-step, internal parts whirring loudly in frustration against whatever invisible force held it. She smelled overloading circuitry and screamed desperately:

"R7! Stop protection! Cancel!"

The drone shut down, and the Omcri came toward her. She backed away, shaking her head.

"This is unnecessary! I came to you freely. I have too much at stake in this to— *No!*"

Her scream echoed shrilly through the chamber as the Omcri caught her forearm. A crystalline knife flashed out, then paused in midair over her wrist.

"Why are you stopping?" demanded the priest. "Cut her!"

Jillian stood there, prisoner to the crushing strength of that gloved hand, her heart thudding with erratic violence. Her eyes could not leave the knife poised above her. There was a certain sinister beauty to it. The blade, curved and hollow, shimmered whitely with the luminescent substance within. *Omcri poison,* she thought and cried out again.

Slowly the powerful fingers uncurled from her arm. She yanked free and backed away, trembling uncontrollably.

"Omcri!" shouted the priest in anger. "She must bleed. Her blood must mingle with the poison in two threads of scarlet and white, entwined as her will must be entwined to ours."

The Omcri turned somewhat jerkily to face him. "Her will not desired. That which this one serves commands it not."

"I am whom you serve, Omcri!"

"Not so, Archus," said the dual-timbred voice. Faceless and implacable, the Omcri stood in the center of the chamber and spread its hands wide. "Your hour, small. That which is greater, comes soon."

"Then give me the knife," said Archus, his face a hellish mask in the flaring light. He snatched the weapon from the Omcri's hand and rushed at Jillian.

Frozen, she watched him come, seeing the madness in his eyes and the spittle spraying through his bared teeth. The jaded boredom of her life seemed suddenly a small complaint. Even her mechanical body, loathesome as it was, seemed precious. The whisper of her breathing regulator hissed in and out, in and out, while almost leisurely, the Omcri turned and spread its arms wide. Twin points of light, green and incandescent, flashed from the black void beneath the cowl, and with a shrill scream the priest crumpled at Jillian's feet. The knife shattered on the dirty stone, leaking the poison which hissed and steamed a cold mist into the air.

The others fled the chamber, leaving Jillian alone with the Omcri which glided forward now. She stumbled back, only the support of her suspensors saving her from falling, and pressed her back against the leprous wall. A thin finger of the poison ran under the outflung arm of Archus, and his body twitched convulsively.

"Archus." The Omcri lifted its palm, and Archus suddenly jerked upright as though pulled by invisible strings. He stood there with his umber robe slipping half off his shoulder, his head lolling horribly to one side. His eyes were open and sightless; his tongue protruded in death.

Jillian pressed a hand to her throat, unable to breathe despite the steady hiss of her regulators. The edges of her consciousness began to fray.

"Are you g-going to k-kill me, too?"

The Omcri did not look at her. "Without necessity, nothing is done."

Her panic lessened. She swallowed, realizing the Omcri had saved her twice now. "Thank you," she said, straightening. As long as she did not look at the corpse of Archus standing in front of her, she could piece her confidence back together. "I am glad you killed the priest."

"Actions can be undone." The Omcri dropped its hand abruptly. Archus swayed as though his body would crumple again, then stiffened. The priest lifted his head, blinked, and instantly closed his gaping mouth.

Jillian bit down hard on a scream. Something within her cardioactivator abruptly burned out. She felt the grind before she heard it. Her heartbeat skittered, and pain knifed through her abdomen. *There are other ways to die than by an assassin's blade,* she thought, clutching herself as Archus turned blankly away from her and walked from the chamber. His eyes were black voids, as Anran's had been.

Her head lifted. "You saved my life, Omcri," she said with a shaking voice that failed to achieve its usual arrogance.

"Will you now let me go? Will you let me have Anran as agreed?"

"No bargain is kept now," said the Omcri, advancing upon her.

"But you must keep it!" she cried, raising clenched fists. "I must have that surgery! I can't go on living like this—"

"Life is of least importance. Reveal true location of Kublai. Previous lie unacceptable."

"No! I won't! Do you hear? I'll tell you nothing!"

The wall jammed against her back, and she nearly slipped on the dust-slick stone underfoot. Her eyes flicked back and forth across the room in search of anything, any weapon which might save her. But it was useless, and her soul despaired at the futility of trying.

"Don't kill me. Please don't do what you d-did to them," she babbled as the Omcri grasped her shoulders.

She felt her own frailty beneath its strength. The coldness hanging upon it seemed to freeze her eyes open, locking them upon the void that should have been its face. And all the expensive training in how to erect mental protection and privacy barriers failed to help her as a cold, black finger of thought probed into the recesses of her brain.

Wob Nogales could not sleep. He tossed and turned, dipping and floating on the elaborate suspensor bed which kept his massive bulk comfortably in midair. The entire past week had been sleepless, but that was natural. He could go round the clock whenever he had a deal on line. Round the clock . . . odd how expressions remained in use long after anyone understood why people used to think of time as circular. But, nevertheless, the deal was completed and here he floated, still wide awake.

He considered worry as a factor. Pros and cons had been weighed. No, he would still have ordered the Kublai abducted if he had this month over again. The men he hired were professionals, smoothly efficient, leaving no survivors in their wake, long since paid and exited off-planet. No one outside the villa knew of the Kublai's presence here, and no one inside had any reason to care at all about the fate of a petty ruler from a system parsecs away. There should be no worry.

Still, he could not sleep. It was not hunger; it was not overindulgence of stimulants. His newest doctor had scared him sufficiently last month to make him follow his prescribed diet. He did not need a woman. And he *was* sleepy. Therefore, nothing of a physical nature was keeping him awake.

Guilt perhaps.

He snorted forcefully enough to send himself dipping toward the floor. Why should he feel guilty? That damnable little Kublai had cost him plenty. Coming here with some ridiculous superstition and stirring up all his Ishut workers as a consequence. Wob had enough trouble normally from the Kanta priests inciting his Ishuts to rebel from the hand that kept them occupied decently, clothed, sheltered, and fed with tranquilized food so that they had some peace from their normal instability. At least with the Kublai's expedition out of the way, he needn't fear being shut down by the safety board. The whole problem was over, or would be once he got the Kublai off-planet. And he had a plan worked out for that, too.

In the meantime, he had to keep the Kublai hidden somewhere. His villa here in Beros seemed ideally bold. After all, Commander Janal of the Planet Patrol had dined here tonight along with seventy other guests of prominence and distinction. As long as he did not act guilty, no guilt would be attached to him.

But the more he thought about it, the less he liked the idea of having the Kublai right here under the same roof with him. Jillian, whose advice he relied upon, had proven to be particularly cross and unhelpful. She was probably going through one of her moods, or else suffering a side-effect from a new drug. But he didn't like her reaction to his little surprise tonight. And perhaps *that* was keeping him awake.

As soon as word of the Kublai's abduction reached Drugh, those inflammatory idiots might decide to attack the city, providing they could get through the planetary defenses. Or, more probable, the Kanta priests might start a search aside from the ceeps'. It would take only one hint, only one slip from his servants to bring everything down.

Wob sat up, rubbing his skull with his knuckles. He reached out for the intercom, then pulled back. It was useless to disturb Jillian again. She was already angry at him. If he woke her twice in one night, she might not speak to him for weeks. He sighed and switched off the suspensor field, sinking gently down to the cushioned floor. Maneuvering his bulk upright, he grunted and threw on a robe before padding out of his suite in the northern wing. Lights flashed on in startled illumination ahead of him as he made his way up into the central portion of the house.

The Kublai, a mere slip of a boy, lay in Jillian's laboratory on a white slab, smiling in his drugged sleep. His ruddy complexion had paled to an unhealthy pink, and his cheeks had sunk in slightly, but otherwise he looked fine to Wob. A wide wristband of gold set with emeralds glittered on one slim wrist. Wob examined it, mentally calculating its worth on the open market, and snorted. Jillian had a boxful of trinkets worth far more.

"May the breath of Hyata wither the flesh from your bones!"

Startled by that venomous whisper, Wob jerked around and knocked a tray of beakers to the floor. The crash echoed through the sterile room, and one of the guards outside poked his head in. Wob waved angrily at him.

"Get the physician."

The guard vanished, and Wob glared at the man stuffed and shackled inside a specimen cage. Bessam's fine clothes hung on him in shreds, and the lines of rank painted on his face were smeared across his torn cheek and mixed with dried blood. He glared back at Wob with bloodshot eyes.

"You are the one behind this," he rasped in a cracked voice ruined from swallowing strifer fire. "May worms consume your sperm, you great mountain of filth!"

Wob's eyes narrowed. He stepped up to the cage and bent slightly to peer inside. "The drug was not supposed to wear off."

Bessam loosed a bitter laugh, then coughed harshly. "I am sworn to the protection of the Kublai. Who will watch over His Glory if I sleep?"

Wob frowned, angry at this foul-up. He could be identified now. And this furious little scrap did not look like the sort whose silence could be bought. Still, he might try.

"No harm will come to you—"

"Harm? Hah! Do not all my living parts burn inside from what I have breathed this day? Have I not seen my Kublai defiled by the touch of violent hands and by the intrusion of chemicals into the Sacred Body? Am I not cramped into torture by this imprisonment in a *cage* for an animal, so that my limbs scream and my organs die from being crushed? I have soiled myself, and I suffer thirst. And you wish to speak platitudes unto me? Begone, fat thing!" He spat fiercely.

Wob jerked back, one broad hand shaking as it drew out a cloth to dab at the stain on his robe. He did not turn his head as the physician came hurrying in.

"You erred, Toine," he said curtly, his eyes burning down into Bessam's rebellious face.

The physician exclaimed in exasperation. "I do not understand this. The effects of mexabenthol are well documented. He should not be—"

"But he is!" shouted Wob. "Check this one." He pointed at the Kublai. "Make sure there are no more mistakes. And get him ready for travel. Guards!" He moved toward the door while the physician hastily seized the Kublai's limp wrist.

"Sir!"

Wob's angry eyes probed the noncommittal ones of the guard. "I want a lytcar, unmarked, ready to fly out within the hour. Take Toine and his patient to my lodge on Lilliput. Keep them there until I send you further instructions. Make sure Toine understands *clearly* that if the Kublai wakes up, the doctor will be Ishut meat."

The guard grinned. "Sir! And the other one?"

Wob's lips clamped together. "Kill Bessam al-zk. I don't care how. And put him through city disposal. It'll take the ceeps weeks to find all the pieces."

By then, sleep was completely impossible. He watched dawn break over the sleeping city from his observation dome atop the villa, his eyes brooding and resentful as he stared north toward his empire lying beyond the gilt-banded horizon. He had carved his fortune with sweat, daring, and a good gambler's instinct. No one else ran amusement parks equal to his. No one else could draw in the crowds like his attractions. It didn't matter that the Directors of Playworld looked down their noses at his humble origins as an engineer and leased him the bleakest, least favored continent on the planet. He had made his parks desirable to the galaxy just the same, and even the Directors could not complain of their share of his profit margin.

One last safety infraction, and all of it would be gone. Forfeited right into the hands of the Directors, to be leased to someone else. Damn those superstitious Ishuts and their inability to keep their minds on their work! And damn the Kanta! That cult was the real root of his problems. He had accepted its interference thus far, despite the money it cost him to meet the priests' demands for the workers. But he would not accept the loss of his empire.

The sun lifted itself over the horizon, a vast brazen ball spilling rays of light over the domed top of Beros, casting fantastic shadows through the fabled lava canyons south of the city. Wob pushed away from the balcony and returned inside to summon his assistant. By the time Ezbell's lytcar landed on the grounds, Wob had seated himself on the garden terrace with his breakfast before him. He watched critically as a drone dropped live scammions into boiling water there at the table and fished them out seconds later to arrange upon his plate.

"Ezbell," he said curtly, not looking up from his observation of this process. The least mistake made the scammions too tough to eat. "I want you to arrange another incident for me."

Ezbell paled and nervously slipped a green tablet into his mouth. "Indeed, sir?"

"You recall the infamous Kanta ruins? We toured the opening of the Archives last spring."

"Yes," said Ezbell warily, sitting down on the other side of the table and shaking his head as the drone started to bring him a plate. "They city is extensive . . . a remarkable site of lost culture."

"Quite remarkable," said Wob coldly. "Hire a demolition team."

"Sir?"

"Blow up those ruins. Especially the temple foundation. And don't spare the Archives."

Ezbell blinked. With his domed head and lashless eyes, he looked skinned and stupid. But of course, he was neither.

Wob tried to be patient while Ezbell struggled to master once again his Ecletian heritage of perpetual shock over human violence.

"Sir, the ruins are . . . ruined already."

"I want whatever is standing toppled. I want dust made of those stones. I don't care about heritage or archaeological loss. I don't want that place left in existence. Is that clear?"

"Quite clear," said Ezbell faintly and stood up. "How soon do you want this done?"

"Early. Now. Before tourists or researchers or whoever is stupid enough to spend time down there burrowing around with superstitious cult rituals shows up at the place. There's no point in having a lot of innocent people killed." Wob's thick fingers gripped the edge of the table. "Mind, I don't care if a few less priests exist in the world."

"Understood." Ezbell blinked in calculation while one boneless hand nervously smoothed the front of his pleated vesture. "It should be relatively simple to locate an implementation team of small scruple. I shall relay instructions immediately."

"Good." Wob smiled for the first time all morning. "Also, about that merger with the Delex Company. I don't think we should jump too quickly— Yes, S9, what is it?"

"Forgive intrusion, sir," chimed the drone, which bore the markings of one of Jillian's personal servants. "Mistress not found in suite."

"Oh?" Wob grunted. "She's up early today. Now, Ezbell, about that—"

"Forgive," interrupted the drone. "Missing. Time for injection past. Cannot be found. Instructions please."

"What?" Wob rose to his feet with a violence that nearly overturned the table. For a moment worry squeezed his heart, then he shook himself. "Nonsense," he said roughly, glaring at the drone. "She's off in the conservatory perhaps. Search for her, idiot."

"Search completed. Not found. Personal lytcar gone from hangar."

"What? Damn the girl, what's gotten into her now? All right, S9, I'll deal with it. Ezbell, go on to the office; we'll discuss the Delex people later. And if the bank reports any large

requests from Jillian today, let me know. If she's run away from home again, she'll need funds. I've already closed off her accounts in Antares, so surely she'll have enough sense not to go there again. F12! Call Commander Janal and report her missing. Tell him to close the space port. And, Ezbell, put a clamp on published ceep reports. If she turns up in some low-grade simulator house on the lower strata, I don't want it publicized all over Beros. Damn her. I don't need another psychological flare-up from her now. S9." He stood on the terrace and shrugged his big shoulders with a helplessness that no amount of rage could dissipate. "Have you checked to see if she took anything? Does she have her medicines with her? Is R7 also missing?"

"Will check."

S9 vanished, leaving Wob to close his eyes while the sun lifted over the trees and struck his back with heat.

Three days later Jillian took her first shaky steps unaided by suspensors. "Look at me! Look at me!" she cried in delight, catching herself against a table in Anran's laboratory. The gloomy chambers and rotting damp about her no longer mattered. She was sore all over, and every beat of her heart caused her pain, but it was beating unaided for the first time in her life. The hope of a normal life was finally becoming real. She turned to Anran, her face glowing.

"This is wonderful! I'm going to walk back to you now." She launched herself away from the support of the table, and carefully negotiated the ten steps across the room to where Anran stood watching, his white face expressionless as usual. She held out her hand to him, laughing in her triumph. He guided her to a chair equipped with monitoring equipment.

"Rest now," he said. "Unnecessary strain is against the purpose."

"Yes." She nodded. The Omcri had not approached her again since that horrible violation of her mind. She refused to think about the creature or what she had done by betraying her father to it. The rewards of Anran's incredible surgical skills justified any action she had taken. Soon she would be whole, and then she would leave this boring planet for the exciting life she deserved. She drew in an eager breath. "Anran, how soon can you operate again? You said you would be able to replace my mechanical organs with real ones, but—"

"It will be done as promised," he said tonelessly. "In—"

A distant boom shook the walls and ceiling, causing a damp, scabrous patch to fall to the floor near her. Jillian looked at Anran in alarm. "What was that?"

But he was already walking away. She struggled out of the chair. "Anran!"

A second explosion, this one very close, threw her to the floor. Dazed, she pulled herself up, her new, still-fragile heart pounding. The floor was vibrating beneath her. She heard a loud crack, and a wall crashed in a cloud of dust that choked her.

"Anran!" she screamed, coughing and unable to see. She crouched, helpless and panic-stricken as the floor continued to shift. Desperately she started crawling forward on her hands and knees, sobbing with fear, and nearly suffocated in the dust. More stone crashed about her, half burying her legs. Screaming from the pain, she tried to drag herself free, but she was caught. She twisted desperately, crying out at the cruel injustice of an earthquake just when life was so close within her grasp.

"Please," she sobbed, falling back weakly. "No. No! Wob! *Father, help me!*"

But the roof collapsed over her in deafening thunder, raining down stone and rubble that crushed and buried her beneath the endless weight of a fallen city destroyed once again, and for Jillian at last there remained only the long, cold nothingness of death.

CHAPTER FIVE

The world shimmered beneath water, sometimes shadow cool and serene, other times sparkling with diamond skips of sunshine. The Ranger lay propped up on wadded tent remains and watched the girl frowning as she wove thorn-stripped vines into some kind of net. She was unaware of his scrutiny, but then it seemed hardly the observant form of study his instructors had drilled into him so long ago. He floated back and away, sometimes seeing her as she sat cross-legged on the broad tree branch with queer balloon-faced animals gibbering in the branches overhead, and sometimes seeing companions of other days and other worlds.

The tree itself was very peculiar. He wondered if it was indeed vegetation or a constructed edifice. The branch supporting both of them possessed a breadth of at least three meters jutting out from a wall of a trunk. It was hollow, he thought, for he often heard creatures scrabbling about inside when he let his head rest against the smooth white bark. Vivid green leaves as broad as two hand spans and veined underneath in purple swayed in the hot air, giving off a pleasant scent whenever they rubbed together. He closed his eyes with a smile and dreamed of the cloved bread of his childhood.

But all the while the girl occupied herself, restless as a caged cadet before a battle. She wove one net, and when she had finished it she began stripping more vines. She saved the thorns, which were as long as his finger, thick at the base, and curved into vicious barbed tips. Her build was small, but compact and strong. She moved with the competence of a born athlete. Her face was narrow beneath the cheekbones and framed by sleek black hair cropped off all around just below her ears. A thin, coiled braid perched coyly over one eye, but it did not have a feminine look to it. He watched her, fascinated by her queer yellow eyes which almost constantly changed color in betrayal of thought and mood, ranging from fiery amber to the chilliest blue-green. She had a way of suddenly lifting her head to the wind as though listening to the steady chuffing of search sleds beyond his range of hearing, and when she listened she grew completely still, not just in movement but in every facet of her being as though even her heartbeat ceased for a second.

He could not remember her name, but he could remember that he had promised to kill her. He slept, waiting for the moment.

Fifteen days later, the soul-piercing howl of a juubjb quavered through the air as the sun slipped behind the wall of trees, sending the last, almost horizontal rays of glittering gold motes dancing off leaf and branch before deep purple shadows lengthened along the rotting jungle floor. Wind, salt-tanged and cool, sliced through the oppressive air to strike Costa's face. She drew in a sharp breath and abruptly hooked the hunting net on her belt before grasping a sawtooth vine and hauling herself up into a spreading tree. In its high branches, she still could not see through the tangled jungle, but the scent of the sea carried strongly on the air.

The mournful juubjb called again, and a flock of carpals screamed across the sky, arrowing down in formation through the treetops, sending lesser fliers fluttering desperately out of the way. Costa's ears fanned out slightly beneath her sweat-soaked hair, straining to hear beyond the clatter of the jungle. Did she imagine a low, cadenced booming or was it truly there?

Pulling off her tunic, she knotted it around her waist by the sleeves and swung out on a vine with a lithe ripple of muscle. In minutes she had recaptured the rhythm of swinging from one tree to the next. Vines were scarce, thinning as the tree themselves shortened and untangled. She snaked out her line, using grappler and stakes with rapid precision. Her spirits rose with the exercise. After days of slogging along on the ground, pushing and fighting a way through the dense undergrowth while the major struggled behind her, to swing out was a delicious freedom.

The jungle ended suddenly, falling away in a sheer cliff to the rumbling sea below. Costa clung to a slender branch, her heart thudding and sweat streaming off her body as she gazed out across an endless expanse of foam-tossed water. The sun was already below the horizon, sinking with a magnificent blaze of cerulean, gold, and purple. To the right she could just make out a dark curve of land. Lilliput Island! It had to be!

She grinned at her own unerring powers of navigation and slapped her rumbling stomach. Hunger no longer mattered. Tomorrow she would have a bellyful of food. Duval always married good cooks.

She wiped her brow with her forearm, only to wince and quickly lower the arm. The cold ache always grew worse with darkness. For a moment she stared at the widening black ring and angry puff of flesh, then shifted her eyes away. She did not know what to do for it; she did not want to think about how the poison was affecting her.

Lights winked on in the distance along the edge of the island. Shivering in the lash of spray and wind, she crouched there in the swaying boughs until twilight blurred the separation of sky and sea. Then she gathered herself to go back into the hot mouth of the jungle. The temptation not to return to the major was nearly as strong as the comer beam the searchers had used to try to bring them out of hiding.

She frowned as she shifted a stake and threw the line to the next tree. At first, while she concealed herself and the unconscious major in the vast hollow trunk of a muyar tree from the first sweeps of the search sleds, it had not been too difficult to believe that if he lived they would strike some point of trust. That belief had faded quickly once he began to recover. He gave her no trust at all, sneered at the fact that she had saved his life, and refused to answer any of her questions. And there was a cold cast to his keen blue eyes which aroused her own distrust. He reminded her of a deadly couchkin, scarlet-banded and coiled to strike. He was the first human she had ever feared.

And yet he was a Ranger, a member of that band of heroes she had worshiped all her life. The Rangers were one of the few elite branches of the Fleet to maintain a tradition of complete integrity. No one fought harder, upheld law and honor more, or stood more firmly in a place of respect. He should be an authority she could look to for help, like Commander Janal. Only Janal had tarnished, too. If his search sleds found her now, she doubted she would ever reach Beros alive.

She paused in the rustling darkness to find her bearings. A

sawtooth sliced her cheek, and she flinched, lifting a hand at once to wipe the blood away. She must move quickly back to camp and get herself inside the beams of the sonic protector before predators caught the scent of fresh blood and made quarry of her.

The dim flicker of a glowlight shone out for a moment, then winked off. Costa drew in a grateful breath and moved toward it. The major must be hungry, she thought as she pulled on her tunic and belted it with a yank. Thus far, they had traveled together in an unspoken truce. But she was not sure how much longer it would last.

"If you go back to Beros you're a fool," he had said on the first day of their journey. He took the medikit from her and rummaged through its small supply of drugs and bandages. "No, I think I am better informed on what injections I should have than you."

"Very well. Cure yourself. I am unskilled in medic lore. I have done nothing but keep you alive for the past five days."

He looked up at her, his eyes intensely blue and far from grateful. "You should have slit my throat and headed out of here at first light."

"Murder a Ranger?" She stared at him in shock.

"I see the inhabitants of Playworld are reared with a strict sense of morality." His lips quirked slightly. "Left me in the other tree, then, for the searchers to find. You could be far away from here."

It angered her to be thought so ruthless, yet at the same time she wished she had been. "Do not judge others by your standards, Ranger. You have answers I want. Why should I go until I have them?"

"You can't squat here in a tree forever. Where's the next city away from Beros?"

She shook her head, smiling a little at his ignorance. "Beros is *the* city. Everything else is little towns or village clusters or agricultural stations. Playworld has less than three million inhabitants. The rest are tourists."

He mouthed a curse. "There are no other spaceports? No other communication centers?"

"Playworld was not organized with a back door according to military specifications. People come here to enjoy themselves." She watched exasperation chase across his hawkish face. "No, Major, I will aim for the coast. I have friends there—"

"Like your commander?"

"No." Bitterness welled up in her eyes. "Better. I hope."

"And then?"

"And then I get my squad together and I go after the Kublai. It's the only way to clear myself." She paused to swallow the roughness from her voice and glared at him. "And you? You aren't my prisoner. Now that you can walk, you're free to go in any direction."

He shrugged, his eyes gleaming like the blue agate beach pebbles found on Maulau Island. "I'm not a fool, Lieutenant. You know the jungle, and I don't."

Costa blinked against the darkness, letting the memory of that conversation fade from her mind. In the morning the sea spray would strike them in the face. None of her expectations of time overcoming his curt hostility had been fulfilled. Her hand brushed against the empty net hanging from her belt, and she grimaced, not looking forward to sitting in hungry silence in the darkness until it came time to sleep with her cutter in her hand. The ration packets were long since expended, and hunger was dulling her sense of alertness.

She moved cautiously, freezing as the light flicked on again. As soon as it vanished, she lowered herself quietly down a vine. She had his scent in her nostrils now and she made a stealthy way through the undergrowth, her wrist held hard by her strifer. When she judged herself close enough, she braced her feet and waited with two eyelids snapped firmly down.

The light came on a third time, shining right in her face as she stood less than a meter from him. He jumped to his feet with an oath, reaching for his belt. Costa dived into the undergrowth and rolled. But he held his fire.

"Lieutenant?" His voice held a mixture of exasperation and relief.

She stood up slowly, brushing crushed leaves from her clothes. "Fool. I told you to wait in the trees. Always get in the trees when darkness comes." She jerked her hand in a gesture. "Up!"

He made no movement, remaining a black shadow behind

the light which would have blinded her had she not kept two eyelids down. "Your face is bleeding."

She frowned, surprised by this small sign of concern. "A scratch. But when the kicats come to lick it we had both better be high out of reach. Climb, Major!"

"I tried to earlier and fell. I think I have damaged myself."

"Mercy of Moii! How badly?" she asked, pushing her way out of the bush to stride up to him.

He shifted his weight behind the light, hopping a little as though he favored an ankle. She bent, then screamed with rage as he sprang and she realized, too late, that the hop was a prelude to a *kaisin* kick. Had his heel connected with her jaw, the force of contact would have snapped her neck. She threw herself up ahead of the blow, grunting as his foot glanced off her chest and took half her wind with it. Her mind raced as she dodged once more. Were he any other opponent, she would go straight in like a fierce slum fighter, aiming for his barely healed side. But she dared not risk getting within his reach. She scrambled back to gain herself a second of time, and flicked out the blades of her cutter.

He tackled her, driving her to the ground before she could throw. She twisted desperately so as not to land completely beneath his weight and then squirmed like a wild thing, chopping at his face in an effort to break free. The glowlight lay on the ground in the midst of their struggle, jostled light bouncing crazily off the fleshy, well-glossed leaves. He threw himself across her, grunting as her knee drove into his ribs, and pinned her arms to the ground.

The pressure of his grip on her poisoned arm shot a white lance of agony through her. She screamed, her body arching with the pain, and saw again the Omcri enfolding itself about her, smothering her with cold, the seared, frosted breath flowing into her lungs, the alien mind probing her thoughts.

"Omcri!" she screamed, her eyes blazing sightlessly in their sockets. *"Iy ket! Iy ket!"*

Only dimly did she perceive the Ranger rolling off of her. He shouted something she could not hear and yanked her up by the arms, shaking her. The pain lanced through her again, worse this time. A thousand times worse. She blacked out.

• • •

Awakening was slow and painful. Costa opened her eyes to the gray light of dawn and found herself sitting upright in the fork of a spindly tree, lashed to the main trunk with her own line. Without thought she jerked against her bonds, and nearly toppled out as they loosened.

"Easy!"

Twigs snapped overhead and the whole tree shook as he climbed awkwardly down and balanced himself on a limb at her eye level. Pressing a hand to his side, and holding gingerly onto a sawtooth vine with the other, he frowned at her.

"Lieutenant?" His voice boomed at her, making her wince. "Costa?"

She turned her head away, shutting her eyes as the world spun. "Kill," she mumbled. A rope burn smarted across her shoulder. She opened one eye and saw fuzzily that she wore only her singlet, breeches, and boots. Her belt, weapons, and tunic were gone. She stiffened, snapping to half-alertness. "You! Take my out . . . Comer worse. Kill me no why?" She shook her head, dimly aware she was making no sense. Her tongue seemed like glue in her mouth.

"It's just reaction to droxyhyazine," he said, balancing precariously. He grasped her chin and tilted her head back to force something into her mouth. "Chew, Costa. Chew!"

He rattled her jaw until she slowly got the idea. The substance was rubbery, wet, and foul tasting. Abruptly she jerked her head free and spat it out.

"Raw carpal! Moii!" For a moment she thought she would vomit, then her stomach settled down and she sent the Ranger a bleary look.

"That's better. The next injection won't be so bad. As soon as you think you're over being dizzy, I'll untie you."

Costa frowned, more bewildered than ever. "You tried to kill me."

"Yes." He stood up on his branch and fished down her pack from an upper limb.

"But you did not finish."

"No." He took the waterskin she had fashioned from a mextle hide out of the pack and splashed some of the stale contents into the cup. "This will help."

She meant to refuse, but thirst won out. She gulped eagerly when he held the battered cup to her lips and did not care about the brackish taste of the water.

"Why?"

He poured himself the last of the water and threw the emptied skin back in the pack. "Why I tried to kill you, or why I did not finish doing so?"

"Both."

"When you went off to hunt, I noticed some carpals flying in with prey obviously taken from the water. The jungle doesn't produce webbed appendages, does it? No. Since we have reached the coast, I no longer need you to stay alive."

"I have done nothing to make you my enemy," she said, unable to keep bitterness from her voice. "I could have let you die!"

"Sentiment has a poor place in the field. You represented a breach of security. I do not want my presence known on this planet."

"Then you might have asked me not to relay it," she said stonily. "In my culture, a warrior is repaid for saving a life."

"Rangers are not permitted the luxury of customs."

"I did not know this. I thought a Ranger was always someone to admire. Well, go on. Cut off my braid and kill me while I am helpless."

"You have become valuable."

"What?" She stared at him, startled by his eagerness.

"You should have told me immediately about your arm."

Involuntarily she tried to draw it closer to her and could not for being tied. "It will heal soon," she said, trying to convince herself as well as him. "My injuries always do. Besides, you gave me no reason to think you would be sympathetic."

"Little fool! Don't you realize you are a link to them now? You can lead me right to . . ." He broke off, a muscle leaping in his jaw as anger warmed her eyes to bright amber. "Droxyhyazine slows down the progress of the poison," he said more slowly, "although by now the stuff will have spread all through your nervous system. They have no current use for you, or else you'd have been summoned. But the drug will protect you to some extent."

She began to shake. "You mean . . . I am one of *them* now, a slave to those faceless *things*?"

"Easy." He touched her shoulder. "Look at your arm."

"No!"

"Costa, look."

Reluctantly she obeyed, and blinked. The puffiness had gone down, and the black ring had faded to a faint mark. For the first time she knew hope. "The drug did this? Will it cure me?"

"No." He sighed. "I'm not sure there is a cure, but you'll have the benefit of the Settle labs when we're through."

"Through with what? Explain," she said sharply, although something told her she did not want to hear.

His cynical blue eyes met hers with unexpected kindness. "We know the Omcris are not of our galaxy, perhaps not of our universe. Look, slinny, Omcris are much more plentiful than they used to be. Mischief around the galaxy has always found them somehow involved. But now major disturbances have been happening in too many hot corners without warning, when political monitors should have been able to post signs of potential trouble. And if you dig long enough and hard enough, there is always an Omcri worm at the root of it. They are no longer mere couriers and assassins for hire; they're part of something much more serious. A few men, mostly in my division, believe these creatures are the vanguard to an invasion; unfortunately we're in the minority. I, for one, don't intend to wait for the axe to fall before I act. So if they are coming in through some avenue the Kanta cults have opened up, I mean to do all I can to plug it."

She frowned, trying to fit it all together. "The Kublai meant to offer you to Kanta."

The lines bracketing the major's lean mouth deepened as he smiled. "Obviously I probed a nerve in my investigation."

"Obviously you were also caught."

He ignored her. "Drugh is always a problem. They thrive on intrigue and delight in causing political turmoil throughout the Commonwealth. The fact that they are placed in a key area only makes them worse. His Supreme Glory is a fool. If he had any inkling of what he is toying with—"

"Do you?"

"No." He dropped his gaze from hers in sudden discomfiture, and she knew he was lying. She realized also that behind the curtness he was afraid.

An orph bellowed nearby, and she jumped.

"Tell me what you know about the cult here," he said.

"Kanta is . . ." She searched for the word. "Primitive. Only people like the Ishuts believe in blood sacrifice and possession—" She broke off in embarrassment, her eyes dropping to the mark on her arm.

"Primitive means are sometimes the most successful," he said grimly.

She swallowed hard. "Recently a team of socio-religiologists applied for a permit to establish an archive of primitive religions on this continent. The Directors granted the permit because they have been accused of running too frivolous a world—as though a recreational planet could be anything else. Consequently the Archives were set up in the name of expanding culture. Visitors are to be permitted to go there and do research by next year."

"By next year there may not be a Playworld. There may not be anything."

"But what will the Omcris do? What do they want? What does the thing they serve want?"

He shook his head bleakly.

She shivered, and the stoniness faded from his eyes. He crouched beside her.

"Costa," he said. "We know how the Omcris recruit people to their side. They either infect them with a chemical substance we call poison, for want of a more specific term, or they possess their souls. The latter are beyond all help or independence. You are the first we've found infected but not directly under active control. Do you understand? Through you we can trace their—"

"No!" she said sharply. "No, I will not trust you. You have done nothing but lie, and evade, and scheme to kill me since I rescued you. How do I know you are telling me the truth? How do I know you are not really the one under their control? How do I know that you are even a Ranger? The Mah Bessam al-zk wore a uniform like yours, but he was not—"

"My name is Haufren," he said, looking at her intently. "Does that mean anything to you?"

She caught her breath. "Haufren. But—" Of course it meant something to her! How could she, who had spent so many years longing to be a Ranger, not know about its founding officer, the legendary Haufren who had led so many successful raids and pulled off more daring exploits than anyone could count? Why, there were visuals in holograph booths in the amusement parks which did nothing but play the "Adventures of Major Haufren" series for children. But if this man were indeed *the* Haufren . . .

She blinked in sudden anger. "Liar! Now you wish me to believe you are centuries old! You—"

"No." His gaze never wavered from hers. "Actually I am Haufren IV, but the traditions of previous generations continue unchanged."

"Oh, how can I trust you?" she demanded fretfully. "How can I know?"

He said nothing as he met her searching gaze squarely. The threat of death no longer radiated from his eyes, and perhaps that was all the truth she could find. She was conscious of an involuntary surge of relief, and hated herself for it.

"Very well," she said softly and shut her eyes. "I take it I have been commandeered, just like a deton-bomb you might need for your arsenal?"

"Exactly so." He untied her. "You may not like the idea, Lieutenant, but you just became an auxiliary member of the corps. Please consider yourself under my command."

Her heart leapt at those words, and for a moment it was possible to forget that he had tried to kill her. "Sir!" she said faintly.

"You mentioned a squad. How many, and is their loyalty to you or Janal?"

She accepted the coiled line he handed her and shakily pulled herself upright. The drug made her sluggish; she felt as though she had no reflexes at all. The strengthening light pained her eyes and she snapped down an eyelid to compensate, but it helped little.

"Two I can trust. The rest are unknown factors now. We'll

find Duval. His *sieghr* is on Lilliput, not far from here."

"We'll move out as soon as you're able."

She sent him a bleak look. "If you had told me this at the start, we need not have become enemies."

Whatever slight warmth had been in his face dropped away. "We are not friends now, Lieutenant. Let's go."

CHAPTER SIX

"We'll have to steal a skimmer," said Costa, wiping the spray from her face as they crouched behind a salt-encrusted pillar near the water's edge.

The sea boomed and crashed along the breakers, making stealth of little importance. About fifty meters away, uniformed guides were marshaling adults and children into lines stretching out from a central ticket bunker. Costa squinted against another lash of spray, trying to see past the throng of squealing children armed with short diglet rakes and rented baskets to the installation beyond where skimmers and other small water craft were moored. It did not look guarded by even the usual Dhurrie sentry. But then the crowd was heavier than usual for this early in the morning, and the guides looked understaffed and harried. She frowned, not certain she wanted to try to take a skimmer in plain sight of a full quota of tourists. And if the guides moved to stop her, could she fire on them? Unhappily she crouched back behind the pillar.

"What's inside those buildings?" asked Haufren.

"The bunkers?" She looked at him, confused by a warring mixture of resentment, gratitude, and dependency. The droxyhyazine he rationed out to her was a leash which she hated. She still could not deal with the fact that this hard, ruthless man was the hero of her youth. "They hold ticket dispensers, refreshment counters, and gift shops. Also rental booths for diglet rakes—"

Haufren held up an impatient hand. "No. I mean, what kind of communication center do they have?"

"Standard short-range. To Beros or to Lilliput. Not much farther. Of course for emergencies they can boost their signal from—"

"I need interplanetary range," he said with exasperation, leaning his head back against the pillar. His stubbled face was gray and drawn with hunger, and sand sparkled across one cheek in a golden arc.

"We can deal with that when we get to Duval."

"I think not. Duval is too much of a risk." He frowned. "I dislike unknown factors."

"And I tell you Duval can be trusted!" The arrival of a wide-bodied transport nearly drowned out her words as it came chuffing up to the pier. She raised her voice. "He is the best squadman ever to serve with me. I have trusted him at my back since my first command—" She stopped, unwilling to make a point of Duval's kinship.

"Trusted him so much you didn't bring him along to guard the Kublai?"

The unexpected barb cut viciously. Costa dropped her eyes from the derision in his and struggled to hold her voice steady as she answered. "You do not understand. There were personal reasons for taking out an unknown squad—"

"Yes!" He grasped her wrist and gave her arm a light shake. "Omcri reasons."

"No! I made my decision before!"

"Did you, Costa?" His blue eyes bored into hers. "Are you sure?"

She pulled her arm free, refusing to look at him lest he see the unprofessional tears stinging her eyes. "This . . . this does not pertain," she said at last. "We need food. We need a safe place to rest. We need allies. Duval is on Lilliput."

"Forget Duval. And forget safety. We need a communications center with long-range capabilities. I don't like the idea of going out there on that island. It might prove to be too difficult to get off of in a hurry."

She frowned, realizing this argument could go on forever. For a moment she stared out across the breakers at the curve of Lilliput's headland. Her friends were within sight; she had no intention of giving up on this.

Suddenly her eyes cooled to a narrow green. "Do you plan to call for help from your own kind?" Without waiting for his answer, she continued: "There is a communications center on Lilliput. It's probably not sophisticated enough to reach Ranger Headquarters in the Settle Belt, but if you have any skills in that area you could perhaps alter some of the circuits on the main boards."

He grasped her by the shoulders. "Why didn't you mention this before?"

She had no answer for that so she said instead, "I am not lying to you. I just don't know if it will serve your purpose."

"We'll find out. Now how do you propose to get out to that rock?"

"By stealing a skimmer."

He sighed. "And you have commanded squads? Don't you ever *think,* Lieutenant? How are you going to do this? Wait until it is dark and everyone has gone home? We don't have time for that. Or are you going to shoot your way through all those innocent people and give away your exact bearings and destination to your pursuers?"

She bit her lip, trying hard not to betray her fury. He was right, but he need not make her feel like *flin.* "What is your suggestion?"

"Zethians," he said, looking past her at the tourists now filing aboard the transport. He nearly smiled. "Well, well." He straightened up to look intently at the crowd.

"What?" asked Costa in exasperation. Not understanding him at all, she turned with a frown to scan the crowd until she picked out the pair. The adult was tall and overweight, heavily furred with a gray pelt. The child was small and round and golden.

She shot Haufren a puzzled glance. "So? What have they to do with our getting to Lilliput?"

Intent on the crowd, Haufren ignored her. The Zethian child balked as its parent tried to lead it aboard the large transport chuffing steadily at the pier. An argument broke out, with the adult tugging and the child dragging back. The wind blew spray high in the air, drenching all who stood on the pier. The child screamed and broke free, dashing hysterically through the crowd, eluding all hands reaching out to snare it. Bored ticketeers suddenly snapped to attention, and a loudspeaker blared. Seconds later, sonic bars slammed shut across the gates.

Costa flung herself back into hiding with a curse as the child veered and streaked toward them.

"May the five plagues smight its growth! It's leading them straight to us."

"Catch it," said Haufren. "We'll use it to get aboard."

"Negative!" She stared at him, appalled. "My ID grid is

flagged by now. They'll know at once—"

"Not with all the furor over this little nib," said Haufren, grunting as he tackled the small fury hurtling past them. He handed it over to Costa, leaving her to struggle with flailing arms and unsheathed claws as the child spat and bit. Haufren stood up and lifted an arm at the pursuers.

"Gengin, unda mot!" snarled the child, kicking at her.

"Sulla," retorted Costa, hanging on grimly. She repeated the reprimand with more emphasis as startled brown eyes lifted to hers. Her own eyes, angry and golden, glared down into that round face. "You shame your parent. You shame your race," she said sternly, hoping the child was educated in the Unise language and behavior code. "You have disrupted order."

The child quivered against her as a wave slopped up against the pillar. It sheathed its claws, and soft stubby hands suddenly gripped hers as two ticketeers and the adult Zethian came running up.

"Not parent," whispered the child in its rough, burred voice. "Tutor. Water I *hate*. Lilliput I do not wish to see!"

"Lilliput is fascinating," she said as Haufren genially accepted the thanks of the others. "And the ocean is equally so."

The child flattened its ears. "It is *wet. Kith!*"

"Thanks to you I give," said the adult Zethian, approaching her. "Great shame the nib has caused. Apologies we do tender."

She nodded, trying to listen to what Haufren was telling the guide.

". . . behind schedule!" snapped someone, and the Zethian held out an exasperated hand.

"Come, Tith! Revoked shall be our tickets if more disturbance you cause."

Tith pressed his short, plump body closer to Costa. She caught the swift gleam in Haufren's eyes, and obediently bent over the child.

"Tith!" she said briskly, masking her alarm at Haufren's tactics. "If you have the escort of a patroller, would you still fear the water?"

"Do not fear. Hate!" came the answer muffled against her leg.

The Zethian snarled silently and lifted his furred hands. "Oh, great Basa, how stubborn is this child! My apologies, good sirs. If kind enough you would be to negotiate a refund, we—"

"Nonsense," said Haufren. "The child must be taught to overcome this phobia."

"Most peculiar it is of him. Never has he manifested such behavior before," said the Zethian with a blink. "But of no avail is it to continue this disturbance. We shall—"

"Tith," said Costa, placing a gentle hand between the small round ears. "What will happen if you do not go to Lilliput today?"

The child shuddered. "Lessons."

"No one should have to do lessons on Playworld!" said Haufren, showing his teeth in a broad smile.

Costa glared at him for overplaying his part.

Tith looked up at her. "Lessons on Lilliput, too," he said bitterly.

"Of course this is so," said the tutor. "It is good a conscientious employee to be. I—"

"Please, sir," said the guide impatiently. "We are behind schedule. It's unfair to delay the other passengers."

"Go with me," whispered Tith to Costa, and she nodded despite the scream of her instincts.

"Come along," she said, keeping a hand on the back curve of his skull. Together they started out along the beach toward the pier. The others followed. She glanced at the guide and noticed his measuring glance at her torn and ill-fitting tunic. "I am on a private expedition," she said nervously and cocked her head at Haufren. Guides were only one grade lower than patrollers. He might easily recognize her from former duty or even, Moii help them, a training video. "You are lucky we happened along today," she continued, afraid that if she did not distract him with chatter he might begin to think too much. "The Zethians can be difficult, and if a complaint were lodged over this—"

"I *know,*" he said bitterly. "My hide is already Ishut meat over this delay. The return passengers will be doubled, and with the wind up this morning, the pilot will give me the two curses for threatening his safety rating. It must be nice, Lieutenant, to pull private duty."

Her laugh held little amusement. "In the jungle? Not so nice."

"No." His brows pulled slightly together, and he glanced back at Haufren in his torn and bloodstained uniform. "Some kind of executive survival course, I suppose."

Costa shrugged, not daring to come up with more lies. They walked out along the pier to the transport already loaded with the rest of the passengers belted in along the padded benches. Everyone gawked, and there were several gasps and nudges at the sight of Costa with her strifer worn in plain view on her hip. More than one adult glared at Tith. His grasp tightened on Costa's hand, but the other children were too excited and eager to pay much attention to anything except the prospect of reaching the enchanted island. The noise made Costa's sensitive ears ring, and nearly drowned out the courteous voice of the attendant drone as it requested them to find their assigned seats.

"Tith," said Haufren warmly, ducking beneath the low ceiling of the craft. "You're a fine young nib. *Shilorr.*" He patted the child on the shoulder, and Tith blinked at him as though in startlement.

"Yes, Tith, come along! Quite enough trouble you have caused." The tutor seized Tith and jerked him away from Costa.

Tith looked up at Haufren. "Sir—"

"Come along, Tith!" The tutor dragged him away.

"Seats please," chimed the drone as the engines whined to impatient life.

The guide, who was still standing on the pier outside, poked in his head through the open hatch. "You can disembark now, Lieutenant."

Alarm speared Costa. She stared at him, ready for the words of arrest, and moved her hand toward her strifer as Haufren stiffened beside her.

"Zethian honor is satisfied. I think they would probably

prefer not to be reminded further of this incident." The guide grinned. "But thanks anyway."

Costa opened her mouth, confused by relief and the sudden scent of warmed refreshments from the minuscule galley.

"Let's go anyway," said Haufren while she struggled to create a reason to stay aboard. "I'm bored with the jungle."

The guide frowned. "The seats are all filled. You'd better wait for the next transport. And the tickets—"

"I'm sorry," said Costa rapidly as the whine of the engines increased. "No time. I know it will make *flin* of your records, but can't we straighten this out later?" As she spoke, she made a rapid hand signal to indicate Haufren's worth as a customer.

"Ten seconds to hatch closing," intoned the speaker above her head.

The guide drew back and said something over his shoulder to one of the ticketeers. "Sure. Just log it in on his account when you step ashore. But the seats—"

"Acknowledged." She lifted her fourth finger at him in a swift exchange and turned gratefully as the hatch whirred shut. "This way," she said, grabbing Haufren by the arm and pulling him back to the cramped cubbyhole where drones were stored between trips across. "It'll be a rough ride."

The transport took off over the bouncing waves with a jolt that set her down more quickly than she had intended. Haufren crouched beside her, grimly hanging onto a bulkhead while screams of delight ricocheted around the cabin interior.

"Will that drone serve us food?" he asked.

Costa carefully tried not to look at the gaily colored packages being distributed along with steaming cups of flavored nutra-gel. "I can't get close to it," she said while her stomach growled its way into a painful knot. "It might scan my ID at any moment, and then—"

With a grunt, he stood up and made his way unsteadily through the cabin to grab several packages off the drone's tray and came back while the attendant was chiming in confusion. He dropped them in her lap and crouched beside her with a swift quirk of his lips.

"Now isn't this better than stealing something and getting

yourself shot at? Always work with a situation when possible, Lieutenant."

She tore open a package with her teeth and bit eagerly into the synthesized fiber bar to divert herself from more violent action. "You are too smug. If luck had not brought along that child, you—"

"I don't believe in luck," he said, chewing as greedily as she. "Opportunities come along, and if we're smart we grab them."

Costa stared at him. "You *made* that child run toward us. You . . . are you an esper?"

"What a parochial term. Let's just say I have many talents," he replied, turning brusque again. "Zethians are notoriously susceptible to suggestion, especially the children who are less trained to protect themselves."

"I see." Costa fell silent and bit into another bar. Under the circumstances it did not seem wise to bring up Playworld's mandates against telepathy. Exercise of it was a felony, but she had to admit it had been useful . . . this time. "And the tutor did not suspect you? I saw him give you an odd look."

"So did everyone else," said Haufren dryly. "We do seem to stand out in the crowd."

"It is impolite to be curious."

With a grunt, he broke the last fiber bar between them and bit into his half with a grimace. "Demos, these things are awful!"

"Food is food. Does he suspect you?"

"Possibly." Haufren's blue eyes flicked to hers then away. "The risk factor was acceptable." A severe jolt nearly threw him across her. He righted himself with a curse. "Our pilot is a fool."

"Currents are treacherous here," she said with a shrug of indifference, enjoying his discomfiture.

"We aren't in the water."

"No, but we're about thirty centimeters above the waves. Do you get seasick?"

He sent her a scornful look and said nothing more until they docked. They were the first ones off when the hatch whirred automatically open, and Haufren led the way down the pier while the rest of the passengers were still being herded into an orderly disembarkment. Costa glanced back briefly at Tith's short round face staring mournfully after them.

Haufren touched her arm. "Come on. Survival and sentiment do not mix."

"You could have damaged that child!" she said, glaring at him.

"But I did not. Come," he repeated with more impatience. "Where is the communications center?"

At the end of the pier, Haufren had to slow down due to the thronging crowd of brightly dressed people all disembarking from a fleet of constantly arriving transports. He threaded a way through, with Costa still following, and did not stop to let her take charge until they were safely through the gates.

"Thank you," she said with irritation as she stepped onto the wide central street of the village. "We'd better go straight to the *sieghr*."

"I am unwilling to argue further about this, Costa."

"So am I. Why are you so distrustful of someone I can vouch for?" She sent him a bitter look. "You have made me dependent on that drug, so I am unlikely to lead you into a trap."

"I wonder. No, listen to me," he said as affluent-looking people eddied about them with brief glances at their stained and torn clothing. "You still do not understand, or else you are unwilling to face the consequences of being frozen out. You are *wanted*. Even if your friends do help you, that makes them guilty too. Do you think they want to face equal accusations?"

She shook her head. "But Duval will listen to me. We need him and Puce. They are both good men. And if we're to recover the Kublai, we need supplies, equipment, and numbers. You're very good, Major, but you are not invincible. You can't do everything alone. Besides, Duval can tell you more about the communications system here."

He stared at her for a moment, his face unreadable. "Very well. How far?"

She shrugged, unable to remember the exact distance. "Beyond the village. Perhaps a kilometer away. It is on the cliffs on the west side. The visitors are not permitted in that area."

"Good," he said with emphasis as a dipcart swerved to miss them by inches. A youth with two laughing girls on his arm was driving. "Lead out."

Lilliput Island was one of the most popular attractions on Playworld. The eastern side had been created in miniature by some freak of nature eons ago. The forest grew no taller than two or three meters, the fairy caves were perfect wonderlands for young children who were small enough not to feel claustrophobic in the little caverns, and the animal life was equally tiny. Pipquets, dox, lullids, and grivers tame enough for petting in designated areas charmed everyone. Flowers of riotous color bloomed year round along the sandy garden paths created by the Playworld botanical crew, and the climate was always mild. The beaches alternated in colors of blue, pink, and white sand, and ceeps assigned to patrol the island reported the primary difficulty of their job lay in keeping children from trying to take some of the sand home with them. Everything in the way of souvenirs could be purchased in the shops lining the central street of Lilliput Village.

Costa turned left onto a smaller track as the street with its mosaic paving of polymer-coated seashells curved out toward the beaches. A few steps beyond, discreetly hidden behind a stand of trees stood a barrier entry point. She stopped to frown at it.

"Automated?" asked Haufren.

"Yes."

"Do you need a special clearance code?"

"No. Any native inhabitant has access." She tugged at her warrior braid and snapped down an eyelid as the sun broke briefly from behind some clouds. "But if my ID flags attention—"

"Not if, Lieutenant," he said grimly. "The question is how long will we have from that mark? Are there active patrols stationed here?"

"No. Just a few ceeps for crowd control and emergencies. They couldn't handle us." She squinted, considering it. "Beros is two hours flight time by rapid shuttle."

"You say this Duval lives a kilometer from here?"

"Approximately."

"Demos, slinny! Slackness won't cut!"

"There has never been a reason to know the exact distance!" she shouted back, equally furious at herself for her ignorance. "I have come here twice on pleasure. It's not a part of my job."

He gripped her arm hard at the elbow. "Your job is to stay alive. When you go through that gate you have perhaps ten or fifteen minutes to reach Duval. That's fifteen minutes back. How long will it take to convince him to help us? If he will at all."

"We can trust him. How many times must I say it until you will believe me?"

"All right. Say thirty minutes talk-time. That's one hour. And that gives us one hour to break into communications, clear this rock, and find a place to hide."

"We can get a sled—"

"And go where? Back to the coast? Back to the jungle?"

"I don't know yet. Maybe—"

"Yes?"

"Maybe there's a chance we can get down to the southern continent. I'll see what Duval thinks."

"Duval," said Haufren grimly, "had better be good."

"He is."

"I don't like trusting my hide to unknown factors."

She looked down at his hand gripping her arm, then glared at him. "Neither do I," she said softly and broke free. "I'll be back quick-time."

"Make it sooner," he said and sat down on a rock to wait.

Costa walked over to the entry point, taking deep breaths in an effort to steady her nerves.

"Lieutenant!" he called.

She glanced back.

"If he keeps medical supplies, be sure you get some more droxyhyazine. What we have won't last much longer."

She lifted a hand in acknowledgment, not trusting herself to speak. Fear, never buried very deep, resurfaced, and she had to fight it down. How long until the Omcris decided they needed her? She pushed the thought away.

Planting herself by the gate scanner, she waited for her ID to be read. Nothing happened. With a frown she pushed the reset button, and a small notice flashed:

> DUE TO TEMPORARY MALFUNCTION, SCANNER INOPERABLE. PLEASE COMMIT MANUAL GRID CODE TO SCANNER MEMORY. APOLOGY TENDERED.

Costa threw back her head with a laugh. "Thanks to Moii! We just gained an extra hour," she said over her shoulder and swiftly punched in her code on the recessed keypad. The wait, only seconds long, seemed interminable, then the sonic gate dropped, and she was through. If there were scanner problems, that meant some drone in the village communications center was having to manually coordinate all data traffic. And if the luck Haufren didn't believe in stayed with her, the drone might be programmed to assign all grid code traffic to a low priority channel. Eventually the flag would be noted, but not for a while. Her spirits rose.

Duval's place was a low, rambling compound overlooking the sea and structured of brown native stone. She ignored the breathtaking scenery and keyed in for admittance at the door. She had not mentioned to Haufren the possibility that Duval might be elsewhere on assignment. Glad Haufren was not here standing at her shoulder, she fidgeted at the delay and re-keyed.

Finally the door slid open. Costa sighed and started to step over the threshold, only to freeze as she realized a scanner booth had been installed in the doorway. Anyone stepping inside would be automatically trapped there until scanning was completed, or until someone decided to let her out. She drew her strifer with a snarl and fried the control panel. Black smoke boiled out over her, stinging her eyes and nostrils.

"Duval!" she shouted furiously. "Either face me or snipe me down. But no more tricks, or I'll fight you to blood-honor!"

A minute later, the rear door of the box opened and Duval stood there. His craggy, square-jawed face was bleak.

"Costa," he said quietly. "If you had been smart you would have run the moment you saw the scanner booth. Now I have no choice but to take you in to Janal." He lifted his big, freckled hand away from his side to show the strifer aimed at her gut.

CHAPTER SEVEN

Xixit crawled through the humming labyrinth of access tubes, barely restraining the urge to rip out sections of circuits webbed in delicate complexity throughout the panels. He refused, however, to let anger affect his good sense. Sabotage would trigger alarms, and he could not afford to be caught.

Pausing at an intersection where illegally bared conduits leaked sufficient energy to make his bald scalp prickle, he gritted his teeth and carefully counted the previous intersections he had passed. Two hours in this place had shown him that his map of the installation was wrong. When he cleared Playworld he would seek out his spy to personally deal him a slow, painful death for this betrayal. The flayers of the Royal House would be too kind.

Xixit twitched violently as the energy waves crawled through his body. Hastily he moved on, shuddering as he went. Finally the spasms eased. He lifted a shaking hand to wipe away some of the sweat from his face. Something near him sizzled faintly, and he crawled faster. How he hated these wires, energy pods, and reactor/generators! This was not a place for one of the devoted. Even the foul sewers with their stench, slime, and sinister filth-eaters had been better than this.

Ah, there!

Gratefully he crawled through the eighth intersection. Crouching beneath a red hatch overhead, he paused long enough to mentally run through his calculations again, then lifted his hands to the metal wheel. It resisted him at first then spun. A hydraulic release lifted the hatch with a soft hiss, and he poked his head through cautiously.

He saw a long, narrow room like a corridor lit by regularly spaced panels. It was deserted. With a snort of relief he grasped the edges of the floor and boosted himself out. He used his heel to push down the hatch, and it resealed itself quietly. The hum that had shook his nerves for so long faded. He drew in a deep breath and walked over to a vast bank of controls, studying them with a frown of incomprehension. To the left was a door. He pressed his ear to it, and gingerly sent out a mental query. Someone was beyond it, but the brainwaves were operating in a low, non-alert beta mode. He set his palm against the activator, and the door slid aside.

A vast gulf of blackness yawned before him, and with it came the deadly scream of a rapid shuttle, bigger than life, its nose aimed right at him. He fell back, and the door shut, closing off a shout of anger. Xixit lay where he had fallen, panting as his panic slowly faded. In its place rose fury. A simulator room! A place of blasphemy against life. He cursed long and thoroughly.

Slowly he picked himself up, recalling himself to his death-sworn purpose. Nothing, not even this maze of nightmares on this disgusting planet, could shake him from it. He had found the Mah, tracing piece after piece of the body through the network of sewers to a villa on the Street of Harmony. He knew now who owned that villa. And he knew the Blessed One was not within its walls. But there he had lost the trail. Already he had combed the vast complex of amusement parks within the Nogales empire. He knew the layout of the rides, of the simulator houses, of the scientific attractions, and of the sensual kiosks. He had even explored the casino, illegally operated and very difficult to access. That left the underground plant of machinery and computers, which he had just come through, and the Ishut quarters.

He closed his eyes a moment to regather himself against the evil of discouragement. Carefully he cleared from his mind the problems, the disappointments, the hunger, and the weariness. He was pledged and full-sworn. He could not eat or sleep full quota until the Blessed One was found. His senses would remain keener for their deprivation.

Moving down the corridor, he found a second door and checked it with more caution than before. Nothing sentient registered. He opened the door and found himself in another corridor. This one was lined in an unusual silver metal, some sort of alloy which deadened every sound. Even his footfalls were silenced, absorbed so completely that the quiet upset his balance. He stepped carefully, hands spread out and eyes squinted in concentration, unable to understand why he should lose his equilibrium so suddenly when he still had other senses to guide him.

Not a single door except the one behind him opened out of that corridor. He had no choice but to keep going. And soon the muted reflection of light off featureless metal began to hurt his eyes, so that he could barely keep them open. He gritted his teeth and kept going. At last he stood blocked by a wall. A hatchway, sealed and painted scarlet, was set into it. He read the sign, frowning as he struggled with the unfamiliar Unise characters:

> WARNING! ACTIVE REACTOR BEYOND THIS DOOR. NO ENTRY WITHOUT ACCESS CODE.

"Hyata, mala din!"

He stumbled back and resolutely turned around to retrace his staggering steps. This accursed place deserved annihilation. How he hoped the Blessed One would order it!

"You!" said a gruff voice just as he made his way out of the corridor back to more stable ground. "This is a restricted area. What is your authorization code?"

Xixit straightened.

"You're an Ecletian." The man came toward him with visible surprise. "How did you get back here? How did you become lost from your guide? Sir, permit me to escort you out—"

Xixit could waste no more time. Discounting the risks, he sprang at the man, who was a big, beefy Ulang armed only with a short, leather-tipped club obviously used to keep the Ishut workers in line. But Xixit was no drugged Ishut. He chopped one wrist sharply at the man's throat and used the other hand to grasp the man's temple. His probe shot deep into that clumsy, unprotected mind. In seconds he had his answer. The Blessed One was not here.

With a curse, Xixit released his captive, and the man sank unsteadily to his knees, groaning. Xixit stared down at him with annoyance. Murder would alert others to his presence here, but he must get out fast and he must get out now. His lips tightened briefly as he drew a needle-thin dagger from his sleeve. His hand flashed down, and the man sprawled limply across the floor. Xixit grasped his collar and dragged him into the blackness of the simulator room, shoving him inside while shuttles caromed and fired on each other with convincing bursts of flame and screams of stressed metal.

Xixit shut the door, sneezing to clear his nostrils of the stench of oxidizing fuel. Then he ran back to the hatch through which he had gained original access and lowered himself into the tube just as echoing footsteps warned him of the approach of another technician. He sealed the hatch and scuttled along rapidly. Besides the well of ignorance in the man's mind regarding the Kublai, he had gained only one other strong impression in that jumble of defiled thoughts. And it had to do with another Ecletian, a real one who possessed some degree of authority over these operations.

Xixit grimaced, feeling ill. To invade the thoughts of an unbeliever was to wallow through incredible filth, becoming equally defiled and therefore lost to the Hope of All Ending. Unlike the simple act of driving a blade into the ground to clean off the blood, to clean his mind would require days of severe purification. If death befell him on this disgusting planet, he would be doomed for eternity to wander outside with the unbelievers.

Xixit paused a moment, breathing heavily. He folded himself up into a tight knot, seeking the right mental terms of imploring. After a few moments, he straightened. He had his purpose. If he succeeded in saving the Blessed One, even at the cost of his own life, the Blessed One would surely reward him by pleading with the great Kanta on his behalf. He need not face doom; he need not fear.

Confidence returned to him. Besides, now that the defilement was done, he was free to use again this swifter, more dangerous form of gathering information. He would return to Beros and seek out the Ecletian. No doubt his own disguise as one of that repulsive species would make access to the creature easier. And if another killing proved necessary, well, he had eaten the decayed flesh of the Mah Bessam al-zk and he had inhaled the sacred perfume of the Blessed One's own garments. If the Ecletian carried the guilt odor of their harm upon his body, then his death would be swift justice, nothing more.

• • •

In his broad office suite overlooking the Golden Plaza fountains, Ezbell paced twice around the circumference of the room, forgetting in his agitation to wince for the pain of the living carpet crushed beneath his footsteps. Had Wob Nogales not insisted he decorate his working area in fashionable status-symbols, he would have been content and far more comfortable in a utilitarian cell, warmly heated and humidified of course. But, no, he was forced into perpetual guilt over his flooring, flooded with light from vast windows, and dwarfed by sheer space and height. He disliked it all as much as he disliked Playworld, but there was the matter of his ambitions and the lack of truly complex work on far away Eclet V.

Normally, he had to be challenged mentally even at the cost of his emotions and morals. But today as he dropped wearily into his suspensor chair and swallowed another green tablet, he thought he did not need quite this much challenge.

Jillian Nogales was still missing. After days of discreet search and inquiry, no sign of her had turned up. His own alarm was quite eclipsed by Wob's, and several delicate business maneuvers had nearly been wrecked by Wob's lack of sensible judgment. The Kublai's kidnapping had been shoved aside, and this worried Ezbell very much. He expected to be arrested at any time. The Kublai should have been released by now, but Wob refused to have the matter brought up. He wanted his daughter home and safe. Even the vital Delex merger had been delayed again.

Merely thinking about that most recent business disaster made Ezbell reach for another tablet. It was mid-morning and already he had lost count of his daily quota. Too many of them had rather unpleasant side effects, but his nerves could no longer stand alone. He sucked at the crumbling tablet between his double tongues and swallowed it as the bitter inside tanged through his mouth. For a moment he longed to be human. Then he could express himself violently. Then he would have teeth with which to bite or gnaw on something more substantial than dry powders and bland liquids. He could even shout. But an Ecletian had no expression for his tension. Indeed, an Ecletian was not supposed to even experience stress.

With a sigh, he answered the call from his reception drone.

"Commander Janal is here, sir."

"*Here?* Not on the viewer?"

"Commander Janal is here in the reception area, sir."

Ezbell recovered quickly from his surprise. Concealing his dismay, he stood up courteously as the commander strode in. Strong, incisively minded, and quick to take action, Janal was an alarming human whom Ezbell avoided as much as possible during Wob's dinner parties where the commander was an invariable favorite. But today Janal looked as tired as Ezbell felt, and his movements lacked their usual snap. There was something odd about his eyes as well. Ezbell blinked nearsightedly, wishing for dimmer illumination so his vision would be better.

When they had both sat down and the courteous formalities were over, Janal leaned forward. "I realize Jillian's absence has become a grave matter. That's why I thought it necessary to come here in person today. We have followed the standard procedures of checking the spaceport and notifying all outlying stations on the planet. She is tied to civilized areas because of her, er, health problems, so I am sure that were she still here on Playworld she would have surfaced by now."

"Indeed. Your concern is appreciated by Mr. Nogales," said Ezbell. One of the two unlabeled disks on his desk contained a not yet erased payroll authorization for the mercenary abduction team. Ezbell spread his webbed fingers nervously over it.

Janal fidgeted, looking impatient. "She has disappeared before. I wonder if Wob is not overreacting—"

"Disappeared, yes, but never in this manner. Sir, may I submit that she has perhaps been abducted?" Ezbell felt himself drying out as he spoke; this conversation was growing too daring for his abilities. The continuing search for the Kublai was well publicized. Carefully he moved his hand from the disk.

Janal smiled grimly. "I'm afraid everyone has kidnapping on his mind. Have you any basis for this theory?"

"Normally she leaves with her drones, medications, personal staff, and a large wardrobe. She is not a clandestine person. And these departures usually follow a family argument of some violence."

"There have been other incidents, however," said Janal with enough acerbity to make Ezbell squirm.

"Yes. I see you have read her file. Those occurred several years ago. I believe—"

"See here. We do understand the importance of finding Jillian. I have both city and planet patrol working on the matter. But I strongly believe she is off-planet. The fact that she took her most crucial drone and her personal lytcar do not point to an abduction. Besides, by now Wob would have received a ransom note."

Ezbell wanted to retort by saying that there had been no note sent for the Kublai, but he could not bring himself to that boldness. He sighed.

"What then, Commander, is suggested? As a parent, the—"

"Yes, I know. Wob will simply have to make an attempt to be calm." Janal stood up. "Off the record, I have notified the Fleet of her disappearance."

"Then you *do* think it is an abduct—"

"No. But I know my job. And with all the trouble here I have to consider the possibility of a move of retaliation from Drugh."

"Indeed." Ezbell slumped in his chair and groped for a tablet. "But—"

"I personally do not believe this is so. Nonetheless, I came today to tell you the Fleet will explore it. They have several special teams which deal with this sort of thing. In the meantime, we shall continue to keep an eye out here on Playworld. Since she has not been found, I think we should assume that she is still, er, healthy."

"But outside forces! The Fleet! Special teams!" Ezbell's voice failed him; he fumbled in his desk for an emergency beaker and gulped down the liquid contents. "Dear me, Commander. I fear this will bring on the very scandal Mr. Nogales wishes to avoid."

"You want her found, don't you?" Janal's jaw clenched. "See here, Ezbell. Wob is a friend of mine. I understand his sensitivity to scandals regarding his daughter. Results are what we want here, however, not delicacy. I have a major interplanetary incident on my hands, not to mention the unexplained destruction of the Kanta Archives on the middle continent, and a subsequent Ishut uprising."

"Our workers . . . yes."

"Quite. If these larger—yes, *larger*—problems continue to escalate, the Directors will no longer be able to maintain the current hush. Tourism will fall off, perhaps forever. That affects all of us."

"I understand," said Ezbell unhappily, not eager to explain to Wob that the search for Jillian had been assigned to outsiders. "At least, I am trying to. Playworld policy has never been—"

"Look, Ezbell. I don't want a crew of shin-nicked Fleeters in here on my planet any more than you do. The Directors are appalled at the prospect. But we all agree that it is better to seek outside help for finding Jillian than for the Kublai. At least for now. Once we submit control of our internal policing to the Fleet or, Moii help us, the Rangers, we'll never be able to get them out."

"Yes. Unfortunately I see your point, Commander. Thank you. I shall relate this to—"

"And tell him to stop hounding my office. I understand Wob's concern. Blast it, *I* am concerned, too! But when I have anything for him, I'll let him know. Tell him." With an abrupt nod, Janal left the office.

Ezbell hastily dug into his desk and brought out a small sprayer to mist himself until his moisture balance was restored. A chime sounded on his desk.

"Yes?"

"There is an unscheduled visitor waiting to see you, sir. His business is unspecified."

"Oh?" Ezbell closed his eyes, wondering how he could successfully pass on Janal's unencouraging message without bringing down Wob's wrath upon himself. "I don't believe I—"

"Forgive, sir. He is Ecletian and said that—"

"No," said Ezbell firmly. "Absolutely not. I will see no one of my race. Not today."

"Sir—"

"Put him off. Schedule him for another time. Tell him I am engaged in a day-long conference and do not say when I shall be free."

"Acknowledged."

Ezbell slumped back in his chair, trembling. The last thing he needed was for another of his race to see him dried out and emotionally shredded. Ecletians told each other everything; he would be discussed all over his homeworld. Ezbell shuddered. No, he could not possibly face anyone at this time. Humans were insular beings, self-contained, resilient. They noticed little around them and certainly had no concern for the difficulties of other races in adjusting to their company. How fortunate they were!

He leaned forward. "Reception."

"Sir?"

"Summon my lytcar to the side entrance. I'm going home and I want complete privacy. No calls, no messages, no interruptions. Tell no one where I am. Not even Mr. Nogales. I shall prepare a message for transmission to him."

"Acknowledged."

Ezbell dictated briefly, then fled with a sense of overwhelming relief, eager to go home to darkness and water immersion where there was only peace and emptiness and no decisions to be made. At least in this way he could be sure Wob's anger would have time to cool down before he had to face his employer again.

His sanctuary nestled in the corner of a small cooperative compound divided into seven luxurious apartments on Stratum Four. As a rule, non-citizens of his occupation and standing had no chance of acquiring living quarters in this exclusive district, but Wob Nogales had intervened on his behalf. Ezbell supposed he was grateful for his employer's generosity, but his fellow residents shunned him as an odd creature likely to lower their property values. He had no friends and no companionship.

At this hour of the morning, no one stirred along the avenue leading to his compound. His drone pilot landed the lytcar with impeccable smoothness, and Ezbell stepped through the sheltered privacy entrance into the polished agate coolness of his home. He paused to gratefully inhale the humid air which enclosed him and condensed on his face in soft warm beads of moisture. Delicate nyacc plants nurtured by him as a hobby turned enormous shield-shaped leaves away from the polarized window toward him. He moved carefully so as not to wilt them, reveling in the dim, slightly green light and dusky pools of shadow spread throughout the small rooms.

Only the bathing area was large. He headed for it, removing his clothes and dumping them into the recycler. Already the home monitoring computer had registered his arrival and was switching on steam jets and water. Ezbell half closed his eyes and walked through the fountains, holding his arms outstretched as the water swirled and deepened around his legs. His limbs grew fluid with the water, and slowly he sank beneath the surface of the pool until only the top of his skull was exposed. Breathing regularly through the delicate parietal membrane, he folded himself together and prepared for meditation.

The attack came suddenly, without warning, and speared his mind with a white-hot lance of pain.

"No!" He ejected himself frantically to the surface. *"No!"*

The alien mind stabbed again, exploding his skull with its power and brutality. He screamed loudly, flailing the water. Beneath his agony staggered immense disbelief. This could not happen here; Playworld had laws against telepathy; as an Ecletian he could live on no other kind of planet.

"Stop! *Stop!*" he pleaded, clutching his skull.

Suddenly the attack did stop, and he fell into the water with a groan of relief. Floating there limply, he dimly saw the nyaccs wilting, collapsing with stately grace around the edges of the pool. He blinked at the figure which loomed over him from the side. The broad-featured, hairless skull looked very similar to his, but he squinted nearsightedly into those blazing dark eyes and realized through his daze that this was no member of his race. Water bubbled in and out through his mouth, and his hands fluttered weakly. Already he knew that if he stayed in the pool he had perhaps an hour of life left.

A strong hand of bone and sinew grasped his shoulder and pulled him partway from the water.

Ezbell moaned. "Why?" he whispered in a voice that jerked and faded. "Mental invasion is . . . equivalent to breaking the spinal c-cord of . . . humans. *Why?"*

His attacker stared at him in silence, then gently allowed him to slide back into the water. Ezbell sighed in relief, knowing he would barely have enough time to prepare himself in meditation for the death throes, then screamed as that strong hand clamped firmly over the top of his skull, closing off his breathing membrane as it pushed him beneath the surface. He flailed once, his weak eyes bulging, then sank down to the shadowy bottom of the pool to move no more.

Xixit drew in a deep breath, shuddering, and stood up, his hunter's face hardening once again with the purpose sworn upon him. He knew exactly now where to find the Blessed One, and when he reached that place he would throw himself down for the Sacred Slipper to be set upon his neck and the Golden Dagger to be drawn through his throat. Only with the blood completely drained from his body could it be pure again and permitted the burial of a believer. Now that he had invaded the mind of a base *thing,* one not Drughan, one not even human, the Hope of All Ending was forever beyond his reach. Water bubbled up from the fountains, and the excessive humidity plastered his clothes to his body. For a moment he stared down into the depths of the pool at the wavering outlines of the pale, naked Ecletian. His body tensed, and he spat. Then turning on his heel, he left the silent, damp rooms to steal the lytcar from its storage hangar.

CHAPTER EIGHT

Haufren stood up as soon as Costa was out of sight. He studied the terrain, squinting against the sunshine which had finally broken free of an overcast sky, and did not find it to his liking. There was too much open ground and not enough cover. He turned back toward the village, walking with a sure, easy stride. With the right training the girl would make a good Ranger, but right now she was too emotional and impetuous. He had no intention of waiting around for her friends. He doubted they could be of any real help; the last thing he needed was to be slowed down by more amateurs. The girl, however, was important. As soon as he had finished his transmission, he would come back for her.

On the central street of the village, he was approached at once by a frowning ceep.

"Forgive me, sir, but have you been in an accident? Do you require assistance?"

Haufren, who had been trying to decide the quickest way to exchange his filthy uniform for cleaner, more nondescript clothing, quickly seized the man's arm. "Yes, a boat capsized—"

"A *what,* sir?"

"Skimmer," said Haufren, amending his story. "I was flipped out just before it crashed in the rocks. It was rented. It should have been in proper working order."

The ceep's broad face looked more bewildered. "But, sir, skimmers are not rented out to . . . I'll have to verify this if you don't mind."

"Mind? Why should I? Where can I send a message?" As he spoke, Haufren started walking, and the ceep absently fell into step beside him.

"Yes, sir. This way. But I don't understand. Where did you, uh, rent this skimmer?"

Haufren lifted his hand impatiently. "I have no idea. Everything was arranged for me."

"Oh, of course. Your guide—"

"Back there." He jerked his thumb over his shoulder in a vague direction. "In the crash. With the others."

The ceep looked alarmed. "How many, sir? I'd better call this in."

Haufren nodded, rubbing his face wearily with his hands. "Yes, you'd better. I must send a message. You understand, don't you?" He saw a squat, utilitarian building ahead of them. It looked slightly out of place amidst the rest of the village's fantasy-inspired architecture. "Is this the communications center? Can I send a message from here?"

"Yes, sir. But perhaps we'd better have a medic see to you first."

"Why?" asked Haufren too sharply.

The ceep pointed at his tunic. "Isn't that dried blood?"

"Not mine." Haufren's eyes shifted as the ceep beckoned to another patroller stepping out of the building. The man ambled over. Haufren sized him up with one look, noting the interlocking Ps on one sleeve, then began studying the shape of the building and its probable internal layout.

"There's been a crash, Puce," said the ceep. "Can you be pulled on duty? Who else is on call besides Rana?"

The man named Puce shook his head. "Not her. Called out to search for a missing child. Duval's here." He was a tall, lanky individual, very pale skinned beneath what looked like a perpetual sunburn. He wore small, tight-fitting goggles to protect his eyes. Haufren started at the mention of Duval, and Puce caught it at once. "You know him?"

"What?" said Haufren, feigning confusion. "I must send a message. It took so long to get here—"

"We'd better take him off the street," said the ceep, placing a steadying hand on Haufren's arm. "Why don't you start a roundup of anyone you can get on call, and I'll settle him inside."

"Better go to the medical center," said Puce.

"He says he isn't injured."

But Puce was frowning at Haufren, who was beginning to dislike the man's sharp attention to detail. "That blood is old. When did the accident occur?"

Haufren lifted his hand. "I got lost. I tried to go around the beach, but there's a barrier past the rocks. I couldn't get through. So I had to come back over the top, but that was blocked, too. I thought this was an unrestricted island, but I guess I was wrong." He blinked and let himself sway against the ceep. "Could I have something to drink? I've been walking for hours."

"Rocks?" Puce exchanged frowns with the ceep. "Think he means the northeast side? What were you doing there, sir?"

Haufren shrugged. "The guide promised us we could get in without being seen. Permits . . . all that bother." He tried a wan smile which bounced off the suspicious faces of the two men. "I shoot scenic videos for the Home Entertainment Network on—"

"So that's it," said the ceep. "And your skimmer got tossed up in the wind currents. Who was the guide?"

"I don't know. It was all arranged when I arrived on Playworld." Haufren coughed. "Please, may I go inside now? I have to call my editor."

Puce looked disgusted. "I'll get started. Take him inside. And find out how many were in the crash."

"Three," said Haufren.

"This way, sir," said the ceep, taking his arm firmly and escorting him into the cool, stone-lined interior of the center. "If you'll wait in this reception area, one of the drones will take charge of your transmission soon. I hope you realize, sir, that you've infracted several regulations. There'll be a fine and—"

"Oh, don't worry," said Haufren, trying to sound meek but his impatience came through. "I've learned my lesson. I just hope you can find the others. They weren't in very good shape."

"We'll find them, sir," said the ceep coolly and walked out.

At once Haufren moved to the counter and signaled for attention. When a drone came over, he broke into its instructions on how to fill out a transmission form.

"Please. First I need to visit a privacy room."

The drone chimed a moment as though searching its memory for the correct response. "There are public facilities located conveniently throughout the village."

Haufren grimaced in annoyance. "I'm not well. I can't go outside and search. Are there no human workers in this building? Would they object? I'm very clean."

"There are public facilities located conveniently throughout the village."

Haufren drummed his fingers rapidly on the counter for a moment, then rephrased himself. "I need to send two short-range messages to Beros and one long-range message to Drugh." That should throw the people who would come looking for him later sufficiently off the trail, he thought. "Do you have the necessary transmission capabilities?"

"Affirmative."

"Location of transmission control?"

"Room seven, corridor two," responded the drone automatically, then chimed, "Public access not permitted."

Haufren sighed. He couldn't pass himself off as a patroller on this overly organized planet because he lacked an ID grid implant. While the drone indicated forms, he turned and frowned at the double glass doors. A young woman stood outside in the street, arguing with two small children. An idea came to him. He squinted and collected his thoughts to give a slight mental *push*. The youngest child's head snapped up and around. They stared at each other for a moment, then the child darted inside toward Haufren, ignoring the woman's call after him.

He planted himself directly in front of Haufren, sent him an accusing glare, and said loudly and firmly, "I need preecy!"

"Oh, dear," said the young woman, coming in with her other youngster gripped by the hand. "There's a privacy room down the street."

The child hopped. "Now!"

"Public facilities are conveniently located—"

"Can that!" snapped Haufren to the drone. "You surely have an override on that instruction for the needs of small children. If you don't you should be reprogrammed."

The drone scanned momentarily, leaving both Haufren and the child gripped with impatience. "Acknowledged. Location is door two, corridor two."

Haufren smiled inwardly and took the child's hot, sticky

hand before the woman could reach for it. "Permit me," he said at his most courteous. "You look as though you could use a rest for a moment. Those chairs are comfortable."

For an instant her eyes regarded him warily, widening as they took in his disheveled appearance. "No, I don't think—"

"I know I look rough," he said, making himself smile. "I was just in an accident and came in to report it. Frankly I could use the privacy room myself, providing the drone will let me pass."

"How dreadful," she said, hesitated again while Haufren mentally cursed her for being such a properly suspicious guardian, then gave the older boy a slight push toward them. "You go, too. Bene will be trouble for this man."

"Now!" said Bene, wriggling, and the three of them trooped off.

As soon as they were past the solid door marked NO ACCESS, Haufren pointed at the second door.

"You go first," he said. "I'll wait."

The narrow door swiped shut behind the children. He heard a brief giggle, then he was striding rapidly down the corridor. Minutes later he knelt in front of a large, slightly obsolete control bank pulsing in purposeful patterns. Through a partition he could hear low communications chatter as a drone manually worked data traffic. He nodded, aware that it was nearly time for Costa to be back at the gate, and started opening the repair access panels. What he saw inside made him frown. The circuit patterns were outdated and not easily altered. Abruptly changing his mind, he sprang up and silently hurried over to the partition. He listened a moment to make sure no human was monitoring the work, then slipped inside.

The drone was not a sophisticated, ambulatory model. It sat, square shaped and squat in the center of the tiny, airless room, plugged in by a tangle of interfacing to a semicircle of banks. Haufren shook his head at such an antiquated mess and waded in to see what he could do about inserting his own unauthorized message to be routed into the programming for Beros' long-range transmissions. He made it short, crammed it into code, and repeated it once.

"Come on, Silta," he whispered, and replaced the connections as he had found them.

A faint noise behind him made him turn, reaching instinctively for his weapon.

"Don't try it," growled Puce, filling the exit. He held a strifer aimed at Haufren, and below the goggles his face was set and angry. "Come out, and make it slow."

Haufren obeyed, arranging his face to show chagrin and disappointment. He hoped Puce would think he hadn't had a chance yet to send anything out. He didn't dare try a *push* with this man. Walking carefully as Puce backed up, Haufren let himself be searched swiftly for weapons. Puce's mouth tightened even more as he took the slim knife from Haufren's boot. He held it up so that the thin blade gleamed in the soft, artificial light then slipped it out of sight up his sleeve.

He gestured with his strifer. "Move."

Eager himself to get outside where he would have more maneuvering room, Haufren gave him no trouble. They left the building by a side door, surprising Haufren as he blinked outside in the bright sunlight spilling down into a dusty alley. A sled was parked there, pocked blue trim and windscreen gleaming.

"Get in," said Puce. "You pilot."

"I don't know how."

Their eyes met in a brief, hard clash of wills.

Puce changed the setting of his strifer to stun. "Pilot or sleep. Your choice."

Awakening from a strifer stun was a particularly unpleasant ordeal, usually involving acute nausea and a splitting headache. Haufren stepped in and fitted his hips into the brace behind the controls.

"Where?" he asked, adopting Puce's laconic tone.

"Due north." Puce swung out a long arm to point.

Haufren barely masked the unpleasant jolt that order gave him. "To Beros? Why? I haven't committed any serious wrong here. Just a little exploration—"

"Wearing a Ranger uniform, failing to present authorization for infringing on local jurisdiction, giving a false report of an accident."

"You haven't had time to check out my story."

Puce looked at him cynically. "Danki is doing that. In the meantime, we go to Beros." He stepped onto the sled and rammed the sharp point of his strifer painfully beneath Haufren's ribcage. The area around the wound was still sore. Haufren winced and bit off an unwise remark. Frowning, he engaged the controls. Talking to Puce wasn't going to do any good. He'd better save his breath and think of a way out.

The air jets whined to life. They shot up with stomach-lurching speed before wheeling sharply in a tight circle and heading north across the sea to the mainland. Puce hung on, seeming unconcerned by the wild ride as the wind bucked them violently.

Finally he said, "Regulations forbid us to fly as low as the transports. Clear the waves by about five meters and cut speed. It's smoother that way."

Haufren obeyed, grateful to have some ease from battling the controls. He glanced at Puce, who was leaning rather casually against his brace, and said, "Not many people recognize a Ranger uniform. Or do all you patrollers get training just to make sure we stay off-planet?"

Puce nearly smiled. Then his pale face sobered. "My lieutenant's main ambition was to be a Ranger. Maybe some of her interest rubbed off on me."

Haufren lifted a brow. So this was one of Costa's friends. One of the two men she had mentioned that they could trust. "Your lieutenant's female?" he said by way of conversation. "I thought Playworld had strictures against bi-gender military service."

"No."

Haufren sighed and tried again. "So she wants to be a Ranger. We've had a few good recruits from Playworld before. You people get fairly thorough training here. What's her name? Maybe she's on my recruitment list."

"You're not here to recruit anyone," said Puce angrily, jabbing the strifer into Haufren's ribs again. "And the lieutenant is marked for the Hall of Accusations as a traitor."

"Serious." Haufren increased speed to lift them over the mainland cliffs. "What has she done?"

"Not your concern, Ranger. Correct your course. That way."

"Ambitious little lieutenants can be tough to serve under. I'll bet you're glad to be getting someone new."

Puce made no response.

Haufren cursed to himself. How was he ever to find out if Puce were sympathetic to Costa, if the damned man wouldn't cooperate? It would be stupid to fly all the way into Beros only to find out, too late, that they should be allies. Still, neither did he quite dare assume that the man was on Costa's side. And if Puce wasn't, it would be an irredeemable mistake to connect himself with the girl. Haufren frowned as they skimmed the treetops of the jungle, worrying over the problem. One thing he did know: he wasn't going to Beros, not alive and not dead. Central HQ would not get their hands on this Ranger.

Puce unhooked his communicator from his belt and thumbed it on. "Field-corporal Puce calling Beros Central. Come in, please."

Haufren glanced sharply at him as a low beep responded from the communicator. When Puce bent his head to speak into it, Haufren eased the sled imperceptibly closer to the tops of the trees. Fleet-admiral Vance would be disappointed, he thought sadly as Puce relayed the fact that he was bringing in an unauthorized Ranger. It would take someone in Beros about ten seconds to remember Costa's earlier transmission about a Ranger. His entire mobility on this planet would be finished. Bungled, as Vance would say with scathing acerbity. Haufren's eyes flicked to Puce then back to his controls as he moved the sled yet lower and increased speed until his hair whipped painfully back from his face.

It did no good now to think about the procedures he should have followed. He should have dumped his uniform immediately for less conspicuous clothing, claimed himself as a tourist lost and robbed of his identification, and sent out a message coded for assistance. Simple.

Only it hadn't been simple. For one thing he hadn't expected to be shot by the Kublai's guard, drugged, and sealed into a stasis box. Waking up alive and on Playworld had been another shock. That unflinchingly competent girl just happened to be bucking for promotion into his own corps, so she immediately recognized one of the most unobtrusive uniforms ever designed for use in the galaxy. Hacking his way through kilometers of jungle had wasted days of precious time without giving him access to any resources so vital for extrication from this mess.

Haufren grimaced to himself. When he fouled up, he did so in a damned big way. Silta would not thank his grave for having to be the next one to come in here and clean up.

They were practically skimming the trees now. Puce snapped off communications and glanced up with a frown.

"Too low. Move up. And north is still that way." He jerked a thumb to his right.

"What's below us?" asked Haufren, looking down at the blackened and twisted skeletons of trees fallen and tossed in a jumble of torn undergrowth. The question was designed to distract Puce from the fact that he was not obeying the order, but then Haufren saw bloody, swollen carcasses of dead animals and vast, powdery mounds of stone rubble. His attention sharpened. "What happened here?"

"Explosion two weeks ago," said Puce angrily. "Set. Probably by Drughans. Search teams couldn't find proof though."

"The fabled city of Kanta," said Haufren with sudden understanding. He slowed the sled, his keen eyes taking in the signs of fresh destruction overlaying the old. "And the new Archives?"

"Gone."

"Damn." Haufren hovered over what he guessed had once been the central temple. The cult had begun to focus here. He might have been able to learn a great deal, but now . . . He sighed. "It wasn't the Drughans, Corporal."

"Their Kublai is missing. We're blamed."

"Drughans are a very devoted people. They would not dare show disrespect to their ruler by destroying the origin site of his personal religion. I suggest you search elsewhere for your culprit."

For a moment they stared at one another, the sled swaying slightly as it hovered over broken stone and dust strewn in dead patterns. Puce's eyes stared into Haufren's with open speculation. This was an intelligent patroller, Haufren realized, one like Costa who could think as well as act. A good man. A loyal man. A man who knew his duty and performed it. Wearily Haufren held down the brief spurt of admiration rising within him. Emotions interfered with the brain. If he should have to kill this man, he would, and whether he wanted to made no difference, just as it never had before.

"You know something of the situation," said Puce, still eyeing him thoughtfully. "Of course. A Ranger here. Because of the Kublai." Puce leaned forward. "You are the man Costa reported in her final transmission. Where is she?"

Haufren's trained ear caught concern underlying that question. Swiftly he seized the chance to save Puce by making an ally of him.

"Are you her friend, as she told me you would be, or do you seek her arrest?"

Puce blinked in startlement behind the goggles. "Where is she?"

"On whose side are you, Corporal? Hers? Or Janal's?"

"You know the commander?"

Haufren did not answer.

Puce frowned. "It is not a question of sides. She betrayed her squad and the Kublai's party—"

"Don't be a fool, man! She did no such thing!" Haufren snorted. "If you believe that, then you can't have served with her long."

Puce reddened. "You forget she is my lieutenant."

"Then act like it! Are you with her, or not?"

"I'm . . . with her. But the commander—"

"—knows her innocence just as you do." Haufren swept out a hand. "She has been framed for this. All she wants to do now is find the Kublai and reinstate herself. Will you help her?"

Puce hesitated, then suddenly lifted his strifer. "*You* are the betrayer! You were with the Kublai's party. You knew the coordinates. You had no other reason to be on Playworld. Did you kill Costa?"

"No, you fool," said Haufren, gritting his teeth in exasperation.

Puce almost smiled. "No. She would not be easy prey, even for a Ranger. Where is she?"

"With Duval."

For an instant Puce's eyes gleamed, then he nodded. "Good. That was wise of her. But she should not have left you unguarded."

"Do you realize the implications of accusing a Ranger of a crime?" asked Haufren, beginning to lose his temper.

"You were her prisoner. For her to bring you through the jungle alone is a feat that will make her even greater among the warriors. Janal will clear her now. As soon as you arrive in Beros."

"My presence won't clear her! We need the Kublai—"

"Move," said Puce coldly, jabbing his strifer back into Haufren's side. "Due north. No more tricks."

Haufren fumed as he pulled back on the controls and shot them up and away from the desolate ruins. "Rangers usually receive respect around the galaxy," he said curtly. "Do you have a reason for doubting my word as an officer of that corps?"

"Yes."

"Official?" Haufren shot him a sharp glance. "I know Playworld is hostile to outside policing forces, but I hadn't heard of an active change in policy."

Puce just stared back at him. "Personal," he said.

"Explain," said Haufren, wondering where this man was from. Not originally from Playworld, not with that pallid, sunburned skin and those nocturnal eyes.

Puce shook his head. "Explain?" he said harshly. "Why should I? You're going to the Hall of Accusations."

Haufren sighed, giving up. A stubborn fool could be offered only so many chances.

"Move up!" said Puce. "I told you not to skim these trees."

Haufren grimly increased speed and lowered the sled until leaf tips slapped against the bottom.

"Move up!"

A limb snagged them, rocking the sled violently as it sped on. Haufren pressed his lean flank hard against the inadequately padded brace, and gave the controls a swift yank. The sled tipped with an angry squall of the little engine and Puce flailed a long arm as he fought not to fall off.

He shouted in anger and fired the strifer point-blank just as Haufren tipped the sled again. Two fierce needle spits of fire burned Haufren's arm, making him jerk, grimacing against the pain. He hung on grimly, pulling up the nose of the sled this time so that another shot went entirely wild. Puce clung with equal determination, crying out hoarsely as Haufren ducked behind the windscreen and sent them diving down into the trees. Branches snapped and whipped around them, raking the sled as Haufren braced himself and kept the insane speed constant. A broad leaf slapped him in the face, stinging it fiercely, blinding him momentarily. The sled wobbled in his hands, and he blinked desperately to clear his sight in time to tip them through a thick congestion of sawtooth vines.

The vines snaked around the sled, blown by the air jets. Puce screamed something, but by this time Haufren realized his mistake as the vines lashed and crossed about them, ripping the shoulders and back of his tunic to shreds. Haufren jerked in agony. The sled bucked in his hands, coughed in gut-wrenching hesitation against a thickening wall of vines ahead, and dipped again. He staggered and slipped to one knee, losing his hold on the controls altogether, and choked off a cry as his wounded arm was thrown against the dash. The control stick jammed, refusing to unlock when he seized it again.

The nose of the sled slammed into a thick limb, making the whole craft shudder as it careened off. Carpals rose up ahead of them in a vast flock of screaming, flapping bodies and razor-sharp talons. One struck the windscreen, shattering it in a brief rain of plexiglass over Haufren as he struggled with the controls.

"Are you crazy?" shouted Puce, clinging desperately with blood splattering from his cut hands and face. The strifer was gone; he was using both hands to hang on. "The intake's choked with leaves. We'll crash—"

Haufren heard the engine cough again and felt a shudder through the deck under his feet. He gritted his teeth and tipped the craft again, knowing that if he didn't dislodge Puce this time he would be forced to cut speed.

Puce flopped to his stomach, grunting as though the wind was knocked from him. One hand came loose, flailed wildly, and grasped hold again. Haufren tipped the sled further on its side to an insane forty-five degrees, feeling his own tenuous balance going. One of his braced feet slipped. He fell, slid, and saved himself only by hooking one leg desperately around the rear support of his pilot's brace. Puce snarled something, taking one hand from his precarious hold to unclip a cutter from his belt. From the corner of his eye, Haufren saw the blades snap out, and knew with a lurch of fear that there was no way to duck. Puce's arm drew back for the throw, and Haufren could see the deadly intent gleaming through the goggles. Then a branch caught Puce and raked him off. Haufren had just enough time to gasp in relief before the engine coughed its last and cut abruptly, plunging him and the dead craft straight down through crashing, breaking, snapping limbs, tipping over until he was beneath the sled. Then his hold failed completely and he was falling faster and faster, caught and bounced by branches only to be dropped a split second later, falling ahead of the sled by diminishing centimeters, and knowing during the long, bitter, terrifying way down that when he hit the ground his only hope was to die before the sled landed on top of him.

CHAPTER NINE

Sick disbelief washed over Costa. She stared at Duval and slowly shook her head, too defeated to even try to get away.

"Not you," she whispered. "Oh, Moii, Duval, not *you*." Her eyes filled with tears, blurring his implacable face.

He frowned, and for an instant his dark, deep-set eyes softened beneath their craggy brows. "Costa—"

Angry at her own weakness and furiously disappointed in him, she dashed at her tears. Her hand, as it came down, brushed against the butt of her strifer, and Duval immediately stiffened.

"Come inside," he growled, gesturing with his strifer.

She obeyed, shutting her eyes as the heavy stone door slid shut behind her. Now she was trapped in the outer courtyard of the *sieghr.* The fountain murmured steadily beneath the sounds of laughter and chatter from one of the upper windows. Costa gritted her teeth, certain Duval's wives were all gathered above to watch. She could imagine their exclamations as they recognized her, and at that moment as everything within her shredded into torn, bleeding pieces, she was glad she could not hear what they must be saying.

"Your weapon, Costa."

Her eyes flew open. Wordlessly she unbelted her strifer and let it fall to the clay tiles underfoot.

"And your sleeve knife. Must I *ask* for it, Costa? Is there not shame enough on this house?"

"I am no traitor!" she said, stiffening. "You cross my honor by saying so—"

"Honor!" He struck her sharply across the mouth with his hand, making her reel back. "You defile the word, *adapt*."

Recoiling from the hatred in his voice, she touched her stinging lip and spat out blood. "Duval—"

"Wasn't it enough for you to grow up under shame, always having to prove yourself over and over, never quite free of the shadow of what you are? For years I have followed you, served under your command, fought for you. And now you have turned on us, all of us. Why, Costa? *Why?*"

He shook her again, until she slapped his hand away. Her bitterness welled up, to be contained no longer.

"Oh, yes, brother, you are indeed someone to depend on. You, the quickest to believe the worst! I have fought my way through the jungle to reach you, thinking I could count on your help, on your belief in me. And *you* have—"

"Can that," he said, gesturing. "Do you think I am uninformed? I know about the meeting with the Omcri courier in the wineshop. I know about the betrayal of the Kublai. I was one of the searchers, Costa. I saw the camp." His dark eyes bored into hers, alight with fury and accusation. "I know you better than anyone. I know about your violent temper and arrogance. I know how quick you are to settle a score. Oh, you are guilty, Costa. I know it, just as Janal does."

"Janal cannot be trusted!" she cried. "His communications lines are snooped, and he—"

The strifer hummed as Duval thumbed it to full charge. He aimed it at her, his eyes very cold. "I won't join your treason, Costa. If you came here for that, you made a big mistake. Throw down your sleeve knife."

Slowly she obeyed, smarting to the third part. But angry and hurt as she was, she could not summon any blood-fury to help her. He was her brother, imbecile or not, and she knew she could not strike at him as she would have any other.

Still, her eyes glared a brilliant yellow, hot enough to sear their sockets, and she kicked the knife across the tiles. A pet juujb leapt from the potted vegetation lining the courtyard to pounce on the knife and bat it away.

"Will you cut off my warrior braid now?" she asked scornfully.

He did not answer the insult, but instead gestured with his strifer. "Into the house. I have a call to make."

"For your sled?" she asked too eagerly. Surely on the way to Beros, she could find a way to escape him. He had never been as clever as she, nor as quick.

He frowned. "I have no intention of transporting you, Costa. Security will come here."

The door slid open as her shoulders sagged in defeat. In her heart she cursed him in the five ways. He gave her a shove, and she walked down the long, low corridor into the interior of the house. Her nostrils singled out the multitude of odors: leather, brien musk, giglan bread, raw fruit, costly perfumes, rugs woven from herendi wool, smoke from the cooking fires, someone's boots worn too long and wet besides. And she could hear quick rustles and giggles as women fled and hid themselves in the shadows of one of the large open rooms as she passed by the entrance. Costa did not even turn her head. She just kept walking, the muscles in her stomach throbbing, her back stiff. But if she did not show her emotions, she could not control them inside. Nor could she stop thinking of how she had always entered this household as a favored guest, to be greeted in a rush of children, women and pets, with Dhurrie servants gliding forward to offer basins of scented water for the ritual cleansing of the hands and mouth, and Duval's heavy face breaking into one of his slow grins at the melee around her. Now there was nothing but an aloof house with furtive watching and whispers, Duval's strifer in her back like a spear of hate, and the coldness of distrust all around her.

She thought of Haufren, waiting beyond the barrier for her. Soon he would grow impatient, then alarmed. She knew he would not try to come after her. But the hunt would eventually close in on him, too.

"Here," said Duval, touching a door activator.

Costa stared in dismay at the windowless, cluttered storeroom. There could be no escape from it. "Duval, please—"

"In." He shoved her ruthlessly inside, sending her sprawling to her knees. The door closed, shutting her in total darkness.

She bumped painfully against something hard and sharp-cornered, jerked in a breath, and flung herself back at the door, pounding until her fists ached. Then she slid down to the floor, and huddled there in complete despair. Without Duval, there was no one to believe her, no one to take her side. In Beros, she would have no chance of defending herself against the charges. They were too neatly fitted, and far too damning. Haufren, who was the only proof she had for the truth of her story, would never come forward in her defense. He had a galaxy to defend, and she was not important enough to make him betray his presence here. For a moment she wondered why he was so set on keeping himself a secret from the authorities, then she shoved speculation away. It didn't matter. She was doomed unless she could get away somehow, and that hope was small. Her reputation was against her. Like Duval, the patrollers who came for her would be on their guard against any move she might make.

Pulling up her knees, she rested her forehead on them. Her right arm had begun to ache with a probing finger of coldness that shot along the bone. It was time for more droxyhyazine, but she would never get it now. Soon she would stand on trial in the Hall of Accusations, or else she would die from what the Omcri had done to her. Either way, her future would be short.

The muted sounds of an argument outside her door awakened her. Costa lifted her head, wincing at her stiff neck, and scrambled to her feet as the door slid open. The light beyond it, dim as it was, blinded her for an instant. She snapped down all three inner lids and squinted against the glare with her hand held up as a shield.

"Oh, Costa, how dreadful!" A gentle, perfumed hand grasped hers and pulled her from the storeroom. "I am ashamed for my house," said Aimlee indignantly, glaring at Duval. A tiny, fragile-looking woman with pale skin and black hair coiled elaborately about her shapely head, she was the youngest of Duval's wives and the most favored. "I leave for half a day to visit my *couiure,* and this is what I find when I return! Dreadful! Duval, how could you treat her this way?"

Duval hunched his thick shoulders angrily. "She is a prisoner of the Directory."

"Perhaps. But does that mean she must be treated cruelly?" Aimlee's eyes flashed at him, then she turned again to Costa. "You look exhausted. And how thin you are! When did you last eat?"

Costa had to think a moment. "This morning . . . dawn," she said unsteadily, rubbing her gritty eyes. "Fiber bars on the transport." Her arm was numb, and she winced as she pulled it closer to her side. *Heal!* she thought angrily. *Why don't you heal?*

"Fiber bars!" Aimlee snorted. "Ocean sand would do you

as much good. Come upstairs with me. I'll have the girls draw you a bath while the bread finishes baking. Then you can have a pot of thick stew and—"

"Aimlee," said Duval as though goaded into stopping her chatter. "No. She must stay in the storeroom. The shuttles will be here in an hour, and she must be given no chance to escape before then."

Something closed in Aimlee's delicate face. For an instant she came perilously near to expressing contempt as she gazed up at her husband. "Escape? *Escape?* Do you expect her to throw herself from one of the upper windows? Do you expect her to hold one of the children at knifepoint? Moii, husband! You speak of her as though she is some dirty Ishut that cannot comprehend what is civilized. Do you forget so easily that she remains your officer and as such deserves your respect? You have denied her the giving of her word of submission while she stands within our walls by taking away her sleeve knife. This is surely insult enough without locking her away as well."

"Aimlee."

"Why don't you cut off her warrior's braid?" continued Aimlee defiantly. "You treat her already as one tried and sentenced. And to put her in a dark room! That is wicked, Duval. You—"

"Woman!" The angry glint in his eyes silenced her, and scarlet-faced, she gave a slight bow of submission.

A taut silence fell over them. In the distance a child screamed with laughter.

Duval cleared his throat, glowered at his wife, and let his eyes flick briefly, uncomfortably to Costa, then away. "Very well. She may eat. But that is all, and then she must go back into the storeroom."

Aimlee brightened. "I shall prepare a tray," she said, picking up the train of her house robe, and hurrying away on quick, soundless feet.

Costa stepped away to put her back against the cool stone wall of the corridor. She felt fuzzy and confused without the drug's support, and now was when she needed her wits to be their sharpest. An hour, Duval had said. So little time!

His sigh broke her racing thoughts. "I have spoken to Janal on the viewer. He feels that you—"

"Oi! Oi! Father, guess what we have seen!"

Two children, a boy and girl of similar ages and coloring, came running up. Their eyes glowed with an excitement so intense they forgot all about pausing to approach Duval with respect.

"Father!"

Duval threw out both hands. "What is this wild behavior?" he asked sternly. "Can you not see there are warriors before you and not a pair of housewomen?"

They stopped, their eager faces falling with dismay.

"Costa," said the girl with a shy smile, but her brother turned red and would not meet Costa's eyes.

"We seek forgiveness," he said stiffly, lifting his palm to his father and nudged his sister in the ribs until she did the same.

"Very well," said Duval, relenting. "Run along to your suppers."

"But, Father, we saw Omcris!"

"What?" Costa straightened from the wall, snapping to alertness. "Where, Mia? How many?"

"On the road, the cliff road," said the girl. "Three of them, in long blue robes. Father, I thought they always wore black."

Alarm shot through Costa. Were they here for her, or were they searching for the Kublai? "Black means only that they are under hire," she said slowly. She and Duval exchanged worried looks, momentarily a team again.

"Heading which way, Ro?" asked Duval. "Toward us?"

"No. Toward the big hill."

"The Nogales villa," said Costa. She blinked, suddenly putting many things together. "He took the Kublai. Of course! Nogales was behind this!"

"You aren't making sense," snapped Duval.

"Of course I am! Listen to me. Don't you remember those reports from the safety board? Nogales has had several infractions recently, ever since we were first informed that the Kublai was coming here on a religious pilgrimage."

"Costa—"

"Listen!" She gripped his arm and shook it. "That has to be it. His Ishut workers were nearly uncontrollable. He has been in danger of losing his licensing from the board. Of course he did it. Nogales is bold and ruthless enough." She snorted. "And Haufren and I were looking everywhere but right in front of us."

"Haufren! Who . . . oh. The Ranger."

"Yes. The Ranger. He's on the island. Maybe he saw the Omcris, too. Duval, we've got to go up there!"

"No." Duval caught her arm before she could stride away. "Children, dismissed."

They blinked and reluctantly scampered away.

Costa pulled free. "Duval—"

"No, I tell you! This is nonsense. Wob Nogales is a leading citizen. How can you dare to accuse him of this? You're insane!"

"But, Duval, it makes so much sense! The Omcri in the wineshop was—"

"Yes, that Omcri in the wineshop who bribed you," said Duval bitterly. "You are a fool to try and make me believe Nogales is the traitor instead of you."

"But I did not betray—"

"Do you realize you are the only survivor of that massacre? Do you know how that looks?"

"Of course I know," she said impatiently. "I'm not a fool. But neither did I escape that attack untouched. Look."

She pulled up her torn sleeve to show him her arm. The flesh of the inside of her forearm was puffed and blackened so severely her own heart jerked in dismay. Duval stared at her, aghast.

"What kind of a wound is that?"

"Omcri poison."

"But you . . . when did it happen? Earlier today?"

A bitter laugh escaped her. "Oh, how well you believe in my recuperative abilities! No, this is a gift from the courier I spoke to in the wineshop." She yanked down her sleeve. "Now you see how I escaped. Oh, yes, Duval, I could have taken the bribe offered. I could have been far away when the attack came. I could have been off-planet with a new identity and plenty of wealth. But I *stayed.* I betrayed no one. And I was marked for it."

"But you didn't warn Janal," he said slowly, frowning.

"I tried to! His line was snooped. And then suddenly I was

under accusation with orders to turn myself in. I couldn't go back to Beros, Duval. I wouldn't have been permitted within a kilometer of Janal. Haufren said—"

"I hear something. Come." He strode down the corridor and into one of the open rooms furnished with hand-woven rugs and leather sitting cushions. Diagonal slats closed the window. He pulled these aside and peered out into the darkness. "Thought I heard a shuttle approach."

Her heart sank. "Duval, you can't turn me over to them! Not yet. If we can get the Kublai back, I'll gladly stand before a tribunal. But I have to help Haufren stop these—"

"The Ranger isn't here," said Duval.

"What?"

"He was captured hours ago. Puce took him in on a sled. Only there's been no report of them. When I called into Beros, Central said they were overdue." Duval stalked over to her, his dark eyes angry. "If that moon-skipper has unloaded Puce in the jungle, I'll hold you to blame for it. You should have brought him in at the first."

"Bring in a Ranger against his will?" she said scornfully to hide her sick sense of defeat. What if Haufren had killed Puce? Oh, Moii spit upon his grave if he had! Puce was the only man she knew who had survived an Omcri assassination attempt. She had counted on him to save her from the poison rather than Haufren's promises of help from the Ranger laboratories. "How good do you think I am? Duval, please. We have to go to Nogales' villa now. Haufren explained to me that the Omcris are preparing for an invasion of the galaxy. Somehow Playworld is the focal point. I don't understand why. Maybe it's the Kanta cult or something else, but they have to be stopped! They're taking over people." She lifted her arm. "I've been infected. Droxyhyazine combats the poison, but without it I may be summoned by them at any moment. Duval—"

He turned away as though she had not been speaking at all. "That *was* a shuttle. It's landing on the roof pad."

Costa frowned, only now hearing the whine outside. She shook her head in bafflement, unable to understand why she had heard nothing before. Her hearing was three times as keen as Duval's.

He started to walk out of the room, but swiftly she planted herself in his way.

"Moii take you, I am your *sister,* Duval!" she shouted in a panic. "Have I no claim upon blood—"

"You will lose your tongue unless you curb it," he said savagely. "When you cut off your warrior's braid and exchange your knife for a ladle, I shall surrender to blood claim for your protection. Until then, Costa, you are an officer of the patrol and you must take full responsibility for the charges against you. My duty is to surrender you, and I intend to do it."

"Duval!" she cried in a fury that suddenly changed to fear as her muscles jerked in a violent spasm. She staggered, nearly fell, and righted herself only by clutching at a table which skidded upon the floor under her weight. Her arm was throbbing, swelling, bursting. Yet when she clutched at it, there was only withered flesh and bone crushed inside her fingers. Coldness pierced her chest just under the heart. She screamed with a shrillness that made her own ears ring and staggered to one side as Duval tried to grab her.

"By the ten mercies!" cried Aimlee, freezing in the doorway, a steaming tray in her hands.

Costa whirled, feeling as though every movement was dragged through clinging mud, and started toward her. Duval's powerful hand seized her shoulder, crushing it, but she scarcely felt the pain as she flung back her arm and knocked him away with a strength far greater than she should possess. He sprawled to the floor, grunting, and Costa found the body she no longer controlled hurtling her toward the doorway and Aimlee.

She screamed a warning, trying to stop herself and failing. Aimlee stared at her in disbelief, frozen and heeding nothing until it was too late. Horror spread across her delicate face, and she opened her mouth to scream as Costa knocked her aside. The tray flew through the air, spilling food and pungent-smelling wine in a bright arc. Costa kept going, faster and faster, unable to stop, unable to combat the force which had possessed her so suddenly.

At the end of the corridor she saw the door solidly barring her way.

"Costa?" Mia darted toward her from one of the rooms, then screamed over and over again in hysterical bursts of sound as Costa ran past her.

Costa plowed right into the door and bounced off with force enough to send her sprawling. Again she felt pain only dimly as she forced herself up and yanked open the panel to the security controls. It took mere seconds to bypass the obedience code that kept the door from responding to her command. She saw her strifer stuffed into a cubbyhole above the control board and pulled it out, tossing away the holster and belt and thumbing the weapon to full charge.

It hummed in her hand as the door slid open, and then she was outside in the rain-slashed darkness, moving in a crouching run across the courtyard. A shape came at her. She fired, and the screaming juujb writhed at her feet. Without looking at the dying pet, she ran on even as that tiny corner of her which was still cognizant cried out in horror at what she had done.

"That's her!"

A torch snapped on, stabbing through the darkness to illuminate her like an insect pinned to a wall. She whirled and fired toward the torch, letting her strifer sweep that section of the courtyard. A man shouted in pain, and she ran on, ducking through the cultivated plants as someone fired back.

"Take her alive, you fool!"

Panting, Costa squinted against the rain stinging her face. She no longer tried to combat the force in control of her. Her will was blending with it. For she had to get *out* and she had to get out now before they boxed her in.

She threw herself at the wall, knowing better than to try for the exit. The torchlight stabbed around her, trying to hold steady as she snarled and fired again. It wavered wildly, and there were more shouts, closer this time. She sprang straight up, hands clawing at the wall to find minute fingerholds. She kept going, mindlessly now, going up by sheer impetus until one outflung hand reached the top. Her fingers curled around the edge with a strength that was incredible. She grunted as a bolt of energy struck her in the back, and for a moment it felt as though her shoulder blade had been melted.

But it was only stun, she realized, and something faint

within her laughed. In mere moments her nerves would jam, and she would be clinging here helplessly for them to climb up and pluck off.

Only the stun wasn't working. She was still moving, still forcing herself up in a last savage squirm that got her stomach across the top. She swung her legs over and let herself drop straight down, scraping her face along the wall. The impact as she landed jarred her to the top of her head. She heard herself cry out as she staggered and fell. Her legs should have been shattered, but they weren't. She scrambled through the mud until she regained her feet, and then she was racing on, hidden by the rain-tossed night from the men cursing behind her, aiming herself unerringly toward her masters.

CHAPTER TEN

Tith paced restlessly back and forth along the narrow confines of the balcony, growling to himself, and pausing only to glare out at the magnificent view of a bronze-ball sun sinking into the white-capped sea, tossing beneath approaching black thunderheads.

Silta . . . Silta . . .

The word drove him mad, spinning around and around inside his brain until he could not even think let alone concentrate upon the lessons Unru Del had assigned to him. That strange, thin human with the blood on his clothes had sundered him and put this word into his brain, worse, into the sending lobe of his brain, where no such thing was permitted. Besides, he now had two of the blue years as well as seven of the standard, and he was too old to be sundered by an adult.

Unru Del was not even speaking to him after his shameful behavior this morning. He had made an assignment of thirty verbs, sniffed, locked the room, and left. While Tith was glad to be rid of his tutor, he did not wish to be alone when his head throbbed like this. He wanted Unru Del to take the word out, but he did not dare ask. Unru Del would probably refuse to believe him and accuse him of trying to shirk his lessons. And Unru Del was not of his line, being of no sibilants. By rights, only Tith's father had the authority to sunder him after the matriarch herself, but this was an emergency. Surely his father would understand.

Silta . . .

The sound of the door opening made him whirl around and run into the suite. He bounded up to Unru Del, who held out a hand before he could speak.

"What means this?" Unru Del's narrow green eyes, slits of perpetual suspicion about whatever a young nib might be up to, moved at once to the table, where the triangular computer screen shimmered blankly. "Nothing you have done! You dare disobey again! For this you—"

"Please, Unru Del!" cried Tith. He butted his head against the tutor's paunch, wrinkling his nostrils at the unpleasant odors of meat grease and scincipi herb clinging to Unru Del's fur. At the moment it did not matter how much he disliked Unru Del. He needed someone to comfort him. He needed an adult to take charge. His stubby hands clung to the tutor's clenched one. "My head hurts. The—"

"A likely excuse." Sniffing, Unru Del pushed him firmly away. "Stand erect. Wicked has your behavior been, ever since permission your glorious matriarch gave to come to this planet. Will you come again? Unlikely."

"Nothing do I care for that," said Tith, his voice roughened with misery. Why wouldn't Unru Del listen to him? Why did Unru Del hate him so much? "Please. The truth I tell you. My head has . . . the human sundered me."

"What?" His attention caught at last, Unru Del bowed his head to peer at Tith more closely. One side of his upper lip had caught on a prominent side tooth, which gleamed whitely as he leaned down.

For a moment the tutor looked as fierce and bloodthirsty as Uncle Simmsa, who had turned pirate and was not permitted to be mentioned within the family fire circle. With his sparse, balding fur, hollow face, and glowing green eyes, Unru Del was suddenly frightening as he grabbed Tith by the shoulder. Tith squirmed, wishing he had never spoken, wishing he had been braver, wishing he dared kick Unru Del and run away, but the tutor's fingers dug in with a hint of claw and Tith could not free himself.

"Lies you speak!"

"No! The human! Strange you said he was! He did it. And now this word will not leave me."

"What word?"

"Silta." Tith heard his voice quiver and despised himself for betraying how near he was to crying aloud. Why must Unru Del get so angry? It was as though he blamed Tith for this, and it wasn't fair.

"A name," said Unru Del as though disappointed. "Well, hurt you it will not. Put thought of it aside and go to your lessons."

"Sent it is to be," said Tith, staring up at Unru Del with anguish. "And *how* I do not know."

"As is well you do not!" said Unru Del in alarm. "Were the honored matriarch of your line to know you are sending, ended my life would be." He shuddered and released Tith to fumble in his pouch for a roll of scincipi herb.

The acrid smell made Tith want to retch. He stared at Unru Del, waiting while the silence stretched out interminably, and finally realized as Unru Del went on nervously rubbing the herb roll across his mouth and chin that the tutor was not thinking about him at all.

Angrily Tith stamped his foot. "Permission you have to sunder me and remove the word."

"Remove?" With a start, Unru Del dropped the herb roll. He looked at Tith with alarm. "Foolish you are. I dare not!"

"You must!" Tith began to pace around the room, angrily kicking a plush hassock out of his way. "More I cannot stand! Take it out!"

"And I tell you I dare not! I have not the power!"

Tith stumbled to a halt, shocked.

Unru Del grimaced in a bitter snarl. "Now, little princeling, you understand that privileged all are not. Your glorious matriarch has no fear that tampered with you will be. To send, I can not; to receive, I can not. Now sneer at me if you dare!"

Tith blinked at him, frightened once again by the blast of hatred emanating from the tutor. He shook his head and with miserably flattened ears, said, "Someone must help me. Find them. Now!"

"Permitted it is not. My duty I know well." He narrowed his eyes to slits and peered thoughtfully at Tith, who barely stifled a howl. "Perhaps the vertu lock—"

"No!" Panic arrowed through Tith. He stumbled back in horror, staring at Unru Del with widened eyes.

"Yes. It was given to me for chance of trouble." Unru Del lifted his chin and sniffed. "Come here!"

His voice rang with authority. Tith quivered, conditioned to obey those in charge of him, yet somehow he held his ground. He would not be tortured by that *thing!* He had done nothing wrong.

"No! Unfair you are!"

"Tith, fear not. For punishment it will not be. The headache it will ease. Come."

The hard gleam in those green eyes belied the softness in the voice. Unru Del started toward Tith, one hand outstretched, his ragged ears slightly flattened.

Tith's heart hammered within his chest. "For this my father will kill you!"

Unru Del bared his teeth. "Your father is far away. Ambassadors to Terra rarely come home before their term is finished. For years you will not see him. By then today will not matter. A lesson in obedience is what you need. Tith! Come here!"

But Tith was already running. He dodged Unru Del's grab at him, and heard the old tutor grunt with the effort. Without looking back, Tith flattened his ears tightly to his skull and threw himself at the door, activating it and hurtling down the corridor to the lift. The doors closed on Unru Del's roar of fury, and with a sob of relief, Tith crouched down on the floor, quivering all over and terrified that when he reached the ground he would find Unru Del waiting for him.

He cried out as the doors slid silently open, but Unru Del was not standing in the midst of richly dressed guests waiting for the lift. Gasping in a breath as a woman murmured something and reached out to him, Tith threw himself forward, his stubby, powerful legs churning as he forced a path through the block of adults. With indulgent laughter they let him pass, and then he was racing like the wind through the silver- and gold-hung lobby, darting past the spun-glass sculptures, spinning holographs of sea globes, and other island wonders. The glass doors were ahead of him, huge and vast and clear. He could see right through them to the courtyard and lytcar pad outside. Beyond them lay safety. Unru Del would never find him again. He could run and he could bite and he could hide. He would find the communications center and call his father, and then he would be free at last of that horrible old thing!

A shout came from behind him. Tith's heart leapt in a violent bound. He heard something behind him and felt the rush of air as arms made a grab. The doors were just ahead, but they weren't opening. He was running too fast; the activator wasn't going to have enough time to sense him and open them. He was going to crash and be stopped and caught and hauled back to Unru Del, who would put the vertu lock on him. Then he would be totally at the tutor's mercy, unable to act on his own, unable to even move without a direct command. Unru Del would torture him. Oh, please, *please* open!

They did, rolling back a split second before he reached them. He sobbed in relief, ducking his head and plunging on into the close, muggy air of dusk and welcome shadows, feeling the whisper of clutching fingers brushing the fur of his shoulder, terrified of how close he had come to capture. Someone shouted again, but the doorman in his brilliant uniform merely stood rooted in amazement as Tith flashed past him, understanding too late the frantic shouts of pursuit. He blew his alarm, making Tith's ears ring, but a slim young man slammed the hatch of his lytcar at that moment, cutting off the shrill sound of warning. Tith made it across the narrow courtyard and out into the heavily trafficked street before anyone else had the presence of mind to activate the sonic gates.

Like a whirlwind, Tith dodged and darted across the street, escaping being run down by sheer luck. Then he was around the corner and into the darkness of an alley off the brightly lit Central Street. He fell to his knees with a gasp, his breath gone and his heart hammering so hard against his ribs his whole chest ached with pain. Only then, as thunder broke open the sky and rain began to pour down with crashing force, did he curl himself into a tight ball and cry.

The rain beat down steadily until he was drenched and shaking with cold. His ears ached from being held so tightly flattened to his skull, and his fur was matted to his skin. Water puddled under him in a broadening lake until the entire alley became a stream of mud. The drumming rain muted the sounds of traffic on Central Street, and somewhere in the darkness at the end of the alley a piece of canvas awning flapped in the wind.

Tith lifted his head, squinting against the lash of rain in his face. The throbbing at his temples was worse. He lifted a hand to rub his forehead and pushed himself unsteadily to his feet. He had to go to the communications center before Unru Del thought of looking for him there.

He remembered the way, of course. Nothing was difficult to find on Lilliput. But he kept cautiously to the shadows as he splashed a miserable way up the street. Few people were out now; most had taken shelter under awninged doorways or had gone inside altogether. Those who were hastening along had their heads tucked down and spared no glance of curiosity for one small nib obviously out where he should not be, without proper supervision.

Tith had never gone anywhere without escort before, and with every step he felt smaller, more alone and increasingly frightened. He thought of all the tales he had been told in the nursery of wicked nibs who had run away and were assassinated when they were beyond the reach of their loyal guards. It seemed to take forever to reach the communications center. He had to resolutely go past several restaurants with enticing smells and lights shining warmly out into the darkness, but when at last he got to the entrance of the low rambling stone building and began with relief to think himself very brave, he found the doors locked and the center closed.

"No!" he shouted, pounding on the glass. "No! No! No!"

But no one responded, not even a duty drone. Tith turned away, unable to understand it. He had distinctly overheard a guest in the hotel lobby asking for the hours. The center *should* be open.

Silta . . . Silta . . .

"Leave me alone!" he shouted, gripping his head. "To send I am not allowed!"

Wearily he sat down in the shelter of the entrance overhang, for the moment not caring that the tiny glowlight there illuminated him. "Oh, Perre," he said with a sigh, wishing with all his heart for his father, "why so far away are you?"

Sneezing, he rested his narrow chin in his hands, remembering the day of his father's departure. To be the ambassador to Terra was a great honor, and all Zethia had gathered to give respect to the matriarch of the Zauran line. Tith, as a nib of the third birthing of the second daughter of the matriarch, was considered too young to attend with his older mates, so he could only watch from afar the rare sight of his perre and matre seated with the matriarch herself. His young heart thrilled at Perre's magnificent auburn mane worn long and full to the shoulders and the star of Zethia glittering on his chest. Someday, as the chamberlain kept repeating to Tith and the awed little nursery nibs, each of them would be old enough and trained enough to receive the privilege of meeting the adults of their noble line, and providing they were found worthy, they could then be permitted the acquaintanceship of their perre and matre.

Would Perre consider him worthy if he knew Tith were sitting here sniveling in the rain? Was that the way a Zauran noble male dealt with his problems?

Tith could imagine the stinging rebuke, and he sniffed in deep shame. There was no one to help him, at least not now. And his head hurt so much he longed to beat it against the wall. He did not think he could wait until morning for the center to open. By then, Unru Del might have caught him again. No, he must do something right now.

He must find the human who had done this cruelty to him and make him take the word away.

With a growl, Tith stood up only to sigh in despair. Where should he look? There were thousands of humans on the island. And he was so cold, wet, and hungry. For a moment the thought of food nearly drove him back into the main part of the village. But he had no money, and he did not know the account number Unru Del used for their transactions. If he went into any place, he would be immediately questioned about the lack of an adult supervisor and turned over to Unru Del. Tith shuddered and turned his back on Central Street.

He dared not risk being caught. And instinct told him the human had not wanted to be caught either. The human had been very strange with his bloodied clothing and intense blue eyes. He had used Tith to get on board the transport. Tith growled again, resentful and angry now of an adventure which had turned into painful misery. He did not think the human would be found in any of the restaurants or casinos or shows. No, the human would be somewhere in the darkness beyond the village. Tith did not want to go out there looking for him, but in spite of the fear that turned him cold inside, he knew he had no choice.

Reluctantly, with his shoulders hunched up, he started walking, making himself go very fast in order not to think about what he was doing. He told himself his perre would not be afraid; neither, for that matter, would his matre. How many stories they had been told in the nursery of her hunting prowess! For a moment it was possible to hold up his head with pride and think of how good it was to be brave. But as he passed the last of the lights and stumbled off the pavement onto a muddy track, Tith's heart sank and he began to walk more and more slowly.

Within minutes, as the wind shrieked and buffeted him, stinging his eyes with needle-sharp rain, he had lost all sense of direction. Even the lights of the village were gone, dimmed to nothing by the violence of the storm. Intermittently, whenever the wind paused for a moment, he could hear the booming crash of the sea. Listening to it, he stumbled into something elastic and intangible which hummed as he fell against it.

Tith screamed, aware that he had fallen against a force barrier, and flailed his arms in a panic, trying to get away before it fried him out of existence. But he had already lost his balance and was falling forward through the barrier, which sang and crackled and spat all around him, stinging him viciously as though thousands of red-hot needles jabbed him all at once. He screamed again, then choked as he landed face down on the ground with cold, metallic-tasting mud filling his mouth.

Spluttering, he jerked himself upright and spat and spat, trying to get the mud out. Then he ran his hands down his body in wonder, dazed at the thought of his survival. The rain must have weakened the signal, he thought, and hastily made obeisance to Basa.

Silta . . .

"Leave me alone!" Angrily he began to run, weaving along as his stumbling feet took him uphill. He tripped and fell flat again, knocking the wind from his lungs. For a long while he lay there, sobbing and retching. His head hurt worse, as though the farther he went the more insistent the command became. Or else, someone was using mind control nearby, and the backlash of it was intensifying his own problem.

He pushed himself up, thoroughly frightened now as he recognized yet another danger of being alone and unprotected. Unru Del was supposed to keep him safe from anyone skilled in telepathy. But Unru Del had not kept him safe from the human this morning; Unru Del had not even realized what was happening.

Tith's flattened ears suddenly sprang up in alarm. Someone was coming his way. He could hear the squishing plops of feet running through mud. Tith's heart squeezed within him. He must hide!

A body, moving fast, plowed into him and knocked him off his feet. It fell on top of him, making him cry out as he was crushed flat. It grunted and cursed loudly, pushing him aside.

Tith gasped. He knew that voice!

"You!" he said, forgetting in his excitement to be afraid. "Wait!" Desperately he grasped a leg as the patroller picked herself up and started to run on. Someone else was coming —several others—but Tith paid no heed to them. He wrapped both arms about her leg and hung on in spite of her attempt to shake them off. "Wait! Please! Tith it is! From this morning! Oh, please! The human with you . . . where to find him?"

A sled was chuffing closer, drowning out his desperate queries. He heard shouts, and a torch stabbed through the rain.

The patroller snarled something incomprehensible and yanked Tith up by the arm. Dragging him ruthlessly along, she ran on so fast he could barely keep up. She did not listen to his cries of genuine panic now, and her hand was like iron on his arm.

The rain eased to a drizzle. He began to make out vague shapes of trees and rocks in the darkness. Apparently her night vision was better than his, for she never stumbled except when the footing became especially slippery. And she was tireless, running on and on at a speed that was killing him. His short legs burned, but he could not catch enough breath to ask her to slow down. Every time he faltered, she jerked him on mercilessly. He could hear the sob of breath in her throat, but still she ran, dragging him uphill now through short trees and bushes that tore viciously at him and whipped him in the face. He cried out, but she never heard, and when he fell down on his knees, she dragged him without stopping until somehow he found the strength to shove himself back onto his feet.

She was relentless, unstoppable. And whatever pursued them could not quite catch up. He did not understand, because a sled properly rigged with search equipment should have been able to catch them in minutes.

Ahead through the mist a vast dwelling loomed up on top of the hill. A light shone from one of the windows. Tith could barely see it, for one of his eyes had swelled shut from being whipped by a branch. His lungs were bursting; his head was splitting. Something about the kind patroller who had been so friendly to him this morning was *wrong* as though she were no longer real. No one could run like this. And even his carefully untrained talent of empathy could detect that all the warmth was gone from her. It was almost like being dragged along by a drone.

He began to fear her as much as he did whatever was chasing them. But he could not break free of her grip.

Suddenly a spotlight stabbed out from the building ahead, blinding him. He heard the patroller snarl, but she did not slacken her speed. The chuffing of the sled grew louder, almost on top of them, as though it had found them again. Tith looked up as a loudspeaker blared:

"Costa! Give yourself up! You can go no farther!"

She stopped and slewed around to face the sled hovering overhead, dragging Tith like a piece of rag. He dropped to his knees, shuddering with the need for air, while she drew her strifer and fired on the sled. They fired back, and Tith cringed behind her leg in terror as a bolt missed him by inches.

In the light he could see her plainly for the first time. Her eyes were wild, blazing almost incandescently beneath wind-torn hair, and she was smeared with blood. The scent of it made Tith groan.

A mental force, as powerful as it was unexpected, flattened Tith to the ground. But he caught only the backlash, for it was not aimed at him. Looking up, he saw shapes from a nightmare floating overhead. Three Omcris in streaming robes stretched out their arms in unison and flew at the sled. The men aboard shouted and fired, and Tith gasped as the bolts blazed right through the Omcris without effect. Ozone burned in the air, making him sneeze, and the Omcris seemed to grow larger.

It was the first time he had ever seen the fabled Omcris, although plenty of stories had been told in the nursery. One of his mates did not believe in Omcris, and Tith thought, *Just wait until I tell you, Mis*. But all the same, his fur was prickling along his spine and his claws came out. His heart hammered in his chest until he feared it would burst.

The patroller grunted and jerked Tith up. "Must hurry," she mumbled to herself. She ran toward the house, still dragging him with her.

A quick, well-aimed blast from her strifer unlocked the circuits of the massive door. She kicked her way inside and shouted at a slim, hairless man descending the long, curved stairs with another human—unconscious—cradled in his arms.

"Defiler!" screamed the hairless man. "By the glory of Kanta does the Blessed One live! By her will shall you die!" He fired a queer, blunt-nosed weapon. The missile screamed past Tith's ear.

The patroller dropped Tith's arm at long last, diving in a quick roll to one side as the hairless man fired again. Tith scuttled out of the way, panic-stricken as the battle began in earnest. The whine and bark of weapons both inside the house and out, the stench of fried ozone and fear, and the throbbing sickness in his head was more than he could bear. He saw the hairless man suddenly fling out his arms and fall in a limp tumble down the stairs. The patroller straightened from her crouch in triumph, but her face was expressionless, almost dead. The slackness there was horrible, but worse were her eyes, clearly seen now in the light. The bright yellow color Tith remembered was dimmed by a murky darkness as though she were being drained away from the inside.

She glanced briefly around as though looking for Tith, but he pressed himself back more tightly into the shadows beneath a table and did not breathe. After a moment she moved away, heading for the stairs, where with a careless nudge of her foot she pushed aside the hairless man she had just killed and went on up to where the other man lay sprawled with equal lifelessness.

A chill prickled across Tith's back. He dared turn his head slightly and gasped as an Omcri entered. It extended a gloved hand toward Costa.

"The Kublai lives," she said in a toneless voice as dead as her face.

"Satisfactory," replied the Omcri.

Tith shivered, certain he would remember that horrible, unworldly voice in his grave.

A second Omcri entered, and beside him walked a tall man of military bearing.

"There is another here," said Costa.

Tith bit down upon a whimper of fear and curled himself up even more tightly, certain the violent thumping of his heart would give him away. One of the Omcris turned slightly in his direction, and Tith closed his eyes.

"Of importance, none," said the first Omcri. "Use of this planet, finished. Costa, we keep. Janal, we keep. Kublai, we recover. Go, all."

"Accord," said the second Omcri.

Gathering up the unconscious Kublai over her shoulder, Costa walked heavy-footed behind the others as they all filed out. Just at the door, however, she glanced over her shoulder in Tith's direction. For an instant, through his throbbing daze of terror and pain, he imagined he saw a look of pleading enter her eyes. Then she was gone, and the house was abruptly plunged into darkness, leaving him there alone with the burned stench of fresh blood curling in on the rain-washed air through the open door.

CHAPTER ELEVEN

Water, cold and incessant, dripped on Haufren's face, pounding against his closed eyes, sluicing down the angles of his face, running into the corners of his mouth. He groaned and turned his head to one side, snorting as water threatened to trickle into his nostrils, and abruptly woke up to the surprise of not being dead after all.

He grimaced, growing cognizant of unbearable bands of pain around both shoulders and across his back as though someone were branding him with a fiery iron. His whole body was strangely immobile and heavy. He opened his eyes with a quick blink against the rain, stared at the gray sky through thickly interlaced branches overhead, and tried to lift his head without success. He tried again, pulled it forward and upright, then let it fall as the effort of balancing it proved too much. His chin slammed against his chest, and the pain nearly snapped his neck.

He grunted, breathing several moments through his mouth until at last the agony stopped shooting from the base of his neck to the top of his skull, and managed to open one swimming eye. The view was straight down this time, and the ground was not close. He stared at his feet dangling in the air, then slowly began piecing together his situation. The limb holding him seemed to be rammed through the back of his tunic, and as long as the cloth held he could go on hanging here.

Gingerly he drew in a deep breath and called, "Puce?"

Muted, irritable squawks made him drag his head up again. He glanced warily around. Row after row of blue-beaked, vicious carpals lined the branches around him, gripping their perches with enormous, razor-sharp talons. They slashed each other as they jostled miserably in the rain, trying to crowd beneath the meager shelter of the leaves. Scarlet-edged eyes regarded Haufren with cold intent. They were flesh eaters, he remembered, and alarm sank through him. Apparently, from their present behavior, they did not feed in the rain, but as soon as it stopped he had no doubt they would strip him to a skeleton in minutes. He shivered, licking some of the rain from his lips to ease a suddenly dry throat. He had to work himself free without falling, and he had to start *now*.

Slowly, with extreme care, he started by lifting his right hand over his left shoulder. At least, he *tried* to do that. His joints were locked up; the effort to pull his hand up higher than his elbow brought excrutiating pain. He gasped, his lips curling back over his teeth in an effort not to cry out. With the pain came unwanted memories of the planet Ruibo, where a certain group of its inhabitants had hung him by the heels for three days in an experiment to see which would happen first: his giving them the information they wanted, or his skull bursting from the intolerable pressure.

This situation is not as bad, he told himself, trying to find some pride to overcome his fear, *and I survived that one*.

Pushing aside the memory of how long it had taken him to be able to walk easily after that mission, he concentrated on forcing his hand higher, inch by slow inch, while his cramped muscles stretched reluctantly. Finally his hand clamped down upon his shoulder, and triumphantly, blinking the tears from his eyes, he paused to rest.

The rain also paused.

Haufren squinted up at the sky, overwhelmed by desperation and a hysterical urge to laugh. Demos, how he hated this miserable planet with its naive population, its ridiculous vacation industry, its refusal to permit proper military protection units, its unguarded gateway point to another galaxy, and its damned, unmanaged weather!

But there was no time to curse the elements. Already the carpals were flapping and squawking restlessly, preening their fur, and stretching out long, scrawny necks to scream furiously at him. He longed for a strifer set on wide beam as he gritted his teeth and forced himself past pain, stiffness, and lack of circulation to grasp the branch hooked under his left arm. Just as his shaking fingers closed around the rough, sodden bark, he heard a ripping of cloth. He froze involuntarily, then shouted as a carpal dived at him with an ear-splitting screech. Startled, the thing veered off, striking him only with a wingtip that stank of vermin and decay.

Grunting with the effort, Haufren twisted himself around. He was definitely slipping; he might as well go for all he could. Trying to gauge the tensile strength remaining in the bowing branch, he grasped it more tightly, tried to catch hold of it with his left hand as well, and failed. There was no feeling at all in his left arm. He might as well be waving around a solid fuel canister.

The branch that was his lifeline snapped with a loudness that echoed off the dripping trees. Panicked by suddenly finding himself in midair, Haufren threw out his right arm wildly, seeking any hold possible. He caught at leaves, which slipped through his hand, and continued falling. A carpal came at him again; this time with better aim. It struck, slicing his cheek viciously. For a second he felt nothing, then an incredible wave of pain swept across his face, and hot blood welled up through the cut.

And he was still falling, twisting, and flailing in the air while the ground seemed to rush at him. He bounced off a branch, crashing through leaves as insubstantial as the air, and could not catch anything. Carpals wheeled furiously in a descent to match his, shrieking at him. Another struck, gouging open his leg with a swift talon. He was nearly to the lowest branches, falling head first now, his wide eyes frozen on the twisted wreckage of the sled directly below like target zero, with the broken point of the windscreen waiting like a massive stake to impale him.

His mind stretched and snapped over into absolute terror, and at that moment he would have given more than his soul to be able to close his eyes, turn the other direction, *anything*, so as not to watch death rushing right at him.

No, no, no, no!

He spread his arms out wide as he plummeted through the last branches, and screamed as the impact nearly tore his left arm from his shoulder. But if the branches slowed his fall, they did not stop it. Still head down, he gauged the final four meters as his shoulders and hips scraped through the latticework of branches, and only then could he clench shut his eyes.

One knee caught on something; he crooked it desperately,

slipped, and screamed as by sheer gut-wrenching willpower he tightened his thigh muscles and clamped that knee hard upon the swaying twig that had saved him. For a long sickening moment he bobbed up and down with the jagged, twisted point of metal waiting below him. Then, finally, he was able to open his eyes, stinging from the sweat pouring into them. Slowly he recovered from his numbing terror. His racing heart eased up, and he began to draw in full breaths again.

His thigh muscles were beginning to quiver from the strain, but at that moment he didn't care. He waited until he had his wits back under control, then he curled himself up, stomach muscles groaning from the strain, and got a solid grasp on the branch. His left arm was still useless, but with his right hand and his knee, he managed to work his way toward the trunk, upside down with blood trickling annoyingly into his ear. Sawtooth vines were wrapped around the tree at this height, and he cut his clothes and himself into ribbons as he grasped the trunk with his good arm and slid by slow, halting degrees down to the ground.

For a moment he stood there gasping for breath, his lungs on fire and his clothes soaked through with rain, sweat, and blood. He took a step, staggered, and went down on one knee as a sled chuffed suddenly into view overhead. It hovered over him while he knelt there in the open, a perfect target too weak to even scramble for cover. Still panting, he did not even bother to lift his head. After what he had just survived, a gibbering corner of his mind could not believe anything would kill him now. The rest of him, of course, knew better.

Move, he told himself, lifting a shaking hand to dash the sweat from his eyes. *Move!*

But all he could manage was to lift his head. The sled landed practically on top of him, blinding him as its air jets blew muddy twigs and leaves into a gale. Then silence fell over the jungle, broken only by the enraged screaming of the carpals flying away in a frustrated horde.

A smooth, silken voice like warmed cream said calmly, "Behold the infamous Major Brith Haufren IV, eight times decorated for bravery beyond the call of duty, due for promotion, well-regarded by senior command in the Fleet, and under serious consideration for desertion-arrest. I presume you have been spending the last several weeks groveling in the mud of this miserable jungle. Surely had you needed a vacation, you could have chosen some less expensive planet and made the standard request for leave in the standard way?"

Haufren blinked stupidly at the lean, elegant Zethian gazing down at him with enormous round eyes of intermingled jade and amber. A thin ray of sunshine broke through the clouds for a second, long enough to cast a radiant nimbus about the sleek, black fur.

"Silta!" cried Haufren gladly and fainted.

"Drink this," said Silta minutes later when Haufren dazedly opened his eyes. He shoved a field cup at Haufren, his big eyes roving the jungle around them.

Haufren drank thirstily, sighing as the liquid spread a reviving warmth through his stomach. It had begun to rain again, but they were dry beneath a tarp spread tent-fashion over the sled. Silta crouched beside him, snarling in distaste at the weather, and intent on the matted undergrowth.

Haufren blinked and suddenly sat up with a wince. "What is it?" he asked quietly.

Silta flattened his ears as a downpour opened up, drumming on the tarp. "We are being stalked."

"Kicats!" said Haufren, recalling those long days in the jungle with Costa when every moment included a watch for the big animals. He lifted a hand gingerly to his throbbing cheek and touched the warm stickiness coating his torn and swelling flesh. "They smell my blood—"

"No," said Silta. "It is a man-thing."

Haufren glanced at him with a frown, only to realize Silta was using the primitive term of his native language deliberately. He held his questions, however, as Silta sent out a delicate mind probe.

"Sistat!" spat Silta after a moment, shaking his head. "What is Ishut? A piece of unpleasantness and what else?"

"Something we don't want to mix with," said Haufren. "Let's get this sled off the ground. It isn't safe to be down here anyway."

"We are requested to wait," said Silta, taking out a strifer and charging it.

"Wait?" Bewildered, Haufren stared at him. "For whom? Silta, you haven't—"

"Local allies," broke in the Zethian coolly.

"Silta! Demos, they can't be trusted. We—"

"Nor can you, Major."

"What?" Taken aback, Haufren stared at the companion and fellow officer who had been a close friend for years. "You can't be serious about that desertion charge."

"Pfit! Haufren, you fool!" said Silta with an angry gesture. He moved to the rear of the sled and opened a storage locker. Curled inside was a sleeping nib, golden pelted, and drawn under the ribs. It moaned lightly, and Silta placed a gentle hand on that small shoulder before closing the locker once again. "Remember him?"

Haufren grinned. "So it did work. I thought it was a small chance at best, but since I couldn't be sure I would be able to break into a communications line, I—"

"When I taught you the process of mind touch, it was not to enable you to sunder a small nib! He is a Zauran, branched from one of the three oldest noble Zethian lines, and not to be tampered with!"

"Silta," said Haufren placatingly. "I thought you had little use for those old-fashioned societal structures. You said you—"

"I have said many things," broke in Silta with a rough burr, his eyes drawn to slits. "You fail to understand. Zauran nibs are extremely sensitive, with extraordinary mental abilities. But they are shielded from any mental training until they are nearly grown. You sundered a nib with the command to send me a message, but he couldn't obey because he did not know how. Do you realize the torment you have caused him?"

Haufren frowned, beginning to understand at last. "No, I didn't realize. I merely saw what I thought was an opportunity, and I took it."

"Yes, just as you always do. This is Playworld, Major! These people are civilians, innocent, *important* civilians, and not scum from a backworld who don't matter! Now how you got here, or what you are doing here is—"

"I was captured on Regus," said Haufren, glancing away with a muscle leaping in his jaw as he remembered that brief second of humiliation at being taken so easily just before the world became black for a very long time. "Simple reconnoitering, but I slipped up and was blasted for it. I ended up in a stasis box and was brought here by the Kublai of Drugh for a living sacrifice to Kanta."

Silta blinked, thrown momentarily by that rapid explanation. "You—"

A soft thud and grunt made them both whirl. Silta whipped out his strifer, crouching in readiness, only to relax as a stocky man in the fatigues of a planet patroller ducked in under the tarp. He was breathing heavily, and his clothes were plastered to his body. His weathered face looked very grim beneath its dripping warrior's braid. Something about his deep-set eyes and the way he moved reminded Haufren of Costa. He hoped she had had a better day than his, and he hoped her friend Duval was more eager to see her than Silta was him.

"Did you find what you were looking for?" asked Silta.

The patroller's craggy face betrayed intense grief for a moment, then, with working jaw muscles, he glanced down and away. "Puce is dead. I found what the jungle left."

Haufren thought of the carpals waiting around him and shivered.

"You were his prisoner."

Haufren looked up to meet those dark, grief-stricken eyes. "Yes."

"What caused the crash?"

Silta stirred restlessly. He knew, thought Haufren. They all knew, but it had to be verbalized just the same.

"I caused it." Haufren made himself meet the swift, incredulous accusation in that gaze. Then he added, "Standard Ranger procedure, Pepe."

The patroller stiffened at the insult, and Silta put a swift hand on Haufren's bruised shoulder, letting the claws dig in slightly.

"Go easy, my friend. This is not the time for an arrogant display of Ranger superiority. The men were close fr—"

"Oh, can that, Silta!" said Haufren, shaking off the restraining hand. "It's about time these people were shaken up. Patrollers? Fleet cadets could do a better job!"

"Haufren—"

"We have protected this planet for three hundred years," said the patroller angrily. "And we have never needed Ranger help *or* the Fleet. It is *you* who do not understand. You think because of your fancy reputation, you Rangers can fly in anywhere and take over operations, but we don't need you. And we don't need the trouble you bring!"

"That is not what you said a few hours ago, Duval," said Silta quietly.

Haufren stiffened. "Duval! You're Duval?" He sprang to his feet without waiting for the man's nod. "Where's Costa? Surely she told you—"

"Costa is gone. The Omcris took her and Commander Janal. They killed the rest of the squad—" Duval's voice suddenly broke, and he did not finish.

"How could they? Did they attack your place? That's not their usual style." Haufren frowned, trying not to remember the fear which had grown daily in the girl's eyes, the fear which he had occasionally fed when it served his purpose. "As long as she had injections of droxyhyazine, they couldn't possess her."

Something in the defeated way Duval shook his head made Haufren's stomach clutch. He gripped the man's arm hard.

"Fool! Didn't you believe her? Didn't you give her any?"

"No."

Furious, Haufren lifted a hand to strike him, but Silta intervened.

"That is enough, Brith! Sit down!" Silta pushed him to the floor with a strength that permitted no argument.

"How could I believe her?" said Duval, anguish breaking through his gruff exterior. He spread out his hands. "She is charged with treason. I tried to do my duty by holding her until a squad from Beros could come. I didn't realize the threat to Playworld, to *all* worlds. She was so anxious to talk to Puce. She knew he would believe her. He was possessed once by the Omcris, a long time ago as a child on Cygni Minor. His family was killed, but he underwent treatment and lived. It damaged his eyes, but he was freed of the poison. She knew he would help her. She thought I would help her, but I—"

Abruptly Duval turned and ducked out into the rain. Silence stretched between Haufren and Silta.

"I never realized," said Haufren slowly, letting the implications sink through him like cold lead. "I thought Puce's goggles were to protect nocturnal-oriented vision. He *was* on our side, would have been on our side if I could have convinced him to trust me. Instead, I tipped him out. I looked no further than the fact that he was hauling me into Beros Central and that once I was officially logged as being on Playworld, the old man would be fielding repercussions on all counts." He pressed the heels of his hands against his eyes. "Demos, I'm tired. I've botched everything."

"Yes, you have," said Silta severely. "Admiral Vance would can you if he could. Did it never occur to you, Brith, that you are human? That when you are ordered to rest it is for your own good? There are limitations to your species which you must observe. How many missions have you gone on this year? How much leave have you taken?"

Haufren sighed wearily, not wanting to hear this. "Twice on the—"

"Twice. Pfit!" Silta spread out his hands, showing the claws. "You were not even supposed to be on that mission to Regus."

"Vance gave me go-light."

"Conditional. You were to observe and coordinate only. Haufren, as a commander, you need to remember that you must obey orders occasionally, too."

"I told you I was captured," said Haufren, leaning back against the pilot brace with a wince. There was not a place on his body that did not hurt. He fingered the burned rips in his left sleeve, finally remembering that Puce had shot him there. That was why his arm would not work.

"Why were you captured?" asked Silta relentlessly.

Haufren lifted his blue eyes angrily to those golden ones. "You can drop the interrogation, Captain. I see your point."

"I hope so," said Silta. "I hope you have learned how much error can be done when you neglect yourself. You lose your reflexes, your timing, your edge, and your wits."

"You sound like a training video."

"Fool!" Silta reached for him, but Haufren was quicker and caught that slim, furred hand in midair. They strained against each other for a moment.

"Slit my throat, you wild-tempered cat," said Haufren breathlessly, "and there'll be no Haufren V in the next century's tradition."

Silta growled and backed away.

"I know I have to account for my mistakes," said Haufren. "But, Silta! Demos! Omcris are crawling all over this planet. We're mere kilometers away from the ruins of the original Kanta site. It has to be a gateway, a transender access point. Now tell me the truth, my friend. Did you come here to drag me home for reprimands from the Fleet Council, or did you hope I'd found something at last?" He held Silta's gaze with the old challenge in his eyes until Silta finally ducked his sleek head.

"Know you already my answer," he said quaintly, humor returning to his eyes, and gave Haufren a mock cuff. "As always you succeed in eluding trouble only because you are so damned good. Do you wish me to play doctor, or do you prefer the medical facilities on Beros? We're cleared now. With Commander Janal abducted, the Directory can't claim we have no justification for being here."

Haufren shook his head, forcing his mind back to the problems at hand. "Do your best patch job. We've got to move out as soon as possible."

Silta met his gaze. "Before the trail grows cold?"

"Exactly."

"No one likes the hunt better than I, my friend, but if we are going to follow Omcris into their lair I think we need more than three men and a sick child."

"There isn't time," said Haufren impatiently. "They took Costa. We have to go now. Beros HQ will ask too many questions before they will raise squads for us. And, Demos, what if they want to go through treaty procedure for cooperation between unallied forces? Costa needs our help now, Silta."

Silta stared at him. "Why should an ignorant lieutenant from a small-scale patrol arouse such concern? You have brushed aside the local patrollers on a dozen worlds. You have brutally used a nib belonging to the line which currently claims the Zethian ambassador to Terra. You have likewise disposed of this man Puce, who could have been of invaluable help in many areas. What is your reason for this sudden change? Is she not expendable like these others?"

"No," said Haufren shortly, hating it when Silta decided to be eloquently scornful. "She's tough, quick, resourceful, doesn't whine, and never gives up. She saved my life a few times. I owe her. Understand?"

"Quite," said Silta, giving him a second measuring glance. "You are—"

The angry spitting of strifer fire brought both of them out from under the tarp. Duval was just rising from a crouch, the smell of burning ozone curling about him into Haufren's nostrils. Lying sprawled on the ground ahead was a skinny, scarred humanoid in a loincloth.

"Ishut," said Duval curtly, slamming his strifer into its holster.

Silta pointed. "You will need your weapon again. There are more coming."

"I know." Duval nodded. "They always travel in layers of advance scouts."

Haufren frowned and cocked his head. "Do I hear something? A sled?"

"Hallucinations, my friend," said Silta. "You have always been the deafest of our—"

"I am afraid your friend is right this time," said an unfamiliar voice from behind them.

A man, grossly fat and caped in green fatigues, rain poncho, and thick boots, shouldered his way through the undergrowth into the clearing. Scrawny Ishuts with feral eyes and aimed spears flanked him, and he carried an illegal Omcri wand that was five times more deadly than a heavy strifer. Small dark eyes glittered from the folds of fat obscuring his face. And every line of him conveyed a man with angry, undeterrable purpose.

Duval drew in a breath. "Wob Nogales."

Nogales gave him a slight nod. "Sergeant Duval. And these men?"

"Rangers," said Duval. "What brings you into the jungle? Where's your guide? Are you on permit?"

"My daughter is missing," said Nogales, sweeping aside the official questions. "Janal can't find her or won't find her. I get nothing from his office. Now I find that patrollers have broken into my villa on Lilliput and stolen personal property—"

"You will be charged for kidnapping the Kublai and starting this mess," said Duval angrily.

Wob colored. "The Kublai had no business coming here with his crazy ritual. The Directors were insane to give him a permit. I couldn't let him ruin my empire, and what I have done to protect it is not the affair of you patrollers!"

"We didn't take the Kublai from you, Wob," said Duval. "Omcris did."

"Omcris!" Wob blinked in surprise. "Nonsense! They—"

"They took Costa. And they took Janal," said Duval, his voice growing ragged. "Don't interfere further, Wob. We have a great deal to do."

"Then perhaps they took my daughter. I have to find her! She can't live without her medical equipment and supports. Her power cells will be drained. She—"

"Go home, Wob. Jillian is probably somewhere having a good time. You won't find her in the jungle."

"I intend to search every inch of this planet until I find her. You, patroller, are hereby assigned to assist me."

Haufren scowled. "You're intruding in military jurisdiction. You—"

Something large and sleek whispered overhead. Haufren broke off in astonished admiration as the gleaming new sled landed beside them. A drone piloted it, and it was loaded with equipment.

"It's practically silent!" said Haufren. "Where—"

"I redesigned the engines," said Nogales impatiently. "A hobby. Now, Duval, it is time to—"

"Are you prepared to shoot me if I fail to comply?" asked Duval flatly. He sounded like a man who had reached the end of his patience. "We are facing an Omcri invasion, Wob. I can't look for Jillian right now, and you would be better off going home before you get yourself lost or in trouble out here. She isn't in the jungle. You know that."

"I am a father, Duval. As you are. Would you leave one of your children until later? Invasion or not, I *can't!* I can't sit at home waiting. I have to do something."

"Go home," said Duval. His dark eyes shifted to Silta. "He

can take the little one to Beros where there are facilities—"

"No," said Haufren suddenly, his mind clicking over into gear. "There isn't time. Mr. Nogales, you said you redesigned that sled's engines as a hobby. Where did you gain the knowledge?"

Nogales frowned. "I began as an engineer on—"

"Fine. You might be useful." Haufren straightened up and began issuing orders. "We'll need that sled. Silta, take charge of unloading its cargo. The Ishuts can do it."

"But my daughter may need that equipment!" said Nogales angrily. "She may be dying!"

"I'm sorry, sir," said Haufren firmly as Silta moved over to the sled and beckoned to the Ishuts. "If we don't find some way to stop the Omcris and what they're bringing, we may all soon be dying. Duval, unload what we need and conceal your sled somewhere in the trees where it will be safe. Can we leave Tith with these Ishuts?"

Duval and Nogales both looked at him as though he were mad.

"No," said Duval.

"My men go with me," said Nogales.

"Not a chance," said Haufren. "Ishuts are too susceptible. The Omcris could turn them against us before we knew what was happening."

Nogales was still shaking his head, but Duval moved closer to Haufren.

"They might eat the little one," he said in an undertone. "He is not human; they might not understand."

"Very well." Haufren sighed, aware that he was not going to get out of his responsibility toward what happened to the nib. Silta had been right to reprimand him, but he honestly hadn't known. Now, Silta might soon have more reason to be furious with him if he hauled Tith into danger once again and something worse befell the child. Slowly Haufren limped back under the tarp and opened the locker.

Tith's round, pain-glazed eyes stared up at him.

Haufren found he could not meet the accusation in that gaze. "I'm sorry," he said quietly and laid a hand on the little shoulder.

Tith spat fiercely and sank sharp milk-teeth into his hand

biting deep until he drew blood. Choking off a cry, Haufren jerked back his hand. He knelt there a moment, watching the scarlet drops well up in fat globules as he tried to reach within himself for more than just words. Down deep, buried beneath the layers of unwanted memory, lay the visions of his own childhood hurt and betrayal. It had been a long time since he had dredged them up; even now, a part of him rose in protest to block them away.

"Tith," he said softly beneath the splatter of rain on the tarp. "I was born on a colony planet very far from here. The people were very cultured and civilized. They abhorred violence of any kind, and my mother was scorned for her alliance with a Ranger. I despised my father too and avoided him when he came to visit us. But when I was about your age civil war was declared on my world. My mother's brother and some of his best friends, men I loved and admired, decided that my mother was a bad influence upon society and that her love for a Ranger had brought violence to our world. My uncle was my hero, but he betrayed my mother and let his friends make a political scapegoat of her.

"It was a day of the growing season, when the sun was shining out brightly and warm. There were few warm days on that world, and I remember pulling on my boots with such excitement I laced them wrong. I remember seeing my uncle from the window. He was coming up to the house with other men. I waved to him, and although he saw me, he did not wave back."

Haufren swallowed, his voice rough. "Tith, they pulled us from the house and they tortured my mother and . . . me. I lived, but she did not. I remember watching my uncle's face while they clubbed my mother, striking her again and again. He felt every blow as though he were being struck himself, but he made no move to stop the atrocity. He wanted people to hate again, to fight again, to undo all the principles of their civilization so that they would follow his new order.

"He was wrong. Peace never came again. Those who did not leave the planet were eventually destroyed with it. I hated him as I have never hated anyone else. Every time I thought of him, every time I looked at something which he had given me, or remembered something he had taught me, there was pain. I could never understand how he could have done that to us, not even when I finally understood *why*.

"I vowed I would spend my life putting an end to evil and to war and to treachery. That's why I went to my father and became a Ranger like him and his father before him."

"But from this what learned you?" cried Tith. "Me, you hurt. What purpose had you?"

"It was not my intention to hurt you. Tith, do you know what Omcris are?"

Tith snarled, sick horror replacing the momentary clearness in his eyes. "Them I saw."

"Then you know they are bad creatures. And they serve something which is worse. That day when I met you, I was just trying to get help in order to stop them."

"But me you hurt." Tith let his head fall back. He closed his eyes, looking drawn. "When I am grown, you will I hunt."

"It is your right."

Tith looked at him in startlement.

"Yes." Haufren met his gaze honestly. "I am trying to tell you that I was wrong in what I did to you. Just as my uncle was wrong. I wanted you to know why I hurt you so you would understand. I don't expect you to forgive me."

"Give I shall not."

"What I do expect is your help. The Omcris have taken Costa away. We are going to bring her back. Will you help? You, like Silta, are a hunter."

For a moment Tith seemed to swell with pride at the compliment, then suspicion returned to his gaze. "She also gave hurt."

"The Omcris have possessed her. They made her do those things. Surely you sensed she was not herself."

Tith's eyes fell. He looked embarrassed. "To know such things is not yet permitted. But . . . yes, this did I feel."

Haufren held out his hand again. "Will you help?"

Tith sighed, looking thoroughly ashamed. "This cannot be done. Blood has been drawn. Between us is challenge. Trust me you cannot."

Haufren cocked his head to one side, not quite able to hide his smile. Deliberately he rubbed the back of his hand across his pants, smearing fresh blood into the old. "Do you know,

I've been cut in so many places today I can't remember whether you bit me or not?"

For a moment there was silence, then Tith levered himself weakly out of the locker and wrapped his short arms around Haufren's neck. Butting his round head under Haufren's chin, he whispered:

"If permitted it were to travel in time, back would I go to help you save your matre."

Without a word, Haufren picked him up and carried him outside where the rain had stopped once again. A pale mist curled around the trunks of the trees. It would be dark soon.

Silta came up to eye him critically. "Brith, your face is wet."

Haufren nodded, letting his arms tighten briefly around the small body curled against him. "It's raining," he said and walked away toward the other sled.

CHAPTER TWELVE

Nogales' sled was slow but uncannily quiet. Duval piloted it with Nogales standing beside him. Tith had gone back to sleep, and Haufren sat at the rear, braced into the corner and wincing while Silta tended his cuts. Darkness came swiftly, and Duval switched on the powerful running lights, thus negating the advantage of the quiet air jets. White tendrils of fog curled back as though melted by the lights, and the warm air condensed on Haufren's face as he glanced up constantly. He kept hoping for a cloud break. Even a glimmer of moonlight would be enough for Duval to steer by, and they could shut those damned lights off.

"Be still," said Silta, dabbing something which stung mercilessly onto Haufren's arm. "Someday you will find yourself without me to patch you up, my friend, and then what will become of you?"

Haufren made himself grin; it was better than groaning. "I have needed you plenty lately. *Ouch!*"

"Be still."

Silta capped the antiseptic and tossed it back into the kit. Haufren sagged with relief, not sure the wounds were worse than the remedies. For a few moments they sat together in the darkness, listening to the gentle slap of leaves against the belly of the sled and the occasional scream of a night creature. Exhaustion lapped around the edges of Haufren's mind. He thought of a good, contour bed in a safe, dry place with genjin wine and meatbread waiting on a little table nearby, and someone warm and gentle to companion him.

"Silta," he said, breaking the stillness. "This *is* foolish."

"Sleep," said Silta sternly.

"We need a full contingent of Rangers. If this really is an access point—"

"We have three good men and a fool," said Silta. "I sense many lies within Nogales."

"But—"

"Exhaustion is speaking, not sense. We both have been in

the corps long enough to know there is never an ideal situation in the field. We never have enough men, or enough warning, or enough supplies." Silta laughed softly deep in his throat. "Are you not ready to be a hero yet again?"

Haufren smiled wryly. "And you?" he countered. "How long until you grow tired of this hobby and go back to Zethia to be lord of the estate?"

"When we face Omcris the boredom of endless protocol and matriarchal domination becomes most appealing." Silta lifted a hand to smooth the fur between his ears. "Did I tell you the Fleet Council has been besieged by a contingent of howling Drughans seeking a direct reprimand of Fleet-admiral Vance? It seems they blame us for the loss of their Kublai. We did not provide adequate protection for His Supreme Glory."

"What?" said Haufren with mock surprise. "Defiled unbelievers protecting the Blessed One? Sacrilege!"

"Mewling idiots," said Silta, opening a ration packet and handing it to Haufren. "How conveniently they forget all their lodged complaints against Ranger activity. Well, this is their own fault. If they had not revived the cult of Kanta, the Omcris would not have had an opening."

"If not the Drughans, then some other race," said Haufren, chewing without much enthusiasm. The contents of his packet were rubbery as well as tasteless.

"Pfit!" said Silta with scorn. "No one else could be as stupid. I tell you, Brith, that my people used Drugh for a hunting ground long before the Kublai's ancestors crawled from the dust. Now they lord themselves over the Commonwealth and cause these difficulties which they expect others to clean up. It is a great pity we cannot give them all to the Omcris, but I promise you this, my friend, they will not escape charges for what they did to you."

Haufren's reply was cut off by the sudden descent of the sled. Perhaps twenty meters above the ground, Duval put the craft on hover, then with delicate maneuvers that had Nogales gripping his brace and Silta leaning forward with excitement, Duval eased the sled into a vast fork of a spreading tree. As soon as the jets cut, Silta inhaled deeply.

"This spicy scent . . . so fragrant. What is it?"

"A muyar tree," said Haufren, frowning as Duval cut off

the lights before he could get safely out of the sled onto a broad limb. He did not want to fall out of a tree again anytime soon.

Silta, whose night vision probably equaled Costa's, jumped out with sure agility. "It is a fine night for hunting."

Duval switched on a glowlight and then set out a sonic protector that made Silta hiss with annoyance. Tith woke up with a muffled cry.

"We dare go no closer until dawn," said Duval grimly.

Ears flattened, Silta made a point of looking at Haufren. "Major?"

Haufren nodded. "Duval is right. The night is no time to hunt Omcris. We'd better get what sleep we can." He heard himself slurring his words and fought back a yawn. "Who will take the first watch? Silta?"

"Acknowledged," said the Zethian, and they settled into their makeshift camp.

Dawn came gray and wet.

Haufren awoke with a start at a touch on his sore shoulder. He sat up, rubbing the grit from bleary eyes, and found himself barely able to move as every muscle protested stiffly. "Silta," he said angrily.

The Zethian stopped arranging the fur over his eyes with a clawtip and shrugged. "What could Duval and I do, Brith? You would not wake up. A log would have been equally useful to us."

Haufren scowled, resentful of being in such bad shape that they had to make allowances for him. He limped over to the end of the branch, glaring out into the dripping jungle. A delicate, rather pretty little creature he could not identify sat in the next tree, busily grooming its scarlet-tipped fur without fear of him. Haufren narrowed his gaze, focusing inwardly. He had to draw on all the reserves he had left. He had to put aside weariness and concentrate on the task ahead. Whatever they were about to face, providing they could find the trail at all, he had to be able to function, to perform. He could not afford to be slow. He could not afford to be careless.

Finally he nodded to himself and turned around to face the others. Nogales and Tith squatted miserably beside each other with no visible friendliness between them as they shared rations. The light was growing stronger; objects were becoming more distinct as the fog curled back.

"Are we ready?" he asked, holding his aching shoulders erect and making his voice crisp. "Then let's move."

Half an hour later the sled landed on the southern perimeter of the ruined city. Haufren belted on a strifer and swung a light pack over his right shoulder. Squinting slightly against the thin spits of rain, he scanned the jumbled stone spreading out endlessly around him.

"Duval," he said. "Do you know the location of the temple or the Archives?"

"I did," said the patroller, frowning as he, too, looked around. "All the landmarks are gone. Whoever blew up the ruins did a thorough job. But we should head that way." He pointed northwest.

Haufren nodded. "You lead. Silta, I'll carry Tith. You bring up the rear. Nogales, stick with me."

"I'll carry on my own search, if you don't mind," said Nogales angrily. He drew his strifer. "You got here; now I'll take my sled back and get on with my own affairs."

"Fool!" said Silta, flattening his ears., "You—"

"Nogales, the Omcris must be stopped," broke in Haufren urgently. "You're an engineer. We may need you to design some way to block the transenders—"

"Nonsense!" snapped Nogales. "Invasions from another galaxy and marauding Omcris are just a fantasy to mask your real activities, Ranger. Well, I'm not some starry-eyed child you can play protector of the universe to; I'm a man of some position. And there isn't a merchant in any system that doesn't know you Rangers are smuggling controlled substances across the galaxy and building up a vast storehouse of bullion on the Settle asteroids."

"What?" Duval blinked, his mouth falling open.

Haufren and Silta exchanged looks, Haufren's amused and Silta's furious.

"You dare much, human!" said Silta, starting for him, but Haufren threw out a hand to hold the Zethian back.

"That rumor is at least a century old," said Haufren. Regarding Nogales with contempt, he smiled and shook his head. "And I thought Playworld was a sophisticated planet with the most up-to-date information."

Nogales reddened, but he did not lower the strifer. "I'm taking the sled. I've got to find Jillian before it's too late."

"If she were on the planet, we would have found her by now," said Duval.

Haufren's eyes caught Silta's. He let them flicker in a brief signal. Silta drew in a breath to show he understood.

"We need you, Nogales," said Haufren, stepping forward. "And we need that sled. I've walked out of this jungle once. I don't intend to do so again."

"Stop there!" said Nogales shrilly, waving the strifer. "No tricks. I—" He broke off with a yelp of pain, staggering back and tripping over a stone block. The strifer clattered to the ground, and Haufren pounced on it.

"Thanks, Silta!" he said over his shoulder.

The Zethian's slitted eyes remained locked on Nogales a moment longer until Haufren had straightened and walked a few steps away, then he lifted his head and blinked. Nogales pushed himself up groggily, outrage and fear warring across his fat-blurred features.

"You . . . how *dare* you! Telepathy is forbidden here. The practice of it is a felony—"

"Definitely a backward world," said Silta, shrugging, and turned away to lift his pack off the sled. "Duval, is there sufficient concealment here or should we park the sled elsewhere?"

Duval, who was eyeing both Silta and Haufren with revulsion, frowned and lifted a hand to rub the back of his skull. "I think it's—"

"Sistat!" shouted Tith. "No! No!" Breaking into a run, he butted his way past Haufren, who snatched at his furry arm.

"Quiet, Tith!" he said, half in annoyance, half in alarm. "What is—"

"Demon things! Before they wanted me. Go I shall not!" Wildly he flailed out at Haufren and wrenched free.

"Tith! Damn it! Come back!" Haufren threw himself after the nib, but Tith darted between two huge stones and vanished.

Cursing in Zethian, Silta leapt atop a leaning wall and

crouched there with his ears flat and his round yellow eyes blazing. "Nothing! May Basa herself eat his dreams. Now I must hunt him—"

"Mercy of Moii!"

Haufren turned at that strangled whisper from Duval and found the patroller staring at the sky. Haufren glanced up, and immediately crouched down behind a rock with his heart hammering against his ribs. "Down! Everyone down! Silta!"

But Silta was already rolling off the wall with liquid grace, reaching out with one powerful arm to drag Nogales down to cover with him. Together they all watched the Omcri float past overhead, pale robes billowing gently as though undampened by the falling drizzle. A thin scream reached them, and a figure writhed and struggled in the Omcri's arms.

"That . . . that's one of my Ishuts," whispered Nogales, gray-faced. "They know—"

"Damn, of course they know." Haufren clenched a fist in frustration. "Or they will as soon as that one gets back to the others. Come on!" He started to jump up, but Duval clamped a restraining hand on his shoulder.

"Are you mad? We've lost the advantage of surprise. If they're expecting us—"

"That's why we must go now, before they have time to organize something against us." Pulling free, Haufren stood up, keeping a wary eye on the Omcri as it floated on. It was heading northwest. "We'll follow it."

"It will sense us," said Silta with a reluctance that showed plainly he agreed with Duval.

"Not if you blanket our mental patterns." Haufren looked at him impatiently. "You can shield us, can't you?"

Silta did not reply for a moment.

"You're not messing with my mind," said Duval sharply.

"Nor mine!" said Nogales.

"You are both fools," said Silta with regal annoyance. He swept out his hand. "The nib, Haufren. What about him?"

Haufren frowned, hesitated, then regretfully shook his head. "We can't wait for a search—"

"Unnecessary," said Tith's gruff little voice. He edged into sight as they all jerked to glare at him. His ears drooped.

"Shame I have. Good hunter I shall never be."

"Indeed it is doubtful," said Silta angrily. "From now on you will stay close and do only what you are told. Understood?"

Tith bowed his head. *"Shilorr,"* he said softly.

"Right." Haufren glared at Duval and Nogales. "Go along with Silta. He won't hurt you. He won't even be invading your thoughts. But if you are shielded you should be safe from the Omcris, even if they try one of their possession tricks." Unsnapping his holster flap, he drew his strifer and charged it. "Let's go." Without looking back, he started after the Omcri.

Within minutes, however, it descended and vanished from sight. Haufren, panting lightly from the quick pace he had set, paused and lifted a hand to wipe the rain from his face.

"Damn," he said under his breath. "Duval?"

The patroller stumbled to a halt and took his bearings, looking strained and nervous under the shield guarding them all. To Haufren, who had been shielded before, it was no more than a slight pressure over his eyes. But the others probably were experiencing a fierce headache, worsened, no doubt, by their refusal to relax.

"We are close to the Street of Souls," whispered Duval hoarsely. Water collected in his thick eyebrows and spilled down into his eyes, making him blink with a violent start. "The Archives were located there . . . underground so as not to disturb the original architecture. And the street led to the temple. The Omcri probably went down there, or close by."

"Good." Haufren shifted to one side. "Take the lead."

Grimly Duval moved ahead, his movements sure and quiet. Nogales stumbled awkwardly after him, hampered by his bulk and lack of fitness.

Panting harshly, he glared at Haufren. "You shall regret this coercion, Ranger. I am a citizen of Playworld, a planet free of your jurisdiction. You'll be taken to court so fast you will wish—"

Haufren gave him a shove, tired of the man's bluster. "Move on. And keep quiet."

Silta, bringing up the rear, glanced at him with eyes that were slightly unfocused with concentration. "We shall be probed," he said softly, moving past Haufren without a break in stride.

Haufren nodded. It was why he was taking up the rear position. His hand curled more tightly about the butt of his humming strifer. "Take care, my friend. And if our two fools go on fighting your help, protect yourself first."

The fur rippled along Silta's strong back. He swept out his hand in an ancient gesture of contempt. "This is an evil place, Brith. Old power lingers strongly here."

There was no need to answer. Haufren felt it too.

In silence they threaded their way through the rubble onto what had originally been a broad avenue lined by stone buildings. At one time it must have been impressive. Now the street was clogged by mounds of stone and petrified support timber from fallen walls and masonry. Ash and dust coating everything streaked and ran in streams of pale mud that clung greasily to their feet and made the going treacherous. Nogales slipped and fell full length, sending up a splash that drenched Silta. His cry echoed loudly down the street, freezing them all until at last an unnatural silence returned to the ruined city.

Haufren could hear his own breathing, ragged and harsh. He swallowed hard, every sense alert as they waited for Duval to help Nogales up.

"All right, Wob?"

Nogales nodded, then bit off whatever he had been about to say and sank down again, clutching his leg. His raddled face paled to sheet white.

Haufren cursed beneath his breath, scanning the clouds hanging low and black overhead. The day seemed darker now than it had at dawn. He shivered from more than cold. "Duval. A sprain?"

The patroller crouched beside Nogales and ran an exploring hand over the ankle. By common consent, no one had dared switch on a field-scanner. They all knew Omcris were attracted as quickly to the energy fields of operating equipment as to living flesh.

"Nothing broken," whispered Duval.

Nogales choked back a moan. "My knee . . ."

"Dislocated. Maybe I can shift it back."

Frowning, Duval moved swiftly, and Nogales jerked with a choked cry. He was perspiring, and his dilated pupils made his eyes look black. But at least he made no further sound.

Haufren kept glancing over his shoulder, hating this delay out here in the open. They were easy targets; he felt something watching and hoped with all his heart he was wrong.

"I'll walk," Nogales was saying hoarsely, levering himself to his feet with Duval's aid. "I'll make it. *Oh*—"

Haufren, who had been limping steadily all morning on a leg that still seeped a little blood through the bandage Silta had slapped on it, frowned but held back the sharp comment he might have said. He was field trained; Nogales wasn't.

Silta growled softly deep in his throat so that only Haufren could hear. "Civilians. We should have left him."

"Agreed." Haufren tried to shake off a growing sense of foreboding and glanced over his shoulder again. "I don't like this place. Too open. Let's move on."

As they hugged what cover they could find, Haufren tried to reassure himself. There had been no attempt to probe them yet. His own abilities told him that. And yet, it was too easy.

Duval stopped so suddenly Nogales nearly tripped over him. He glanced back, his weathered face revealing fear for the first time. "I just remembered," he said, glancing at the strifer in his hand. "These won't kill them. We haven't got a chance."

"A strifer does more than you think," said Haufren.

Duval grimaced in exasperation. "I *fought* them—"

"Easy," said Haufren, but with the snap of command. He glanced at Silta, who nodded, and then dug into the Zethian's pack. "Use this." He tossed Duval a charge pack of special manufacture. "Our lab has done some research."

Duval caught it with a frown of anger. "This is rather late to rearm us, Major."

"And what of me?" demanded Nogales in alarm.

Haufren scowled at him. "You can always pull out that Omcri wand you're hiding."

"Its power is exhausted. I use it only for effect."

Haufren raised both brows and said curtly, "The supply is limited. If you load your strifer with that charge pack, Duval, you go in first."

Duval glared at him for a hot moment, then surprised Haufren by tossing the pack at him. "You go first, Ranger. This is your show."

Silta made a faint sound of admiration. "It is time for the scanner."

"You always claimed you could smell Omcris." But as he spoke, Haufren was already pulling a field-scanner from his pack. He set it to low power and cautiously switched it on. The reading blips were faint but steady. He took a directional swiftly and shut it off. "Follow me. Take the rear, Duval. Silta is going to have to concentrate more than ever."

Tucking Tith under his arm, Haufren set off in an unsteady run diagonally across the street, trying not to favor his leg. He could hear Nogales puffing and blowing loudly behind him, laboring to keep pace, his feet slapping the ground with the noise of a blundering orph. The building indicated by the scanner as having the strongest readings stood closed to them by a high wall scarred by the recent explosions but not breached. Its door was immovable, and Haufren did not have the patience to try to unjam its circuits.

With a grunt of impatience, he put Tith down and moved to the corner where roughly forty-five centimeters separated this building from the next one. If he took no deep breaths and kept his head pointed over his shoulder, he just fit between them.

"Haufren—" began Silta in alarm, but ignoring him, Haufren started making his way through, scuttling sidewise as fast as he could and trying not to think about what he might find at the other end.

All he found was a gigantic crater with the rear of both buildings fallen in. Climbing with caution over the rain-slick stones, Haufren made his way like a shadow into dark, empty chambers smelling of bitter herbs and cold. When he reached the front courtyard and stood outside in the mist once again, he released a breath he had not realized he had been holding and found the controls to the street door. The panel was modern, though filled with dust, and everything still worked. Moments later, Duval, Silta, and Nogales stepped warily into the courtyard.

Tith wrinkled his nose. "There is a stink here."

"Come," said Haufren and led them inside. He dared use the scanner once more as they paused inside a vast round chamber containing only a single chair in the center. Silta prowled about the circular archways, running an exploring finger along the damp stone, and stopped with distaste at the small pile of clean-picked bones before him.

"Jillian!" said Nogales suddenly. He rushed past Haufren to stoop behind the stone-hewn chair. "She has been here!"

"Quiet," said Haufren, but Nogales was glowing with excitement.

"Look!" he cried, thrusting a fist-sized cylinder at Haufren. "A spent power cell. She must be close by, or else she was . . ." His voice trailed off uncertainly, and he looked pale again. "No," he whispered.

"Come," said Haufren to the others. "Behind this room." He could no longer contain his impatience. The lack of guards here where he had expected the trap to be sprung convinced him that the Omcris had gone. And if they took Costa and her fellow prisoners beyond reach . . .

He quickened his steps, whipped through the archway and into the next room in a swift crouch, his weapon ready but unneeded. There he found a trap door set into the floor.

"Through that."

"Moii," said Duval, staring at it.

"Jillian wouldn't be down there," said Nogales, still clutching the power cell. He turned about as though he would walk off, and Silta grabbed him by the sleeve.

"Stay close," said the Zethian. "There is no one living in this building besides ourselves."

Haufren heard him and looked up sharply from his efforts to pull open the trap door. "Beware of that, Silta. No mind scans while—"

"Scanning is unnecessary for something so elementary the senses pick it up," replied Silta haughtily and dragged Nogales over to the others.

Grasping the cold iron ring, Haufren crouched down, set his feet, and pulled until the muscles in his back and legs quivered with the strain. The massive wood panel moved slightly, giving Duval enough room to get hold of the other end.

"Now," he said, giving a hard push.

The panel grated back over the stone floor, and a dank miasma lifted up from the blackness yawning below them. Haufren sat down, daunted in spite of himself, and Duval made a furtive sign of warding.

"If they are gone, then why don't we let the matter be?" asked Nogales shrilly.

Silta glanced at Haufren, who sighed and said wearily:

"Because if they are convinced this is an easy access point, they will return through here. We assume their plans are not complete, that they are still searching for the ideal route in. They have explored other planets. So far we have been alerted by increased numbers or activity and have been able to drive them away. But I think here they have made their choice."

"No," said Duval.

"Playworld is perfect. It is in an isolated system, yet all space lanes lead here. Its native population is small. It is deliberately kept undeveloped, its natural state preserved so that vast areas of the continents are either uncharted or never visited. Patrollers can't cover everything all the time. There aren't enough of them. And sooner or later, every important personage of this galaxy comes here. They could wait, ensnaring heads of state as they chose, or they could mass here. I don't know. But they are coming." His eyes stabbed to each man as he spoke. "If we can stop them—if there's the slightest chance of it—then we can't turn back now. So it's up to us."

Silta lifted his head. "We are ready. I sense nothing ahead."

With a nod, Haufren took out the special charge pack and loaded his strifer, hoping that this time the lab had the right power base. The last time he had used these charge packs against Omcris, they had failed, and half of his squad had been killed. But now was not the time to mention that. Taking out two miniature deton-bombs from his pack, he fitted them carefully into his pockets and clipped a small torch to his belt along with the field-scanner.

Drawing a deep breath, he groped his way carefully down the crumbling steps into the hole. For a few moments the faint light within the chamber overhead lit his way, but his body blocked most of that inadequate illumination and then he was in complete darkness, moving down one slow step at a time with both hands pressed to the wall on his right. The smell of shadow and age and damp clung inside his nostrils, and the farther he went the stronger another scent became, a scent of something ripe and tainted. The darkness seemed almost alive; it was thick and impenetrable. He passed through levels of air with variant temperatures, and always they seemed to grow colder. It was almost like entering the space between galaxies, into a complete void with no stars, nothing material, nothing of matter existing.

He stopped, panicked by his own thoughts. Was that what he was going into? Was this darkness the actual gateway he feared he would find? For an instant he imagined the air was thinning, disappearing, that the oxygen was going, that he could not breathe.

His fingers clawed at the wall, scraping on the stone. The faint sting to his flesh brought him back from the numbness of fear. He drew a deep breath, thinking again. He was standing on solid matter. He could feel the wall under his palm. There was plenty of air; it simply stank. And stone always held cold for a long time. Nothing else could be expected down here where the sunlight never reached.

He could hear the others groping their way cautiously after him, trying to be silent and failing, their breathing harsh. It was foolish not to turn on a light. They lacked the advantage of surprise, and if a fight came the darkness could only help the Omcris. His fingers moved to his belt; the torch snapped on, flooding the remaining steps in its clear light.

Six steps down lay a pool of water that shimmered opaquely like molten silver. Haufren drew in a swift breath, thanking whatever watched over him. He had learned long ago never to trust water, or what might live within it. Warily he shone the torch across it, trying to measure its width. Beyond jumping reach rose a wall carved with worn markings and leprosied with pale dank patches of fungus. A landing jutted out from it over the water, and there was a rusted grate standing ajar within a doorway.

"There's the way across," said Duval.

His voice, though pitched low, boomed through the quiet, startling Haufren. He turned, shifting his gaze to follow Duval's pointing finger. A tiny ledge wide enough perhaps for a toehold crooked its way up and around the wall circling the pool. Haufren swallowed, considering the risks.

"Shine your torch up again. I thought I saw something," said Duval. "Yes, there! A support beam end. If I can hook my grappler into that, and if the wood isn't rotted, we can use my line for support. I'll go first."

Haufren started to tell him he was insane, then remembered Costa's skill in the treetops. These patrollers must be trained acrobats. He stood back to give Duval room to throw.

The first try fell short, and the grappler landed in the pool with a sullen splash. Duval hauled it back and threw again. This time the grapple held. He yanked down hard on it, and gave a nod. Haufren lifted a brow with respect.

"Very good."

Duval's teeth showed briefly in a smile, then he was busy tying the rope around his stocky middle. He eased his way cautiously onto the tiny ledge, slipping slightly on the damp surface, but keeping his balance with remarkable agility. Haufren watched, holding his breath, and took note of how far Duval's heels hung over the ledge. The least slip . . .

"These patrollers have many talents," said Silta admiringly as Duval jumped lightly onto the landing and waved. "Shall I go next?"

Duval swung the line back, and Silta caught it. Deftly knotting it around his lean flanks, he knelt and spoke quietly to Tith, who climbed onto his back and clung tightly there. Silta scrambled up onto the ledge and tested it.

"Pfit," he said with scorn. "Whoever carved this had no thought for tall persons. The holds are positioned at wrong intervals." But already he was moving on along the ledge with his usual gracefulness, undeterred by Tith's weight.

"I can't do that!"

Nogales crowded Haufren at the water's edge, sweating and glassy-eyed.

"My weight. And . . . I am afraid of heights. No. I'm going back, Haufren, and this time you won't stop me!"

Turning, he started up the steps rapidly, puffing and wheezing, as though afraid Haufren would hold him back by force.

Haufren let him go a short distance, then said flatly: "Jillian is beyond that door."

Nogales stopped short. "What? How can you say that? How do you know?"

For a moment Haufren almost pitied the man. "If that power cell was hers, then she was here. And if she was here, the Omcris have her. Simple logic, Nogales."

Silta was safely across. He swung the line to Haufren, who caught it and gazed up at Nogales' stiff back.

"Well?" he asked. "It's your turn."

Nogales turned and came blundering down. "Damn you!" he said and seized the line with a shaking hand.

Without a word Haufren made the knot for him, then stood motionless, avoiding looking at Nogales as the man's thick lips quivered. Nogales stared at the pool for a moment while impatience crawled through Haufren. He started to speak, but Nogales sidled along the last step and hoisted himself with a series of grunts onto the ledge. Once up, he pressed himself against the wall for dear life, his thick arms spread wide. He moved a few centimeters, stopped, then moved a few more. Across the pool Silta signaled for them to hurry. Haufren glanced at him and shook his head. He had goaded Nogales all he dared.

The sound of crumbling stone followed by quick plops of water brought up his head sharply. His breath caught in his throat as he saw the stone breaking away under Nogales' feet. The big man clung frozen halfway across with his face pressed against the wall.

Haufren took a step forward and shouted: "Move! Damn you, Nogales! Move!"

With a whimper, Nogales remained where he was. "It's going!" he said. "I can feel it. I can't swim! *I can't swim!*"

"Wob! Come on!" shouted Duval from the other side.

Haufren exclaimed and reached for the ledge with the idea of going out after him, but just then stone broke with a loud crack and the ledge fell, crumbling away along the wall like dried plaster. Screaming, Nogales plunged toward the water only to be jerked up short by the line which twanged like a cut bowstring as it snapped. Arms and legs flailing, he hit the surface of the pool with a tremendous splash and promptly sank.

"Damn!"

Haufren took time only to switch off the charge on his

strifer before diving into the water. The icy coldness numbed him instantly. His outstretched hands scraped stone, and he knew relief. So the pool wasn't bottomless after all. He arched his back, sending himself up for a gulp of air, then shot down again. This time he ploughed into Nogales and grasped him firmly as he kicked his way back to the surface. As soon as his head cleared the water and he got a breath, Nogales began to fight. Expecting this, Haufren chopped him across the throat, then nearly bobbed under as he struggled to roll the limp Nogales over onto his back. Haufren grasped him by the chin and began to swim with short, powerful strokes.

Duval knelt on the landing, ready to help. He and Silta reached down to grasp Nogales. They heaved, groaning, while Haufren treaded water and did his best to push.

"Got him?" asked Haufren at last, flipping his dripping hair back from his eyes. From this angle all he could see was the slime-coated underside of the landing and one of Nogales' big feet.

"Mercy of *Moii,*" came the exhausted answer. "It should be a crime to weigh so much."

Silta peered over the edge of the landing, baring his side teeth in a swift grin, and held out his hand. "You always did enjoy swimming. A most disgusting exercise."

"It's freezing," said Haufren, grasping Silta's hand and giving a strong kick to boost himself high enough to grasp the edge of the landing.

He was half out of the water when powerful pincers clamped upon his leg. The pain was immediate and overwhelming. With a shout he arched his back, helpless in that initial moment of blinding agony. All he could think of was that something had severed his leg below the knee.

"Brith! *Brith!*"

Bile, intensely bitter, spilled from Haufren's mouth as he fell limply back into the water, and then he was choking, unable to breathe or swallow. He knew he was not yet free when the pincers clamped next around his waist and squeezed with intolerable pressure as he was dragged down into the depths of the pool.

Something plunged down beside him, buffeting him with

rapid bubbles of water. Dimly he was aware of a violent struggle going on around him, and he was yanked this way and that as the need for air drummed within him. Then suddenly he was released and floated lower while his body convulsed in one last struggle for survival against the water filling his lungs. *I should have scanned the pool,* he thought vaguely. Then he sank down deeper into the water, and knew no more.

CHAPTER THIRTEEN

"I have him!" said Silta with a grunt as he grasped Haufren's limp arms and pulled him onto the landing. "Get out of the water, Duval. Quickly!"

Duval needed no urging. He climbed out with alacrity, water streaming from his clothes, and knelt with a gasp as Silta rolled Haufren onto his stomach and began resuscitation procedures.

"No, I know a better way," said Duval. "We're trained for this sort of thing."

Moving Silta gently but firmly aside, he rolled Haufren over onto his back and began pumping his arms with skilled rapidity, pausing at intervals to breathe into Haufren's lungs. Silta crouched there miserably, his eyes never leaving Haufren's face. Inside, he had to battle down the keening of grief rising within his heart. Not yet, he told himself. He must not give up yet. But, oh, my friend, you look dead. You look worse than dead. And he thought, there is nothing harder to gaze upon than the face of a drowned man.

Haufren's cheeks were colorless in the glare of the torchlight. His shut eyes were sunk into their sockets. Silta pressed the backs of his hands together, the soggy lumps he had felt within Haufren's side still impressed upon the memory of his fingertips. Internal injuries . . . crushed ribs . . . so little life left . . . the remaining spark so low. *Live!* he thought, sending the force of his will into Brith.

At the other end of the landing, Nogales groaned and stirred. Silta turned his head a fraction, and swift anger burned through his veins. "If Brith dies," he said softly, showing his fangs, "so shall the fat one."

Duval looked up from his efforts. "Then you negate Major Haufren's sacrifice."

Silta spat. "Sacrifices are for humans! Upon me such things do not bind."

"Even a friend is not worth killing for."

Silta slitted his eyes and estimated how long it would take to slice the flesh from this human's bones. "So does your law say. Brith is more than friend. He—" Silta broke off, still unable after all these years to speak of that day of horror and chaos with the palace burning and collapsing around them, the females screaming, the crunch of sword thrusts through the bony chests of young nibs, himself cowering in the rubble—too young to fight, too old to run. Even now his dreams still brought him vividly the strength of a hand grasping his shoulder and drawing him away to safety. Brith's hand. Silta shut his eyes, biting down hard so as not to utter the wail of grieving.

A faint cough jerked him upright. He stared intently, watching with delight as murky water bubbled from Haufren's mouth. Then he helped Duval roll Haufren over onto his stomach and held his head as Haufren retched violently again and again. Without a word Duval moved away to the fat one.

"Gently, my friend. Gently," murmured Silta, wiping Haufren's face. "You continue. You live."

Haufren's eyes flickered open and focused slowly upon Silta's face. Death hovered within their blue depths. Silta sought to erase it, but Haufren's hand clamped down hard upon his wrist.

"Leg . . . gone . . ." he said with a gasp. *"Silta?"*

"No, Brith. No!" Silta quickly, seeking to soothe away that terror. "Both are with you. Lost them you have not!"

Haufren frowned at him, disbelieving, still terror-stricken. Silta sent him a light mind touch of reassurance, and smiled when the strain suddenly faded from Haufren's face.

"Demos," he said, letting his head fall. "I thought—" Violent coughing racked him, and this time blood splattered the stone landing as well as water.

Worry pierced Silta like a knife thrust. He ran his hands lightly down Haufren's sides, feeling for the broken bones, and stopped his examination at the quiver in Haufren's face.

"We can't stay here," whispered Haufren hoarsely.

"Agreed." Silta shifted Haufren's injured leg and decided that by some miracle it was not broken. "I shall help you."

As gently as he could, he pulled Haufren upright and

slipped a steadying arm around him when the major swayed.

"Some hero, eh, friend?" said Haufren with a grin and coughed.

"Do not talk," said Silta, letting annoyance mask his worry. "We must turn back. We must go to Settle at once."

"No."

"Brith, do not argue. You will die without medical attention. We know where to find the Omcris now. We can come back when you are restored."

"No!" Haufren's fingers gripped the thick black fur covering Silta's chest and twisted it painfully. His blue eyes bored into Silta's. "We never leave Rangers in the field!"

"Agreed. But you present us with a paradox, my friend." Silta's gaze could not meet the intensity in Haufren's. His voice roughened as he said: "They are not Rangers. You are more important."

"Don't be a fool," said Haufren sharply enough to make himself cough again. He sagged against Silta, fighting for breath.

"You see?" said Silta, steadying him. "What would we do without you? Brith, you *are* the corps. And you are my—"

"The Rangers can continue very well without the great-grandson of their founder." Haufren gripped Silta's arm, his fingers digging in as he struggled to pull himself erect. "As can you."

"Continue without my spear-brother? My friend? No—"

"Silta, you fool, I don't intend to die yet," said Haufren with exasperation. He shoved his wet hair back from his face. "We go on! Commander Janal is too valuable a personage to be left in enemy hands. The girl may not be one of us, but she is worthy of that honor. You can sit here and light my funeral pyre in this water-logged hole if you wish, but I am not through with the Omcris yet. Now get your mental shields up and let us be moving!" He paused to spit blood into his hand, then met Silta's worried eyes. "That was an order, Captain."

Silta's throat closed with the effort of holding back what he could have said. The long years of discipline enabled him to drive down his personal feelings. It was the Zethian way to be inscrutable; it was the Ranger way to follow orders.

He blinked at Haufren, trying to imagine him as a piece of

food rather than as someone to whom he owed his life many times over. "Acknowledged," he said.

"Good," said Haufren, glancing at the others. He saw Tith staring at him with enormous, frightened eyes and with a wan smile took the nib's little hand in his.

"Gentlemen," said Silta for him. "Let us move out."

Duval took the lead now, and Nogales the rear. Silta greatly disapproved of having the fat one at his back, but there was no help for it. Haufren could barely walk even with his and Tith's assistance. Silta nodded to himself. In minutes Haufren would collapse. Then he would be free to take command and turn them back. Haufren had always been stubborn, a risk-taker, a defier of odds. Silta, on the other hand, had more regard for the sanctity of a whole skin. He preferred to crawl through these dank tunnels for the blind with a full contingent of men and plenty of deton-bombs.

After several minutes of walking through a low, noxious-smelling passageway dotted with puddles of slime, they came to a door. Duval checked it with the scanner, nodded, and put his shoulder to it. The panel was of a type Silta had never seen before save in archival pictures: thick and hung on hinges that shrieked alarmingly as Duval pushed it open. Beyond was a laboratory.

Silta, who had no interest in chemicals and distillation flasks, did no more than glance briefly around and note that it was hardly a sterile place or an orderly one. He pointed at the far end of the cluttered room. "Another door."

"Wait!" said Nogales, pushing past Silta and Haufren to kneel awkwardly beside a crumpled heap of metal. "Duval, shine your torch here." When Duval complied, Nogales gasped. "R7! My daughter's drone! She's here! She must be here." Snatching the torch from Duval's hand, he began flashing it here and there about the room.

Silta nudged a battered metal arm with his foot and sniffed. "Obviously scrapped for parts."

Haufren suddenly stirred. "Under the table."

Duval dragged the body out. It was the corpse of a tall humanoid resembling the giants of Tamar. The eyes were missing, and one hand was swollen black. Moving it stirred up the smell of death, which quickly tainted the air.

"Pfit!" said Silta, wrinkling his nose. "One of their creatures."

"Poor devil," said Duval, frowning in an anguish of his own. "That's what will happen to Costa, isn't it?"

"Not if we find her in time," said Haufren.

"We've got to hurry!" Duval turned to beckon to Nogales who was kneeling in a corner piled with objects and tools of every kind. "Come on, Wob. There is nothing here."

Nogales rose slowly and turned to face them. His face was streaked with tears, and he held something in his hands.

"Her heart-box," he said, then shook his head. "Her cardio-protection unit. It's all here. All of her equipment. The suspensors that helped her walk. The thing that prompted her lungs . . . all of it. Except her. Oh, Jillian! Those devils dissected Jillian!"

"Incorrect," said a double-timbred voice that made Silta spin and Haufren reach for his strifer. Silta scanned the room swiftly with eyes and mind, and found nothing. Cowering beside him, Tith choked back a whimper. Silta cursed himself yet again for bringing the nib into this.

"Dissection not performed," continued the disembodied voice. "Human destroyed in explosion. Salvage unsuccessful."

Silta flattened his ears and flexed out his claws, his muscles twitching in readiness to pounce. For a moment there was only silence in the room, broken by the faint hum of Haufren's strifer as it charged to maximum.

Then Nogales let the device in his hand fall to the floor. His eyes widened in horror. "I set those explosions. I ordered them to get rid of those damned Kanta worshipers once and for all. I . . . *killed* Jillian! No!"

Duval reached out for him. "Wob, try to—"

"No!" Thrusting Duval aside, Nogales ran for the door at the opposite end of the room and wrenched it open.

"Follow him!" said Haufren hoarsely. "Clear this room before it—"

But Nogales had taken the torch, leaving them blind in the dark. Tith suddenly screamed. Snarling to himself, Silta pulled another from his pack and snapped it on in time to see an Omcri vanishing through the door with Tith struggling in its arms. Another Omcri waited before Silta, hovering a few centimeters off the floor. Silta stared into that void beneath the cowl, felt himself going mad, and howled in fury, lashing out with swift strifer fire as the thing reached for him. Haufren fired, too, and the Omcri crumpled at Silta's feet into an uninhabited pile of cloth.

They stared at each other for a second, panting.

"Go!" said Haufren.

The three of them moved, aiming for the door that Nogales had gone through. Something shoved a table aside behind them, the legs scraping on the floor.

The fur prickled up Silta's spine. He paused, glancing back, and spat in fear as he saw the dead humanoid coming after them, arms outstretched, head dangling at a crazy angle, the sightless sockets aimed at him.

"Sistat isk surrur!"

Silta fired at it, saw the bolt hit the body squarely and cut it open. The stench of burned flesh filled his nostrils, but the thing did not falter.

"Silta!"

With a cry, Silta whirled and ran after the others, catching up and seizing Haufren's arm as the major stumbled and nearly fell. Haufren clung to him.

"Strengthen your shields, Silta," he whispered, his face gray. "They'll try that next."

"Run," replied Silta, his heart pounding wildly within him. "Run!"

But Duval balked at the mouth of another tunnel. "This is a trap," he said, looking back. "They are trying to force us down there. We must go back."

"No!" The scream of protest tore from Silta's throat. He whirled, panting, and could see the dead thing slowly, relentlessly stalking them, coming closer with every ponderous step. "Not past that thing! Don't you see it? We have to go forward."

"Silta." Haufren gripped him by the arms and shook him. "Silta! What is it? What do you see? Silta, there's nothing following us."

But terror had become a tangible thing coiling about him. Silta felt himself shaking violently.

Haufren stepped back, bracing himself against the wall. His eyes met Silta's and widened. "They've got him, Duval. Demos, they've got him!"

Silta opened his mouth, but no sound came forth as he watched Haufren slowly raise his strifer and aim it at him. In horror Silta thought: *He thinks I am possessed!* He tried to reach out to Haufren, to stop him, yet all the while the dead thing was coming relentlessly closer. Silta threw back his head and screamed as something within his mind snapped, and all his shields came crashing down. Every thought and emotion in all its violence poured from him in a powerful onslaught that sent Haufren reeling back and wrung a cry of pain from Duval.

Then suddenly the Omcris were there, six of them robed in sickly white, the color of decay. Still screaming, Silta felt an invisible, powerful pressure push him back against the wall and hold him there despite his thrashing struggles. Haufren fell to his knees with a groan, but managed to fire in a broad sweep at the Omcris. One staggered, and for an instant the pressure eased off Silta. Then it slammed back in full force, and not one of them collapsed.

"They've adjusted already to absorb the charge," said Haufren as though in disbelief. "Damn it, how did they know? How do they communicate?"

Duval shouted something and snapped open the blades of his cutter, hurling it with all his might. An Omcri lifted its hand, and the cutter was deflected in midair, passing within less than a centimeter of Silta's face before clattering harmlessly against stone. The Omcri stepped forward, and twin flashes of green light blazed from the void that should have been its face. Duval screamed and crumpled to the ground.

"Brith! Run! *Run!*" shouted Silta, but the words were only in his mind. Nothing came from his throat but those constant, terrible screams.

The green lights flashed again, and Haufren fell.

Something cold and incredibly loathesome squirmed deep into Silta's brain. Silta writhed violently, struggling with all his might, but the mental power of these creatures was too great to resist. Pain ground through him.

"Serve us," it commanded. "You will serve us."

"Never!"

"Then watch how we create playthings from your companions. They will make you wish to die."

An Omcri hand stretched out, and Haufren jerked puppet-like to his feet. His eyes were open, but there was no life at all in them. His face had the slackness of the dead. Duval joined him, and then suddenly the corpse thing stood between them. The three of them reached out to Silta, who panted and jerked to no avail against his invisible bonds. The touch of their flesh was cold and slightly moist, leaving little trails of slime upon his fur from their fingers, slime which seconds later began to burn his skin like the fires of hell.

He screamed, maddened with the pain.

"Serve us, Silta."

"No!"

Haufren approached him again, curling cold fingers loosely around Silta's throat. He made no further move, but soon that continued touch became an agonizing heat that scorched Silta's throat and mouth and seemed to flame up through the bones of his skull.

"Silta? You will serve us!"

Tormented beyond endurance, Silta beat his head back against the wall in an effort to crush his skull and thus die. Zethians served no one as slave. Zethians could not beg for mercy. What was demanded he could not give. No! He was an officer, a warrior trained in the strictest, the proudest, the most elite corps of service in the Fleet. He would die before he let himself be broken. He would die before he betrayed his race.

"Then die," said the voice in his brain and laughed. "You will still serve us."

CHAPTER FOURTEEN

Costa huddled next to a delicate geometric structure no taller than her shoulder. The chilly, rarefied air cut through her body, making her shiver, and whipped away the final vestige of cloudiness from her mind. Suddenly alert, she blinked and leaned forward slightly as she gazed upon the wonder of alien surroundings as fragile and lovely as glass sculptures. She was sitting outside with a silver-colored sky arching above her. A dim, barely seen glow radiating from that cloudless expanse told her the sun was either dying or far, far distant from this world. She had no more than the faintest outline of a shadow, blurred and indistinct, around her. The muted light seemed only to add to the hushed quality of the air. She frowned, unable to understand what was missing, then caught her breath. On Playworld there were always sounds; nature was never quiet, and Beros—especially its slums—roared with activity. Here, nothing moved. Nothing made sound, save for an occasional, far away tinkling as though wind chimes were stirred by the gentle brush of a hand.

She sat enclosed by a webbed mesh of hand-length crystals, eight-sided, rectangular with pointed ends, and no wider than her finger. The enclosure was shoulder height and perhaps two by eight meters in size. The interlocking crystals were open enough for her to slide her fist through at any point, yet despite the seeming fragility of the formation, she could not snap it. Climbing out would be easy, but she hesitated, staring at the buildings nearby. Dotted in seemingly aimless patterns of circles and triangles rather than in intersecting or parallel lines like the cities she was used to, the buildings were all small but unique examples of breathtaking architecture, built with a delicacy of scale and a brilliance of geometric design. One which her gaze kept returning to again and again as though she were mesmerized was directly across from her enclosure, and larger than the rest. It was a conglomeration of domes, spires, and pyramids formed from tiny blocks of pale blue quartz.

Her gaze narrowed as a piece of memory fell into place.

Somewhere inside there was the access point through which she had been brought. She must go back.

She reached out and grasped the crystal mesh with both hands. But before she could fit her foot into a toehold, the once-faint tinkling sound was suddenly loud and right behind her. She spun, her heart beating absurdly fast as she saw two shapes outside the enclosure.

Only then did her bruised mind permit her to remember all that had happened. The Omcris had taken her from Playworld and brought her here. Dozens of fragmented impressions swirled through her mind. Was this, then, the origin point of the devil-things?

No, she thought decisively, gazing at the shimmering entities before her. There was beauty here and exquisite, precise order. This world, with the clarity of its cold atmosphere, its clean scents of polished stone and ice, and its odd gravitational pull which made her feel squashed and heavy as though even her lungs were too flattened to breathe, had not produced the Omcris. Their sickly, decayed taint was not here.

"Who are you?" she asked, only to be startled by the change in her voice. Its tone was muted, flattened almost to a monotonic quality. She took a step closer to the mesh, frowning at the entities in an effort to see them better. Their shimmering, unstable quality made them seem to fade in and out of her vision as though she were trying to peer into a liquid mirror that could not hold its reflection. "Who are you?" she repeated. "What is this place?"

They made no reply, and the eerie silence of the world pressed around her. Then a single musical note of such volume and purity it brought pain struck through her. Clasping her hands to her ears, she reeled back, falling just as the crystal mesh of the enclosure shattered around her. Tiny shards embedded themselves in her arms as she cringed, covering her head as best she could. Panting, she looked up, lifting herself unsteadily to her hands and knees. Hot little rivulets of blood ran down her cut arms, but she barely noticed as the things rushed at her.

She tried to rise and was knocked down again. Then one of them was on top of her, its weight immense, crushing. She cried out as she was pressed into the frozen ground, cutting her cheek on the shards of crystal littering the earth like snow. The gentle tinkling noise grew more agitated as she heaved and struggled. Something gritty scraped across her shoulder blade, tearing through her already tattered tunic and abrading her skin. She felt fierce stinging, and smelled blood, her blood, as though her hide were being peeled away. The scraping came again and again, almost eagerly, and she felt it rasp bone.

It was feeding upon her!

"Mercy of Moii!" Furious and terrified, she flung herself aside, rolling beneath the weight of the creature with an effort that snapped a rib. Her breath caught, and for a moment she thought she would be sick, but she pushed herself on, squeezing free of the creature, dragging herself to her knees, dodging its rush at her, and scrambling to her feet.

The two of them moved to cut her off and pin her between them, but she lashed out with hands and feet in desperation, cursing them with the full fury of an unleashed temper. It was like kicking solid rock. She staggered back a little at the jolt of impact, realizing she could not fight them. One of them knocked her down again, and she cried out as she landed on the broken rib. Flecks of black danced across her vision, but she gritted her teeth, making herself move before the things could pin her again. Her fingers clawed the ground as she fought to keep going, scrambling, dodging, half falling, her breath sobbing in her throat as she eluded them again and again. Then at last she gained her feet and sprinted between them like a mad thing, feeling one last glancing blow as she drove herself against the heavy gravity that made her feet like lead. She ran without daring to look back, the memory of that horrible, sucking greed upon her flesh driving her on as she aimed herself at the building of pyramids and spires ahead.

None of the buildings, however, were as close as they had originally seemed. When at last she stumbled to a halt, her breath rattling in her throat and a searing pain gashing through her side, it was to find herself no closer to them than she had been before. Were they real, she wondered in despair, bending over in agony. Or were they illusions? She had nothing else to aim for.

She looked back, dreading pursuit, but saw none. Perhaps the creatures had not been hungry enough, or perhaps they had some other means of cornering escaped game. Shuddering, she made herself stumble on. The gravity was becoming heavier with every step, and she felt far too exposed out here in the open with no vegetation of any kind for cover, nothing but occasional geometric shapes like queerly formed sculptures that might or might not be living things and more of the enclosures such as the one that had held her.

At first those she passed were empty. Then she came upon shattered ones, with clean-picked bones lying amidst the glittering shards of crystal. Sickened, Costa hurried on, her eyes constantly scanning, her ears straining for that betraying soft chime of tones. Her instincts told her she was watched, making the skin along her spine prickle. And yet, she saw no one and heard nothing save the crunch of her feet over the metallic earth.

By the time she drew near the buildings, sweating and shivering in the icy air, she began to pass larger enclosures. They were all full, many containing species she did not recognize. But the reason for their presence was more than clear.

A scent suddenly filled her nostrils, one that she knew too well, one that made her back arch in revulsion.

Omcris!

She threw herself behind one of the enclosures, holding her breath and ignoring the inmates reaching for her as her eyes apprehensively followed six of the devil-things herding prisoners like bleating herendis into a long crystal chute which fed into a tall, isosceles-shaped building. The noise here after the previous silence made her ears ring. She crouched lower as an Omcri sailed within a few meters of the enclosure shielding her, and fought off a mindless urge to run. They would not possess her easily again, she vowed, but she dared not venture out into the open so close to them.

A snarling scream, shrill and piercing, caught her attention. In the largest enclosure a black-furred Zethian male stood a head taller than most of the other prisoners. Screaming again, he made a wild swipe at one of the Omcris floating above him. His claws ripped through the hem of the Omcri's robe, and he snarled as he jumped in a mad effort to sink dripping fangs into the devil-thing.

Pitying the demented one, Costa swung her eyes away, only to blink as she suddenly glimpsed a human. Surely it was not . . .

"Duval!"

The word tore itself from her throat. Heedless of the danger, she raced forward and sprang at the crystal mesh, climbing up and over with a rapid bound. Omcris whirled and sailed toward her, but she ignored them as she pushed and shoved her way through the milling crowd in an effort to reach Duval. Jumping up to try to see past an orb of pulsating flesh, she saw Duval going into the chute and passing from sight.

"Duval!"

Her voice was drowned out in the roaring confusion of terror around her. A tentacle snaked around her arm. She chopped it viciously and pulled free, reaching the chute just as a section of meshwork slid into place, cutting her off.

She struck at it in frustration. "No!"

But the Omcris herded Duval's group through the gateway at the opposite end of the chute, and he passed from sight into the building. Her eyes aflame, Costa tossed the warrior braid out of her face and began climbing the meshwork. She had to follow him; she had to find out what fate awaited him and all his fellow prisoners.

A furred, claw-tipped hand grasped her arm and pulled her down as easily as though she were a doll. Furious at this interference, Costa whirled with her fists curled to attack, only to find herself facing the mad Zethian.

His amber-jade eyes glowed into hers. He bared his fangs, still holding her fast despite her attempt to jerk free. Something whispered along her mind, and she screamed, flinching back.

"You are the one called Costa," he said in hoarse Unise, and for an instant the madness cleared from his gaze. "Haufren . . . for you searched."

"Haufren!" Her hand tightened on his arm, hope warming her. "Where is he? Did he find the access point beneath the temple? There is an ancient trans—"

"Transender," said the Zethian in a hollow voice. "A highly dangerous device used in the past to disassemble the corporal body into tachyon particles and beam them to another access point on physical wavelengths of . . . shall we carve also the flesh from their faces and dance upon their hearts? Shall we bite upon their entrails and strew the hollows of their bones? Fight! Let us fight!"

He whirled as though to pounce, and although she shrank from his madness Costa held onto his arm.

"Wait, Zethian!" she said, putting all the bark of command she could into her voice. "Do you know Major Haufren? Haufren! Do you know him?"

The Zethian's eyes widened, staring at something she could not see. She heard the breath catch in his throat.

"Touch me not!" he said to the air, hysteria in his voice. "Duval! Haufren! Touch me not! *No!*"

He broke free of her and plunged into the crowd, snarling and scratching in utter terror. Costa stared after him, her heart thumping. Who was this Zethian? Was Haufren here as well as her brother?

"Duval," she whispered, turning back to gaze at the chute. Urgency burned through her. She dared not wait until the Omcris returned to force more of them into that building.

Wincing as pain ground anew through her side, she climbed over the gate and dropped to the ground on the other side, crouching there a moment to see if anyone noticed her. The prisoners watched apathetically with the Zethian screaming at the inhabitants of the next enclosure. Costa drew in a breath and hastened along the chute to the far gate standing in icy shadow. Glittering like spun glass, the building loomed over her. She hesitated, then climbed over the gate.

At first she thought she was entering pitch darkness, but as she snapped open her innermost eyelid she was able to discern a faint glimmer of illumination in the distance ahead. Cautiously, moving with all the stealth she possessed, she eased her way ahead, feeling the downslope of the floor with every groping footstep. The farther she went, the warmer the air became, and only then did she realize how thoroughly chilled she was. She shivered, rapidly running her hands up and down her arms, and longed passionately for a weapon.

The faint but steady hum of distant machinery alerted her. She caught disturbing scents of death, fresh and hot, and she quickened her pace. A light glowed at the first corner she came to, and beyond it a broad series of steps descended to endless depths. She set her hand against the wall and felt the vibration there, traveling vertically as though lifts were working through the building above her. But she had no curiosity to explore this place beyond the need of finding Duval. Swallowing hard against the urge not to go any farther, she started down the steps.

A broad chamber, blindingly lit, opened out at the foot of the steps, leaving her exposed with nowhere to dart for cover. She stood there a moment, blinking and deafened, as a vast network of generators roared and metal clanked and shrieked in swift efficiency. A vast belt, black and stained, conveyed past her a multitude of packaged cubes from the maw of a gleaming, silver monster which shook from the violence of its own working.

Costa swallowed down her nausea and swiftly scanned the chamber. She saw no one, neither guard nor prisoner. Duval could not be one of those packages. He could not be! Desperately she plunged into the room, threading her way through vats of noxious-smelling liquids which bubbled thickly and coated everything around them with greasy steam. She passed more belts, these bearing things not yet completely processed, and had to avert her eyes lest she lose all control of her already heaving stomach. Finally she came to a wall and eased through the doorway it contained, only to stop in astonishment.

Acoustically padded walls blocked off the cacophony of noise behind her. The air was warm and pleasantly scented. She heard the shriek of laughter and a rapid babble of children's voices. Slowly she climbed the steps to a grillwork extending over a vast play area containing hundreds of children, all plump and healthy, divided by species with glass walls that permitted them to see one another but not to mingle. Their laughter stilled as Costa walked overhead with a lump choking her throat and rage blurring her sight. Were these the delicacies of an unknown galaxy?

She could bear no more of it. Throwing aside caution, she ran the rest of the way, her boots ringing out on the metal grillwork. Using both hands, she wrenched open the door on the other side and flung herself through.

She found herself knee-deep in grease-coated mud. Nauseated by the stench, she retched uncontrollably until there was nothing left in her stomach. Trembling, she slowly straightened and began to make her way through row after row of bodies, hung up by lashed wrists. Some were dead; some kicked feebly, moaning. Costa stared at them in horror, then began running, her eyes scanning every face.

There! Thank Moii herself, there he was!

Sobbing gratefully, she ran to him, nearly slipping in her haste, and pressed a hand against his chest with desperate hope. He lived!

"Duval!" she whispered, her voice choking. "Duval!"

Slowly he dragged open his eyes to look down at her, and she screamed, stumbling back in horror. Where his eyes should have been were swirling black voids of space and madness.

She spat, tears burning her face. The Omcris had taken his soul! He was only a hulk, one of their dead things to be used as a puppet and then discarded.

"Oh, Duval, no. No!" she said. Gripping his tunic, she bent her head against his side and wept.

"Sufficient."

Startled, Costa whirled and saw beyond the rows of hanging bodies two enormous faces floating in holographic transmission. Neither were humanoid; instead the skulls were long and narrow, tapering to slim muzzles. Tall pointed ears projected upward, and the eyes were cold and lidless, unblinking with reptilian intensity.

"Yes, Hosahkt will be pleased with this test subject. It has performed well."

"Agreed. It must be taken before Hosahkt. Since it is the first of its kind to recover unaided from Omcri tampering, evidence suggests it can be utilized in many ways. Come, subject." The second creature beckoned to her.

Costa stood her ground. "Identify yourselves."

They exchanged startled glances as though not expecting anything other than immediate obedience from her.

"Unnecessary."

"Agreed."

"Who are you?" repeated Costa. "What is this planet? How long—"

"Oh," said one in amusement. "It desires statistical information. Answer it."

"For what purpose?"

"Another test. Hosahkt will be curious."

"We are Gerend. This planet is unimportant, serving merely as cold storage for food purposes which serve five systems of Hosahkt's third sector. It has been labeled Storage Facility Nine. Previous to Hosahkt's occupation of this galaxy, the planet had another designation. We do not know it, any more than we know or care about the original inhabitants who built the structures you have so admired today."

"I am not food for you, *flin!*" shouted Costa. "Those other things did not eat me and neither will you!"

Again the two faces exchanged looks.

"It refers to the Vestiges. They are not governed by us. They exist by stealing. Omcris are charged with destroying them on sight, but a few manage to survive."

"Enough explanations. It is time to present the subject before Hosahkt. He desires the Ranger's secret. If this one provides the key, we shall be amply rewarded."

"Recovering the Zethian Ranger from madness would have been preferable," muttered the other.

"That failure we need not immediately report. Come, subject! Walk forward."

Every sense within Costa quivered eagerly. Haufren had not abandoned her! Somehow he had learned of her capture, and he and Duval had come after her. Her grip tightened on her brother, who had believed too late in her story.

Head high, she made no move to obey. "This man is my brother. Can you reverse what the Omcris have done to him?"

"Irrelevant. Come!"

"I do not leave without him! Can he be cured?"

"Your species has great belief in the power of Omcris. They are, in fact, minor beings of little importance to Hosahkt."

"Then he can be—"

"Unimportant. You will come now, subject, or be hung here for processing. Other keys can be found."

Costa faced them with steel in her eye. "Then you do not care that Duval also has information about the Rangers? Isn't that what you want? Information about the Rangers? Where their primary base is? What their numbers are? What their capacities are for striking against you? They've held you out of our galaxy for quite a while now. That must make them your greatest enemies."

"Hardly. You are but a small—"

"Time is wasted," snapped the other. "It delays us and shall pay for its arrogance."

"And if it speaks truly? Let us err on the side of caution, Phobis. Let us take the second creature."

"And the Zethian," said Costa, afraid of her own boldness, but not daring to leave the mad one behind if he truly were a Ranger as well. She had heard of the Ranger rule of never abandoning someone in the field. They lived by it. She would not break it if she could help it. "He is also a Ranger—"

"Useless. The Omcris have broken its mind with their games."

"Then let them mend it!" shouted Costa. "Bring these two men, and I shall come willingly."

"You will come, willingly or not."

"Agree to its terms, Phobis. Other uses can be found for them besides meat."

"Indeed," said Phobis darkly. "But I shall personally see this subject carved, spiced, and served to Hosahkt on a tray of its own bones as soon as its use is expended."

"You would be wiser to dissect it to determine why it has been able to withstand so much of Omcri direction. Come, subject. Your terms will be met, for now."

Costa swallowed, her throat dry. She wanted to run, but there was nowhere to go. Besides, if there was the slightest hope of restoring Duval. . . . She stepped forward through the greasy mud, walking with the confidence of a patrol officer, but she had never been more frightened in her life. There was something sinister about these jackal creatures who spoke to her so easily in Unise yet regarded her as though she were not even sentient life. Haufren had spoken of the masters of the Omcris; plainly these Gerend were, but who commanded them? What was this Hosahkt? She did not really want to know.

"Stop there."

Obediently she stood still between the flickering holographs with the rows of hanging bodies behind her. The chamber was very warm, making her sweat beneath her tunic. The stench of ripening flesh filled her nostrils, sickening her.

It came as a sharp blow between the eyes, numbing her just before she seemed to be wrenched in half. And then she was spinning through a void, nowhere and everywhere, parted and together, nothing and all things.

"Welcome," said a deep, resonant voice.

Costa twitched, suddenly realizing she was standing with her arms hugged tightly about herself and her eyes clenched shut. The horrible stench was gone, and the muggy heat had been replaced by the sere breath of the desert. Slowly, not yet willing to face whatever might be before her, she opened her eyes.

CHAPTER FIFTEEN

"I am Ephemeron, coordinator of the maze of Hosahkt. Is it correct that you have been sent here by the Gerend, Phobis and Tumult?"

Costa slowly turned, trying to locate the source of the voice in the shadows. She was standing in an alcove of stone, one of many ringing a circular chamber lit by guttering flambeaux. "Yes," she said, and her voice echoed loudly.

"You are the subject which has excited them, the subject which has recovered unaided from the effects of Omcri injection?"

"Yes."

"Excellent. Please step down from the transender."

Costa obeyed, only to start, reaching for the weapon she did not carry, as an enormous Omcri robed in scarlet glided into the chamber toward her.

"Do not fear! Do not flee! I am coordinator. It is not my function to attack."

It took a moment for Costa's thudding heart to slow down. She straightened, wincing, from her crouch and stared at the Omcri. Unlike the others of its kind, this one displayed faint, pulsating patterns in the cloudiness beneath its bright cowl. She frowned, aware of a slight pressure against her mind. The other Omcris, she realized, were simply directed tools. But this one was far different.

"Yes, you indicate understanding of higher functions," said Ephemeron. "Good. The Gerend were right. You adapt and assimilate very quickly. Hosahkt will be intrigued. Please follow."

Costa obeyed as the Omcri turned and glided from the chamber, noting how the flambeaux nearly flickered out as the devil-thing passed yet flared high at her approach. The air was very dry, and reeked of sulphur and other noxious gases that made her nostrils burn. Her eyes burned too, but from mounting anger. Was Ephemeron the thing which intended to conquer all that she knew? She would not serve something like it! No human ever could!

"Phobis warned us of your arrogance," said Ephemeron, startling her. The Omcri glided smoothly on as her footsteps faltered.

For a moment she knew despair. How could she ever manage to escape if these creatures read every thought? "I don't intend to be your slave, mind-slasher," she retorted.

Ephemeron stopped. "Be very careful, human," he said, geniality vanishing from his voice. "You amuse for a moment, but that can quickly change."

The passageway through which they were walking widened to a long, rectangular chamber lined with stone benches that had crumbled with sheer age into rubble heaps. Interspersed between them were obscene statues possessing living eyes that watched her pass. Reptilian life forms slithered everywhere, pausing to peer at her with red, glowing eyes that were disturbingly mesmerizing. She hastened on after the Omcri, beginning to pant a little from the heat, her throat dry and parched, the skin over her cheekbones stretching uncomfortably.

Beyond the chamber lay another crooked passageway lined with tiny cells. Each held a prisoner, most of them human or of species she recognized. Her heart began to drum. Her eyes flickered rapidly into each cell, searching.

Abruptly she stopped. "Commander!"

Janal sat slumped on the dusty floor, his uniform torn, his hands bloody. He gave no sign of hearing her.

She moved to the doorway of the cell, caution making her wonder what undetectable force served in the stead of sonic bars. Her keen ears picked up no hum of an energy barrier.

"Commander!" She reached out her hand, ready to flinch back. But nothing stopped it. Her breath eagerly caught in her throat. They must guard minds here, not bodies. Once again hope lifted within her, which she hastily tried to crush down lest Ephemeron sense it. "Commander Janal!"

He did not stir, and she was about to step inside when Ephemeron said:

"Do not interfere, subject."

Green lights glowed fiercely through the swirling patterns beneath the Omcri's cowl, and Costa hastily moved back.

"He is known to me. He is my—"

"He has been designated. When the time comes for his use, he will be reactivated."

Chilled, Costa opened her mouth, then shut it with her questions unasked. She dared push no further right now.

Two cells down, they passed Duval, slumped and lifeless as Janal was. Her heart leapt, but she said nothing and gave no sign of seeing him. The cell opposite Duval's held the black Zethian, who lay curled on his side, twitching convulsively. They ascended crumbling steps, Costa's boots scuffing quietly over the stone. Here, the cells became cleaner and larger. Only three were occupied: One held a figure in the royal livery of Rigel, the second held someone in Fleet uniform, and the third held the Kublai of the United Worlds of Drugh. His Supreme Glory reclined on a gilded couch, attired in face paint and scarlet robes. He was the first prisoner Costa had seen awake. Smiling vacantly with dreamy fascination, he watched the pouched serpents undulating languidly around his couch, their eyes glowing into his.

Ephemeron paused here. "Hosahkt is very pleased with this one. It met all his greatest expectations."

"In what way?" asked Costa, half-afraid to hear the answer.

"It is naturally in the best interests of Hosahkt not to war with a galaxy he wishes to assimilate. There is less damage done when certain key figures can be persuaded to assist in the conquest."

"And the Kublai has agreed?" asked Costa, cold inside. She thought of Drugh, centrally located, controlling vital space lanes, economically superior to so many other, poorer worlds which depended upon the Kublai's wealth for survival.

"The Kublai," said Ephemeron with amusement, "thinks it has found complete unification with its deity Kanta. The Kublai is willing to do anything to maintain its blissful state."

"You are tricking him!" said Costa angrily.

"So shall we deal with the mighty Zethian empire through the assistance of a wellborn child. So shall we deal with the Directors of *your* planet, subject, when they are brought to us by you, the subject Janal, and the subject Duval."

"Never!" whispered Costa, the word sticking in her throat.

"Come," said Ephemeron and glided on.

At the end of the passageway rose a pair of massive stone-banded portals. The Gerend stood guard there, jackal faces turned suspiciously toward Costa as she followed Ephemeron between them into what lay beyond.

"Hosahkt!" Ephemeron's deep, resonant voice boomed with reverence.

The chamber was cavern-sized, so vast Costa could not see the walls. Flaring torches stuck everywhere flamed and smoked in myriad colors, contrasting and mixing all the bands of light. The floor was polished to the sheen of glass, its hue blood-purple obsidian. Serpents, these magnificent cousins to the lesser reptiles in the dusty chambers behind, glided everywhere. Most were larger than Costa and banded in brilliant shades of green and magenta and black-speckled silver. Their hissing breaths expelled sulphur and dioxides. Eyes the size of Costa's head glowed at her with spellbinding fascination, never blinking, beautiful colors swirling in their unwavering depths as they mesmerized her, making her breath shorten until the flesh of her thighs and arms tingled. She swayed as they swayed, became dizzy as two circled her more closely, turning so that eyes met eyes without interruption.

And then some instinct of preservation within Costa snapped to life. She shut her eyes, forcing herself to stand still as a part of her longed to continue with them.

"The Gerend were right. It possesses a remarkable independence of will. Are you certain it is human, Ephemeron?" The voice was liquid purity, rushing thunderously yet gentle. Underlying each word were other words half-spoken, half-heard like distant echoes of multiple languages all blending in a harmony that made Costa shiver.

"Aside from certain adaptations in the genetic structure, yes, Hosahkt."

Not yet daring to open her eyes as she listened to the serpents slithering around her, Costa heard a sharp intake of breath.

"So the humans begin experiments in that area! Interesting! There must be more such as this one—"

"Many more," said Costa, keeping her eyes firmly shut

against the temptations beating against her. "We are called adapts."

"How original. I wonder if the taste will be altered. Approach us, subject."

Warily Costa permitted one eye to squint open and saw the serpents moving away from her. In relief she strode forward, tired of tests and mysteries and ready to find a way to blast herself out of this place.

The dais rising before her was backed by a semicircle of twisted pillars fashioned from smoky quartz with tiny, spidery creatures imprisoned forever inside them. Torches blazed unsteady flickers of green and purple light. Braziers wrought in the shape of serpent skulls burned bones like incense. Scaled things, narrow and furtive, slithered into the warm shadows or coiled arrogantly in her path. And other things gathered here as well, furred things, or hairless ones, humans, and suffering Merriads from the cold ice system of Thanos. Delicate crystals shone with gemlike splendor from atop short pedestals lining Costa's path, now and then flashing brilliantly in the torchlight. At the jewel-studded steps leading to the dais, Costa stopped to gaze at the sight enthroned beyond the ring of Omcri guards standing motionless in robes of bronze and amethyst, deadly wands pointed at her. Tith crouched there, his fur wet and matted and his eyes closed. He was chained to the throne as a pet would be.

"Come to us, subject," said Hosahkt.

Costa swallowed against the intense heat, longing for water. Whatever hideous monstrosity she had expected to find, Costa realized she had never imagined anything that came close to the vision of Hosahkt himself. A face that shone with pure beauty, as delicately etched as a woman's and radiant as though light emanated from within, lifted itself to gaze at Costa. It was not a human face, being both alien and indescribable. Such beauty so near absolute perfection was frightening to behold. The radiance poured over Costa as she stood there stunned, warming her until she writhed against the urge to kneel.

I am food to it, she thought grimly and pulled herself back from the precipice of worship.

"Yes, very strong of will," said Hosahkt.

The feeling of *interest* washed over Costa, swaying her with its intensity. Beads of perspiration trickled down her forehead as panic seized her. How could she hope to cling to her own identity against such a forceful personality? It wanted to crush her, to absorb her, to make her feel as it did and to feed on her emotions in turn. Desperately Costa shook her head, stepping back in readiness to flee.

Hosahkt rose from his throne, gracefully unfolding a slender shape that glistened in shades of palest mauve and gold. Enormous, gossamer-thin wings spread out from his back, lifting him up with an ease that belied their fragile loveliness. He had neither arms nor legs. He did not need them. He had legions to serve him.

"Costa," he said in the voice that rushed and babbled like mountain streams. "Our servants have spoken to you of the importance of conquering your galaxy by quiet agreement. Your area of origin is rich in resources, containing many varieties whose nutrients will bring a high price. Damage must be minimized. We have Drugh to serve us in this matter. We have the Directors of Playworld . . . as soon as you and your fellow subjects bring them to us. We require only the cooperation of the Fleet. The subject called Haufren has closed itself to the probes of Ephemeron and other servants. It releases no information. It has long been our enemy, but still we would not desire its flesh to be baked in the ovens of Kahnjoor if it would be persuaded to cooperate."

A chill broke out over Costa. Some of her awe faded. This was no god! Hosahkt was nothing but a meat merchant, haggling over condition and price like the skin-sellers in the Beros slums.

"My legions have many weapons," continued Hosahkt. "Unfortunately their power is so great that nothing of your resources would remain. This is to be avoided. We might destroy only the Rangers, but they are a rare, priceless delicacy. The flesh of warriors is usually tough and unpalatable, but there is something unique about the radiation on their asteroids which makes them tender. We do not wish to destroy those asteroids; therefore, we seek the defense keys which Haufren can provide us. Settle must be maintained. We can grow many varieties there, reaping outstanding prices for flesh which does not age or wither. You, subject, will persuade him to assist us."

"No!" Whirling, Costa started off the dais, but the Omcri guards faced her, closing off her path.

"You reactivated yourself, subject," said Hosahkt, and his voice thundered at her with such force the floor shook and some of the torches extinguished. "But remember that you can be deactivated permanently! Serve us, or go to the ovens!"

Costa shut her eyes a moment, seeking to master her rage and revulsion. She had no weapon yet; she must calm down; she must wait for her chance. Somewhere inside she found the old discipline and forced it into place. Then she turned to look back at that glowing face with an accompanying Omcri cloud floating beside it as a familiar.

"Where is Haufren?" she asked.

When she saw him she thought he was dead. He lay sprawled on a slab of dusty stone in a hot, airless cell where the stinking torch was busy burning what little oxygen seemed to exist. His hair had dried in tousled strings, and his face was bloodless gray. She started to touch his shoulder, then drew back in remembrance of Duval's eyes.

"Activate him," she said to her Omcri guide.

"Activation completed previously," it replied. Lifting a hand, it glided out.

Costa gave him a slight shake. "Haufren!" she said, glancing involuntarily over her shoulder. She wondered how many unseen eyes, ears, and minds were scanning them. "Haufren, wake up!"

He groaned, and his eyes flickered partially open. They remained blue, but were clouded over as though he floated half in and half out of Omcri possession. Alarm gripped her. Not Haufren, too! She had been hoping he had the means to protect himself.

"Haufren!" she said again. She started to pull him upright to a sitting position, then some instinct made her leave him as he was. "Haufren, it's Costa. Can you hear me?"

His mouth worked. "Affirmative."

She frowned, seizing on her training in rescue and revival. "All right. You can hear me. Who am I?"

He mumbled, his face growing slack again. She shook him.

"Haufren! You must wake up. We have to get out of here. Come on, Major, take grip!"

He blinked, trying to lift a hand to his head. "Who . . ."

"Costa. Do you understand? It's Costa." Keep talking, she told herself. Say something he'll start to pick up on and follow. Get his brain working. "You came after me, didn't you? You and Duval? He would not believe me. I guess you convinced him." She felt the bitterness coming through her voice and squelched it. Puce would know how to cure Duval, if she could only get him out of here. "Did you leave Puce behind? He gets shaky around the Omcris. No one hates them more. Come on, Major, talk back! How did you find me?"

He was trying. She could see the effort behind those glazed eyes. "Street of Souls—" Abruptly he coughed, spitting up blood.

"Easy!" She held his shoulders, despair welling up through her. He was probably dying; he should be left to rest. But she dared not. She had to have his help if any of them were to get out of here.

Drawing an unsteady breath, she tried again. "Major, how many men did you bring with you? I have seen Duval. Was there a big Zethian?"

"Silta." For an instant his eyes cleared. "Need him."

"He is insane." She watched the frown of dawning comprehension come, and winced at the raw pain in his face. "I'm sorry. I'm not good at saying things gently."

Haufren made an effort at sitting up and failed. "Must get him back to Settle . . . cure . . ."

"The radiation there?" she asked, holding her breath. She had never heard of any such thing as Hosahkt spoke about. With all of her information so eagerly gleaned over the years regarding the Rangers, she had not even come across a rumor. "You mean you don't age?"

He frowned at her. "Of course we do! Don't be absurd!"

"Hosahkt believes otherwise. He—"

"Who?"

"Haven't you been questioned yet?" It was her turn to frown.

Haufren expelled a ragged breath. "Yes. I think so."

His voice quavered, and she gripped his arm, willing him to hang on.

"Listen to me," she said in a low, rapid voice. She knelt beside the slab to put her lips on a level with his ear. "Hosahkt is the one in charge here. The one you've been trying to keep out of our galaxy. He wants to sell us—humans, everyone—for meat. Do you understand?"

Her tone got through. Haufren's mouth tightened.

"Affirmative," he said.

"Good. He doesn't want war. According to him, he can wipe us out in one attack. But that would also destroy his profit. He has the Kublai mesmerized into a treaty with him; probably it guarantees the Kublai's safety in exchange for a certain quota of bodies every year. Hosahkt intends to use Tith as a hostage to blackmail Zethia into cooperation. He also claims he has Playworld, and you know that through us he can reach any other head of state who happens to be vacationing—"

"Yes."

"He also wants Settle. As a special breeding ground." She swallowed, revulsion leaving a sour taste in her mouth. "He claims the radiation there makes Ranger flesh a real delicacy. Do you *understand*?"

Haufren closed his eyes. "The defense keys."

"Yes! He expects me to get them from you."

A ghost of a laugh lifted from Haufren's throat. "Don't sound so grim. It's all a lie."

"What is?"

"Settle radiation. Your Hosahkt's no fool. He knows that no matter how many key planets he coerces, the Rangers will never surrender." Haufren frowned. "By Demos, we'd destroy worlds to keep from surrendering! So that's why they were probing me so thoroughly. I'm sure they would like the defense keys. Wouldn't that make eliminating the Rangers easy?"

"Haufren, we may have to give them to him."

"Never!'

"Haufren, we need time enough to get out of here. Until he has something, Hosahkt will have us watched every moment. We—"

"And once he has the information he wants, he'll just throw us back to the Omcris."

"Maybe not," she said urgently, angry that he was refusing to trust her judgment yet again. "Listen! We must use anything we have to get out of here. Your commander can always change the keys if we can reach him with sufficient warning."

Smiling in what was more a grimace, Haufren grasped her arm and shook his head.

"Damn you, Haufren! Have you got a better idea?"

"No." He coughed. "It would work. But, Demos, slinny, I don't *know* the keys."

CHAPTER SIXTEEN

"What?" Stunned, at first she could only stare at him. Then rage engulfed her. Did he have to go on playing games? Couldn't he trust her just once? "What do you mean you don't know them? That's *flin,* Major! Of course you know them! How do you get home?"

"We pass through a pick-up security scan, just like everybody else. You have an ID grid implant. We have something similar. The defense keys are too vital to be entrusted to field operatives."

She sighed, her shoulders sagging in defeat. "Then what do we do?"

His eyes met hers with a faint grin. "It may look hopeless to you, but this is common for us. We call it Situation B or Imprisoned in a Tough Spot. Situation C is Tortured in a Tough Spot."

She looked up, supposing she should be grateful for his attempt to cheer her. "And what is Situation A?"

"Lost."

She smiled, then sobered quickly as she gazed at the stone walls surrounding them. "That may apply, too. I remember the way back to the transender here. But if it's just a link to the last planet I was on, then I—"

"Don't worry. Silta has an unerring sense of direction. If we can find him, we'll be—oh, Demos. You said he is insane." Haufren rubbed his eyes wearily. "And Tith? I should never have brought him into this. Where is he?"

"I last saw him with Hosahkt."

"What about the other man? Duval?"

"Deactivated," she said, her voice choking. "And so is Commander Janal. I don't know how we are going to get them out." Despair made her voice shrill, and she hastily lowered it in shame. "You should not have come in after me."

His eyes met hers, but appalled by what she had just said, she jumped up before he could speak.

"I am a fool!" she said bitterly. "Of course you did not . . .

you came to destroy the transender access points and—"

"We could have come back with a full contingent of Rangers and shock troops," he broke in with a quietness that cut through the self-pity strangling her.

"What?" Startled, she turned back to face him.

"Captain Silta made strong recommendations against this move. I overrode him in favor of rescue. Costa . . ." Haufren's blue eyes burned into hers. "Rangers don't leave their people behind."

A sob half broke from her. She forced it back, only now realizing how frightened and exhausted she was, and how desperately she wanted someone else to take charge. "Thank you," she managed, dropping her eyes in the old, ever-burning disappointment that even his kindness could not quench. "But I am not a Ranger."

His lean strong hand grasped hers hard. "Costa," he said, the authority in his voice forcing her to meet his eyes. "Get us, *all* of us, out of here and back to Settle, and you'll have your commission as a buck cadet in the corps."

Astonishment drove the weariness away. She gasped, laughing in disbelief. *"What?"*

"And if you manage to also destroy the transender access points, you'll enter at your present rank." He gave her hand a shake. "Take grip, Lieutenant! There isn't much time. Do we have a deal?"

Her eyes glowed warm gold, and her heart came close to bursting with every beat. A chance! No matter how overwhelming the odds might seem now, at last she had a chance! Then doubt crept in, and she frowned, dropping his hand.

"My contract. The Directors won't release me."

Haufren's eyes chilled, and her heart seemed to shrink.

"Slinny," he said with some of the old scorn. "You aren't on Playworld now. If you don't go back, what authority can they hold over you?"

"I'm not a fool! You know the legal entanglements!" she snapped. "Or you should. I am an adapt. I cost them a lot of money to develop and train. They don't want adapts free and attracting the attention of GSI."

He frowned, looking angry, and started to retort only to

cough and spit blood. She reached for him, but he waved her back.

"I'm sorry," she said, not knowing how to explain. "I'll still do it. Somehow." She swallowed hard, her vision blurring with the old pain. "There just won't be any reward. Your recommendation, Major, won't be good enough."

Sagging, he closed his eyes. She drew in an unsteady breath against the hurt. For a moment he had been friendly; she had been accepted for the first time. Now she was the outsider again. Well, she would get him out; she would get them all out. She would show Major Haufren IV that the Rangers weren't the only corps to have pride. She would show him what a provincial planet patroller could do.

"Where are you going?" he asked weakly as she reached the door of the cell.

She paused but did not glance back. "To locate a weapon. Try to pull yourself together and be ready. If you can, move left along this passageway and wait at the main intersection."

"Costa—"

But she left without waiting to listen.

In the passageway she shoved her burning emotions down, trying to think as hard and quickly as she could. Hunger, thirst, and the grinding pain in her side must be ignored. Haufren had said they did not have much time, and whether he meant that was because of Hosahkt's plans or the fact that he was dying made little difference at the moment. She *must* hurry.

But how? What was she to do?

Create confusion, she thought, making sure her feet made no sound as she passed the cells. Again she felt as though she were being watched, and she expected an Omcri to return and take charge of her at any moment. Oh, Moii! Was there no way to destroy those devil-things? Logic dictated that since they had been created, they could be destroyed. She must not believe them invincible.

"Well, subject?"

As though from nowhere, Ephemeron suddenly stood before her, blocking the passageway. His scarlet robes billowed lightly in the parched air, and vaguely disturbing patterns pulsed rapidly beneath the cowl. Although several meters still lay between them, she could feel intense eagerness radiating from the Omcri.

She paused where she was, not wishing to close the distance yet. "Well, Ephemeron?"

"We shall probe your pitiable mind for our answers!"

It took all the willpower she possessed not to flinch back from that threat but she held her ground and even managed to shrug in apparent unconcern. Attack, she thought. Give him the unexpected.

"The Kublai has made a deal of cooperation with you. Do you, er, does Hosahkt expect the Directors of Playworld to do the same, or does he intend to simply have them possessed?"

"You waste time! These questions are irrelevant!"

"No, they aren't. I have coordinates, mind-slasher. You don't— Wait!" she said, holding up a hand as a slight stir from the Omcri warned her she was about to be probed. "I am an adapt, remember? Not the usual kind of human you are used to dealing with. Probe me, and you won't get what you expect." And that was certainly the truth, she thought wryly. For the first time in her life she began to see the force of certain arguments in favor of mental techniques. She still believed that telepathy was wrong, that to invade another's mind did more than destroy privacy, but to bury oneself on a planet where its practice was forbidden by law and expect that law to protect one was foolish and definitely naive. If she survived this and ever got out of here, she vowed to find out if she had at least enough talent to learn how to shield herself.

"Very well," said Ephemeron angrily, and she tried to hold back a sigh of relief. "But do not delay. Relate them!"

"I want to make a deal."

"You are not—"

"Hosahkt wants what I know, doesn't he?" she broke in, showing her teeth. "And he is growing impatient. I, however, do not want to be meat for some piece of *flin* here. I want out. And I want continued protection when I do get out. That, in exchange for Settle."

There was a long silence. "You dare a great deal, subject."

She shrugged. "Go on. Go and ask Hosahkt. I'm sure he

thinks the defense keys are the important issue here. And I'm hardly being greedy."

"We have observed your pattern," said Ephemeron. "You ask now for your safety, but next you will demand the same for other subjects."

"No," she said coolly. "I don't think so. One Ranger is dying; the other is mad. My friends from Playworld are deactivated. There is no hope for any of them. I am intact, though, and want to stay that way." While she was speaking she had been moving by imperceptible degrees to the wall. She reached out and scratched her wrist on the stone hard enough to leave a drop of blood. The scent would bring her back to this place should she need to find it.

"It is not the time when approach is permitted to Hosahkt," said Ephemeron. "Yet he has commanded implementation. You dare much, subject."

She said nothing, hiding her smile. She had him now, and they both knew it.

"Go into that cell behind you and wait," commanded Ephemeron.

She obeyed, though not without reluctance. "I want a strifer," she said. "When you send me back to the jungle on Playworld, I must have a weapon to survive."

Amusement radiated from Ephemeron. "That is your concern, subject, not mine. Wait."

But she did not wait. As soon as Ephemeron disappeared, she expected something to arrive to guard the door. But not even one of the lesser Omcris came. Costa frowned in astonishment. Were they truly so complacent in their own power they believed she would obey without enforcement? Had they perhaps become so used to dealing with possessed individuals held under the power of activation they forgot she was different? It seemed so, and she thanked their carelessness fervently.

Leaving the cell, she hastened down the passageway, stepping over a serpent without much attention. Then she paused, frowning over the dig of an instinct she dared not ignore. She whirled and pounced in a swift leap, coming down with one bootheel upon the serpent's head and the other on its neck. It writhed violently, lashing its tail about her ankle, but she had heard the snap of its spine and after a moment she stepped away, leaving it in its death throes. So much for one spy, she thought grimly, and took down a torch from its sconce. Flame was an effective weapon against certain things. She felt better with the knobbed twist of burning wood in her hand, scorching her arm and face as she hurried on with it brandished before her.

She met nothing else, and began to feel the temptation to gather the men and break for escape. But she fought it back, knowing better. The Omcris would stop them before they got to the transender. No, she had to go on the offensive. The best way to create confusion would be to destroy Hosahkt.

Something large hissed at her from the shadows, and she flinched aside, hastening on with her heart thudding. Rubble littered the way ahead of her, and she could hear the furtive scratching of claws and the faint rasp of scales over stone. She wished suddenly she had not yet formed that thought about killing Hosahkt. Her mind was wide open to anyone who desired to read it. She must be careful.

"Stop."

Startled by that double-timbred voice which seemed to come from nowhere, Costa jerked to a halt and whirled in a half-crouch. The fire of the torch roared and crackled, shooting up sparks as her eyes jabbed here, there, seeking the Omcri.

Suddenly it was before her, less than an arm's length away, floating, sinister in its black robes, faceless. "Area unauthorized. Intrusion denied. Return to cell of assignment."

Costa thought of being herded back to the cell by this Omcri and held there while time and the advantage of surprise ran out. With an inarticulate cry, she sprang at the Omcri and plunged her torch straight through its center.

It was an action done purely on reflex. She had no hope of fire being any more effective than strifer bolts. And when she heard the muffled pop that signified the torch had been extinguished completely, her heart sank like a stone. It would attack her now. It would kill her.

She backed away as the Omcri raised its arms. But instead of rushing at her, the creature suddenly whipped as though jerked on an invisible string and screamed with an agony that pierced her as no death cry ever had. Harsh pain lanced through her poisoned arm, making her cry out and stagger to one knee. But even as she rocked back and forth, clutching her arm to her middle, triumph laughed within her. She had destroyed it! The shadows pressing around her did not frighten her now. She had found their first weak point.

As soon as the pain eased in her arm and she could catch her breath again, she reached out gingerly to the crumpled robe on the floor and drew forth the Omcri's wand. She grinned to herself in the gloom, snapping open her innermost eyelids. Now she had a real weapon.

Soundlessly, exulting in her warrior's heart, she ran on until she came to the next torch, which she also took down. She left her mark of wrist blood at selected points, understanding now why Ephemeron had mentioned a maze. She did not remember so many twisting passages before, but she refused to be daunted. She had a hunter's instincts, and she followed them.

When she reached the area where the Kublai dreamed contentedly in whatever fantasies the serpents provided for him, she paused to catch her breath, ducking out of sight as two massive, armor-plated quadrupeds with tiny heads no larger than her fist rumbled past. She had her bearings finally. Without hesitation she turned toward Hosahkt's audience chamber. Haufren had to get himself this far. She did not think there would be a chance to go all the way back for him. Swiftly she examined the Omcri's wand to be sure she knew how to fire it. Then she slipped it out of sight in her sleeve where she usually carried the knife Duval had taken from her.

Anger, unbidden, rose within her. If only he had *listened* the first time! And then she remembered that if he hadn't felt guilty enough to come with Haufren, he would not now be something neither living nor dead.

She shoved the thoughts away. She had to go on. She had to concentrate on boldness. She had to make sure Hosahkt and his slithering spies did not sense the death in her true purpose. The range of an Omcri weapon was fairly extensive, but she had to get close. She had to make sure nothing intercepted her aim.

"Disobedient fool!"

Ephemeron blocked her path, glowing fierce green beneath his cowl. He was flanked by a smaller, black-robed Omcri pointing a wand at her.

"You have strayed from your cell. A messenger Omcri has been reabsorbed. You are d—"

Costa jerked the wand from her sleeve and fired two brief bursts of precise death. Again agony shot jaggedly up her arm as the Omcris died, but this time she had braced herself to withstand it. Grimacing, she staggered past their remains, pausing only to take another wand, and pushed herself into a run. She had to hurry now. She must give Hosahkt no further warning.

But the decayed chamber of reptiles waited ahead of her, and entry was blocked by the two gigantic quadrupeds which roared at the sight of her. The whole passageway shook, and little splatters of dust rained down from overhead. Costa fired, then threw herself flat as the deadly energy ricocheted off their armored hides. One stamped forward, roaring loudly enough to deafen her. She still held the guttering torch in her other hand. Fighting off the blindness of terror, she made herself stand her ground, crouching on the floor until the thing was nearly upon her. One thrust of its enormous stubby foot could crush her into a stain upon the dust, but she waited, making herself face those tiny, red-maddened eyes until the grotesque mouth opened, giving her the chance to ram the torch down its throat.

Its roar of rage shrilled to one of agony. Shaking itself madly from side to side, it knocked her into the wall and blundered on, amok now and gaining speed until it ran into the wall where the passageway turned. It stood there hammering itself into the stone.

Costa lay limp, barely conscious from the force of impact, and tried to bring herself around. She sat up, gasped for the breath her flattened lungs could not provide, and fell back. But as soon as she got some air, she pushed herself up, clawing at the wall for support. Where was the other one? She had to get on her feet before it charged her.

It came with a roar, shaking the ground so she feared the roof would fall in. Adrenaline shot her to her feet, pressing her against the wall in a hopeless attempt to escape, but to her surprise it charged past her with its small head down and its powerful legs thrusting it faster and faster until with a savage howl it crashed full tilt into the first beast, now bloody and staggering from its fight with the wall. They faced each other, screaming in rage, and with a gulp Costa limped on, weaving and nearly falling as one leg tried to fail her. She clung to the rough stone wall, dragging herself on without heed as she scraped her hands.

Inside the long chamber with its crumbling benches, some of the noise from the awesome battle behind her faded slightly. But she did not notice this as she scanned the place with a frown. The gruesome statues had closed their eyes and the serpents were gone. Why? Where did they await her?

At the huge, stone-banded portals to the room of audience, the two Gerend still stood guard. As one, Phobis and Tumult swung their jackal heads in her direction as she appeared and lifted their hands to throw. Costa fired, sweeping both in one blast, and the black spheres in their hands uncoiled into long, whip-thin snakes that darted frantically away as the Gerend crumpled to the ground.

Costa swallowed hard, panting, and wiped the sweat from her forehead. Now there was only Hosahkt left to face, and with him the best and strongest of his defenses. There was but one of her, and no matter how good, tough, and quick she was, one was not enough. She faced failure and death, and for a moment she could not go in. Pride and fear held her trapped between them. Then she thought of Haufren, lean and tough and hard as a damned Ishut club. Rangers never gave up. As long as they could move or think, they weren't beaten. And neither was she. Costa steeled herself. She had to do it.

Holding her breath against the sick nausea of fear crawling through her gut, she stepped over the sprawled Gerend and walked through the portals into the vast audience chamber, expecting to be fried from existence.

Emptiness awaited her. The rich, sumptuous beauty was gone. All the torches with their multicolored flames had burned low or were dying, guttering deep in blackened sockets with faint pops of sound. The gigantic serpents of fascination, banded in brilliant color, did not appear. She limped forward, every sense straining as her adrenaline dropped by slow degrees. Disbelief washed over her, and with it disappointment and half-hysterical defeat. Where were they? Did she have to hunt them, and go through this again?

"I remain, subject."

Costa jerked, startled, and stared at the shadowed dais where a winged figure slowly drifted up into sight. The aching, indescribable beauty glowed more sharply in these subdued surroundings, striking her harder than before. But she had no admiration left. She was too tired to be swayed by emotions she could barely control. She let it come toward her, her eyes dispassionately studying that mauve and golden body and those gossamer wings for the place of vulnerability where she must strike. Hosahkt bowed his head for a moment, and only then did she notice the dark wisp of Omcri cloud wreathed about his throat.

"Where are your Omcri guards?" she asked, and her hoarse voice echoed loudly through empty space. "Where are your creatures?"

"Destruction is a factor of your species," said the voice like rushing waters. "Here, we have always sought continuance—"

"Yes, by feeding upon other sentient beings!" she snapped, in no mood to listen to philosophy.

"It is our right to survive."

She snorted. "We could argue forever by using the same position against each other. Where are your guards?"

Hosahkt folded his wings and sank down before her, coiling his limbless body with smooth grace onto the floor. Even thus, they were of a similar height. "You fear they have gone to destroy your companions. Yet Omcris are not sentient. They possess no emotions or thoughts of their own which we do not transmit through them. You have caused two to be reabsorbed and have destroyed my coordinator. Do you not realize the difficulty in creating coordinators? Gerend sentience must be grafted into symbiosis with Omcri life force. Without a coordinator Omcris require severe energy expenditure to control. I have found it necessary to release all my Omcris in an effort to reestablish equilibrium. Only a portion of this one remains to serve me."

Costa let out her breath, wondering if she could believe him.

"You will sense no lie within me, subject."

"I am not your subject! Let us go from here!"

Amusement radiated toward her. "I do not keep you."

"Janal and Duval must be reactivated. You—"

"If I summoned an Omcri you would cause it to be reabsorbed. Oh, yes, the emotions are strong within you. So much hatred, so much arrogance, so much misunderstanding. We are higher beings. We require survival, even at the cost of yours."

"No," she said, gritting her teeth. "That is falsehood. Your species could live on manufactured foods as we do. You choose to sell us as luxury goods for a higher price. You wish to *breed* us on Settle so we will be tender! Don't speak to me of arrogance and misunderstanding!"

He began to sway gently from side to side before her, glowing in his beauty, soothing murmurs humming from him. "Yes, yes," he said, his voice slowing and becoming soft. "Settle. Tell me about Settle. Tell me what you found out from the Ranger."

"No." Her eyes watched him sway back and forth. She blinked fiercely, but the movement continued, gently back and forth, back and forth. "There is nothing. It is a . . . lie. They . . . age . . ." She felt herself sway as he did, and tried to stop. "You want to . . . destroy . . ."

"Yes, of course. You believe you are very clever to see through my little ploy. But it is foolish indeed to try to deny me the information I seek. The Rangers guard their place very tightly, but you know the secrets. The Rangers trust you, little one. As does Hosahkt. Hosahkt knows his subjects will never harm him. Will they?"

A deadly lethargy crept over her. Dimly she perceived the danger, but it was too late. She swayed from side to side, her eyes gradually losing focus as his voice bored deeper and deeper into her.

"No harm is ever done to Hosahkt. No harm."

"No harm," she echoed dully.

"Put away your toys, subject."

No! screamed something within her, but her hands uncurled

and let the wands drop to the polished blood-purple floor. Her foot moved in a slow kick that sent them spinning far away behind her.

"Approach Hosahkt," murmured the gentle voice, rushing over and around her. "Approach. Yes. Hosahkt hungers. Lie down, subject, and feed Hosahkt. Now."

She folded bonelessly to the floor, her scream no more than a soundless little sigh as he uncoiled his heavy body and unfurled his wings until he hovered directly over her. Her eyes stared, mesmerized by that widening, gaping mouth which stretched itself unbelievably. And then she realized through the fog holding her that he was going to swallow her whole.

Everything left within her strained to its utmost, and she succeeded in moving only one fingertip. Hosahkt noticed, and radiated a warmth akin to love toward her.

"Such spirit," he murmured and dropped to the floor by her feet. The horrible mouth stretched further, nudging her into place, and then it closed about her boots. She felt the grinding of innumerable teeth through the tough leather and writhed, screaming.

Tith lifted his aching head with a jerk that rattled the chain binding him to Hosahkt's throne. He blinked, free at last from the crushing mental pressure Hosahkt had held over him, and drew a shuddering breath, wanting to be sick. Then he saw Costa lying helplessly on the floor and the monster stretching itself to swallow her. Beyond them Haufren clung weakly to the doorway as he aimed a weapon. Tith's heart thudded with violent alarm as he saw the grim expression on Haufren's face. The major couldn't fire yet! He would kill Costa too!

The harsh restraints of Zethian law cracked apart as raw instinct surged through Tith. Baring his small fangs, he forced himself to his feet, straining against the collar which choked him, and loosed a shrill version of the death cry as he hurled his untrained mental powers at Hosahkt.

It was enough to rock the monster. Turning a bloody shade of purple, Hosahkt pulled away from Costa and flew furiously at Tith. Haufren fired, engulfing Hosahkt in a crackling nimbus of raw energy. Hosahkt's scream mingled with Costa's, then he was gone, the invisible fetters upon her falling away as he collapsed into a smoking heap of ooze and charred remains.

Slowly, shaking all over, Costa sat up and drew her mangled feet toward her. She stared at Tith, who was snarling on the dais with his teeth bared and his young eyes blazing fiercely. For a moment she was too numb and dazed to comprehend what had happened, then her head snapped around in time to see Haufren stagger to his knees. He let the Omcri wand drop, and the noise of its clattering fall brought her back to reality.

"Haufren!" she gasped. "How did you get here?"

He was white, spent, and clinging to the leg of one of the braziers with desperation, but he managed to lift his head. "Your blood," he said, "smeared all over the walls. A few people besides patrollers can follow a trail, you know." He paused for breath and his eyes traveled to Tith. "Well done, little warrior."

Heartily agreeing with that praise, Costa lifted an unsteady hand in a grateful salute to the nib. "Very well done," she said. "I owe you my life."

Tith's small bony chest swelled proudly. "To home now can we go?" he asked.

Haufren grinned weakly at Costa. "You heard him, Lieutenant. Take us home."

EPILOGUE

Costa stood at ramrod attention in the small reception chamber of the infirmary building at Settle HQ, faced by an impressive delegation from the Zethian government. Five adult males, heavily maned and attired in the glittering robes of public office, flanked the Zauran matriarch herself who was regal, battle-scarred, and white-furred with extreme age. To one side stood Tith, his golden pelt sleek and glossy once again, his eyes gleaming jade. A slim, competent tutor held him tightly by the hand, but there was no need. Tith was absolutely motionless through the matriarch's long speech translated carefully into Unise by a clerk in the Ranger service. His huge eyes shone alternately at Costa and the tallest male in the Zethian contingent, furred a dark tawny gold with a magnificent auburn mane that brushed the collar of his white robe. The order of the Ambassador to Terra gleamed upon his chest.

". . . and so as a token of gratitude for Lt. Costa's courageous endeavors toward preserving a royal nib of the House of Zaura, descended from the Matriarch Istisse and born of the House Daughter Sheatha, most excellent warrior of the female line, the government of Zethia hereby bestows the title of Spear-bearer of Zethia upon Lt. Costa and grants her honorary citizenship with all rights due that position."

The matriarch opened a small medal case and handed it to the ambassador, who hung the shining emblem of crossed lances about Costa's neck. He shook her hand, permitting himself a smile which revealed his side teeth.

"And I wish to add a personal thanks," he said, *sotto voce*, "from Tith's matre and myself. Impetuous children make the best warriors, but raising them safely is sometimes difficult. Consider our home yours, Spear-sister."

Costa smiled back, then snapped a crisp salute as the ambassador stepped to one side. She remained in place as the Zethians filed out after their matriarch. But as the others vanished, Tith pulled free of his tutor and came running back to butt her in the stomach with his round head.

"Costa, miss you I shall!"

"I'll miss you too, Tith," she said unsteadily, hugging him tightly. *"Shilorr."*

"Shilorr," he whispered. "When I grow up I shall be a Ranger just like you and the major!"

"Tith!" called the tutor sharply. "Time it is to go!"

"Just as strict as Unru Del," said Tith with a sigh and obediently ran out.

Costa stood there a moment longer, fingering the medal, then she sighed and picked up her cane to slowly make her way to the lift.

High on the observation deck, she seated herself in one of the chairs that was more comfortable than its utilitarian lines suggested, and gazed out through the plexibubble protecting the main complex of Settle HQ. The view behind her showed a fascinating network of plexitunnels containing the supply lines, with all the activity that work entailed, supporting the shuttle field out of sight beyond the second wing of the complex. But Costa kept herself facing the view of the wind-raked plains containing nothing but rock ridges and dust dunes shifting in aimless patterns. Her mind moved back, still trying to piece together the fragments of memory: dragging Tith and an unconscious Haufren through the passageways, unable to walk herself, yet walking, running, crawling, then going back for Duval, who was weak but himself again, and Janal who helped her struggle to subdue the mad Silta; the desperate moments in activating the transender, not knowing how to set new coordinates, hoping the old ones were correct, losing consciousness only to wake up in some formless place glazed with cold, and dying inside moment by moment with fear until the next link of the transender was found; the moldering remains of the Kanta temple, where they stumbled across the picked bones of Wob Nogales; finding a deton-bomb in a discarded pack and timing it for delayed explosion as she sent it back through the transender; little Tith, muddy and scratched bloody from sawtooth vines as he helped her break out the sled from its hiding place in the ruins.

Costa blinked, realized her cheeks were wet, and angrily brushed them dry. Tith thought she was a Ranger, but of course she wasn't. It was her last day on Settle. She had been told this morning that she would be dismissed from the infirmary at 1200 hours.

The memories did not take her much further. Duval and Commander Janal had been left behind on Playworld. But she could not recall how she had found a ship or who had piloted it. She had since speculated that Playworld authorities had let her go off-world to prevent Rangers from coming onto the planet to pick up Haufren and Silta. But it was all unclear.

Drones and an elusive medic had tended her in the stark infirmary on Settle where she had fully awakened at last. She was soothed with meaningless words like a child, and told only that the two officers she had brought in were making satisfactory progress. She had seen no one else; no one had come to her. Twice, a drone had wheeled her about unclassified parts of the complex, which were few, consisting primarily of the library reception area, the cafeteria, which nauseated her, and some of the walkways overlooking service areas. From the observation deck she had once seen lean men in silver, striding easily along, laughing with each other as they greeted an incoming shuttle piloted by two women. Even from that distance the camaraderie had been apparent. Costa stared at her hands with eyes that burned. Being there, shut off though she had been, was like seeing glimpses of home. The viewer permitted for her use had played texts of the history of the Ranger Corps, outlining backgrounds and achievements of selected officers. All she had worked for, all she had stretched and yearned for was here. This was where she belonged, and yet, the ache of being an outsider continued.

Today had brought the stark announcement of dismissal at 1200. Her eyes moved reluctantly to the wall chronometer. A few minutes left, and then she would have to go. The coldness of the Rangers overshadowed the honor given to her by the Zethians. Obviously it was not Ranger tradition to commend or celebrate, or else Haufren and Silta had died and she was being ignored because of official mourning. Surely if Haufren were able he would have sent *some* brief message of farewell.

The chronometer clicked again. She heard the doors at the far end of the observation deck slide open and sighed, leaning down to grasp her cane. It was time to go. She would not embarrass these unfriendly Rangers or herself by lingering. She would go back to her contract on Playworld with dignity, and no one would see the ache of her dreams ever again.

"Attention!"

Even as her body responded automatically to that command, her heart leapt into her throat. That was Haufren's voice! He was alive!

Gladly she stood at crisp attention, holding discipline as Haufren and a white-haired man walked toward her. Haufren moved a bit stiffly, but he was obviously whole and well. The lines of pain and hunger were smoothed from his face, and being rested made him look younger. His blue eyes were fairly snapping with vitality and they raked her up and down critically as they stopped before her.

"At ease."

She snapped to rest, holding her cane at her side as unobtrusively as possible.

"Sir, this is Lieutenant Costa."

"Yes." The white-haired man was stocky and very fit. His gray uniform was tailored perfectly, and he wore silver stars on his sleeve. Costa's eyes widened. "How do you do, Lieutenant," he said. "I am Admiral Vance."

"Sir," she said faintly, awed to the third part.

"I understand you are to be dismissed from the infirmary today."

"Yes, sir."

He glanced at her feet. "Healthy again? Everything satisfactory?"

"Yes, sir."

"Good. The medic has written in his report that you should be fit for duty within two weeks. At that time you will report to Section Four for active training. In the meantime, you will assign yourself to the library for passive training. That course usually takes four weeks, but if you apply yourself—and we have reason to believe that you are a remarkably bright and able individual—you should be ready in a shorter time."

She blinked, not understanding, not quite daring to understand. "Yes, sir. But—"

"Official swearing in doesn't take place until passive and active are completed," said Haufren, grinning at her. "Think you can make the grade?"

"You *did* it!" she exclaimed, forgetting discipline. "Haufren, how—" She broke off in confusion, clearing her throat. "Sorry, sir."

"That's quite all right, Lieutenant," said Vance with a dry smile. "I've seen your Playworld record. Commendable."

"Thank you. But—"

"Well, Major? Don't keep her in suspense forever. You've had your surprise. Now fill her in!"

Haufren's grin faded slightly. He shrugged, looking discomfitted. "We made a deal, remember? I, er, have a little influence in the service. I persuaded the admiral to intercede personally on your behalf."

She stared at him in bewilderment, not daring to say what she thought. No major, however good, had *that* much influence.

"She doesn't believe you, Haufren. Better spill it all." Vance laughed at Haufren's expression and quirked a bushy eyebrow at Costa. "Excuse me, Lieutenant. Buck cadets aren't made too much of around here no matter what their past record is, so you'll have to prove yourself all over again. But you've made a good start by bringing home two of our best. Make us commend you; that's all we ever ask."

Smiling, he returned her salute and walked away.

"Well?" demanded Costa as soon as he was gone. "Haufren, you must explain this! I can't believe you actually managed it. How did you? I feel as though I've been quarantined for the past six days since I woke up."

"You have. Checks had to be run on your records. Negotiations made and—certain transactions."

"For me?" She blinked. "Am I that valuable?"

"Probably not," he said dryly, while she flushed at her own unintentional arrogance. "But you see, I keep my end of bargains. My so-called influence has to do with that legend—"

Her eyes widened. "You mean—"

"I am the direct descendant of the founder of the Rangers," he said with an embarrassed shrug. "The tradition of the corps values that more highly than I care for. So I rarely use the influence I have around here." Haufren raised an eyebrow at her. "I don't often recommend cadets, but you've proved yourself in my book. I think you'll find that Silta and I stick by those who save our lives. Besides, we can't afford to let people of your caliber stay on backwater planets."

"Major," she said, struggling to hold down her excitement, struggling to find the right words to thank him. "I—"

"Call me Brith," he said with a smile and stuck out his hand. "We're all on the same team now, Costa. I think we work pretty well together, don't you?" He laughed, crushing her hand in his. "Don't worry, saving the universe never gets to be an ordinary job. Now cut line, Lieutenant! Get moving! Report to the library and start studying double-time. My team goes out on basic maneuvers in two weeks and if you want to be on it, you'd better know those manuals inside and out! Clear?"

Grinning, she snapped a salute, tossed him her cane, and raced out with a whoop.